A SOLITARY BLUE

Books by Cynthia Voigt

THE BAD GIRLS SERIES

Bad Girls
Bad, Badder, Baddest
It's Not Easy Being Bad
Bad Girls in Love
Bad Girls, Bad Girls, Whatcha Gonna Do?

THE TILLERMAN SERIES

Homecoming
Dicey's Song
A Solitary Blue
The Runner
Come a Stranger
Sons from Afar
Seventeen Against the Dealer

THE KINGDOM SERIES

Jackaroo
On Fortune's Wheel
The Wings of a Falcon
Elske

OTHER BOOKS

Building Blocks
The Callender Papers
David and Jonathan
Izzy, Willy-Nilly
Orfe
Tell Me if the Lovers Are Losers
Tree by Leaf
The Vandemark Mummy
When She Hollers

A SOLITARY BLUE

CYNTHIA VOIGT

ATHENEUM BOOKS FOR YOUNG READERS
New York London Toronto Sydney New Delhi

ATHENEUM BOOKS FOR YOUNG READERS
An imprint of Simon & Schuster Children's Publishing Division
1230 Avenue of the Americas, New York, New York 10020

Also available in an Atheneum Books for Young Readers hardcover edition
Book design by Debra Sfetsios-Conover
The text for this book is set in Baskerville.
Manufactured in the United States of America
This Atheneum Books for Young Readers paperback edition March 2012
8 10 9 7
The Library of Congress has cataloged the hardcover edition as follows:
Voigt, Cynthia.
A solitary blue.
Summary: Jeff's mother, who deserted the family years before, reenters his life and widens the gap between Jeff and his father, a gap that only truth, love, and friendship can heal.
ISBN 978-0-689-31008-9
[1. Divorce—Fiction. 2. Fathers and sons—Fiction] I. Title.
PZ7.V874So 1983
[Fic] 83-6007
ISBN 978-1-4424-5062-2 (hc)
ISBN 978-1-4424-2880-5 (pbk)
ISBN 978-0-689-84799-8 (eBook)

To Gail Paris

Editor ludorum,
editor egregia
et fidelis

PART ONE

CHAPTER 1

When Jeff Greene was in second grade, seven and a half years old, he got home from school one Tuesday afternoon in early March, and found a note from his mother, saying that she had gone away and would not be coming back. He could read the note all by himself:

Dear Jeffie,
You know I love you best, better than anything. I love to come into your room when you are in bed, and read The Lorax *to you, and then kiss you on each big gray eye before you go to sleep. I am going away, but I'm not really going away from you. I will hold you in my heart, and you will hold me in your heart, and we can't ever be very far from each other then, can we?*

There are some hot dogs in the refrigerator. If you don't remember how to cook them for bread sandwiches, you will have to ask the Professor for money when he gets home and go get some rolls. But you shouldn't bother him for unimportant things, so try hard to remember. You're my helper, my best assistant, you remember everything. You won't need to ask, will you?

I will think about you tonight, eating hot dog sandwiches, and I will be very sad and missing you. But you are old enough now, and there are people everywhere who need me, little boys like you who don't get enough to eat and are hungry every night when they go to bed. Imagine that, Jeffie. You know how I feel about that. Or children with no parents at all to take care of them and grownups who can't help themselves and little animals hunted down and wiped out and air and water made dirty. I have to help the people who need me. I have to try to make things better, for you and for all the little children. You are big enough to understand. It is such a big job that I will not be able to come back to see you, so I have to say good-bye. Good-bye, little boy, my own sweet Jeffie, from your sad

M.

M was for Mommy and for her own name, Melody. Jeff read the note twice. He did understand about all the work she did, because she had explained to him about how people had made the whole world sick, all of nature, and it was the last chance to make it better, or little children like Jeff wouldn't have any world when they got big. He knew how sad it made her to think about rivers or the lion in his cage at the zoo or the dirty sidewalks and streets. He knew she couldn't be happy unless she was doing something to make things better—she said so.

But he didn't know why she had to go away to do that. And not come back. A cold, frightened feeling lay all over his body like a wet blanket, and he started to cry. He wrapped his arms around himself and cried.

Jeff knew he shouldn't cry, he knew he had to stop. The Professor, his father, didn't like crying, because he wanted things regular and even. He wanted a boiled egg every day for breakfast and his usual times in his study when nobody disturbed him. He had all of his classes in the afternoons so he could stay home and study in the mornings. After supper, he went back into his study to do more. Melody had explained that and Jeff knew how to keep the kind of quiet house his father wanted, the kind Melody always kept.

When Jeff was too young to go to school, his father took him to a day care center, every morning. Melody picked him up in the afternoon, when she was free. Usually, that was on her way home to get supper. Sometimes, if the weather was nice, she would be free early and they would go to the zoo or to a museum or shopping together. If the day care center was closed, she would take Jeff with her to her work, and he would color at the table where she was talking. Once he started school, he could spend all day there. He even went to both kindergarten classes, the morning one and the afternoon one.

Melody wasn't free most of the time because she worked to make the world better. As he got older, she explained to Jeff how people were making the world worse. Industries dumped their garbage into the water, into the rivers and into the Chesapeake Bay. Because of the garbage, the water got too dirty to swim in, and the fish couldn't live there, and the animals who ate the fish died. People put dirty smoke into the air. Politicians and countries fought wars and murdered people with bombs and fire and even, if they wanted to, poisons. Not everybody was as lucky as Jeff, not everybody had a mommy and a daddy, not everybody had enough to eat, not everybody had their own rooms or got to go to Ocean City for a week every summer—but Melody could help those unlucky people. It was her job to help make things better because if she didn't, things might get worse.

That was sad and scary. It was that picture of the world getting worse that came to haunt Jeff when he woke up in the middle of the night and tried not to think about it. Sometimes, at night, Jeff wanted to go into Melody's room, just to hear her breathing, just to see her. But she had explained to him that the Professor didn't like to have his sleep disturbed, so he couldn't.

Melody didn't talk to the Professor the way she talked to Jeff; she didn't talk to him very much at all. When she tried to, he asked her questions that she answered unhappily until he finally said, "It's not as simple as that."

Jeff, still crying, thought about his father now. He wasn't sure what his father liked. He knew what Melody liked, she liked lots of people at her meetings, she liked Jeff to know about what was going on in the world, she liked to hold his hand outside of the lion's cage and tell him about how the lion's life used to be. She didn't mind if he was sad or cried, because she would hug him. She liked new people and new ideas, and sometimes she worried about Jeff because he was too much like the Professor, no matter how hard he tried.

All Jeff knew about the Professor was that he liked things regular and even. He didn't like feelings, and crying. Melody said he wasn't much of a father, and now—Jeff cried quietly, alone—he was all Jeff had. Jeff would have to stop this crying.

He had stopped before the Professor got home at five. He had stopped with a glass of milk, looking out the window over the sink through a cold, sleety rain to the row of houses behind the row of houses they lived in, looking out to the taller buildings behind them, sticking up into the gray sky like irregular teeth. The rain spattered on the tin roof of the back porch.

When the Professor entered the kitchen and put his worn briefcase down on the table, Jeff turned around, holding the empty cold glass in his cold hand. He watched his father open the envelope she had addressed to him and read the short note once. He watched him throw the note and envelope away, crumpled up, into the yellow plastic wastebasket. His father didn't look surprised, his father didn't look unhappy, his father didn't look worried. His father didn't look anything.

"Did she leave you a note, too?" the Professor said to Jeff.

Jeff nodded. "Do you want to read it?"

The Professor shook his head quickly. "Is there anything for dinner?"

Jeff nodded.

"Can we eat at six-thirty?"

The Professor left the kitchen, but he forgot his briefcase. He didn't come back for it. Jeff heard him go into his study, which used to be a living room, back down the hallway at the front of the house. What used to be the dining room was the living room. They ate all their meals at the Formica table in the kitchen. Jeff did his homework at that table too, because there was no room for a desk in his tiny bedroom tucked under the eaves at the back of the house.

That evening, after his father had left him alone, Jeff did homework. He did a page of mixed addition and subtraction problems; he copied out sentences into his French notebook, being as neat as he could. He boxed in all the verbs in the ten English sentences and then went back to find the subjects and label them with an S. He wrote a paragraph about lizards for science. He filled in the names of the original thirteen colonies on the social studies map, then memorized it. He worked carefully, because teachers liked neat, careful work. When he was finished, he gathered his books up into a pile and set them on the counter by the refrigerator, for the morning. He looked at the clock: six.

Jeff knew how to set the table and how to get a hot dog dinner for himself and his father, because Melody often could not get home for dinner, when she had a meeting, or when she had a lot of work to do with a committee, or a demonstration to plan. Jeff and the Professor were pretty used to getting themselves a hot dog dinner. Jeff set the table, then cut up lettuce and tomatoes for a salad. He split the hot dogs and piled the slices of bread up beside the toaster. He put the bottle of salad dressing out on the table and the mustard, catsup, and relish. He kept himself busy except for just a couple of minutes when he had nothing to do but wait; for these minutes he stood at the sink and looked out the window into the darkening rain. Across their little square of cement yard, blocks of yellow light shone from the kitchens of the row of houses a street up. The tall shape of the humanities building of the university was all dark, and in the rain its edges merged fuzzily into the clouds. "But what will I do?" Jeff asked himself, inside his head.

He knew that if he stayed there, looking out, with room for questions to rise up in his head, he might cry again; so he took a warm sponge and washed down the drainboard by the sink, scrubbing it with Comet. He had lost his mother, he didn't want to run any risk of losing his father too.

When supper was on the table, Jeff went down the hall to knock on his father's door and say that everything was ready. Then he went back to sit down. The Professor always came right away and poured himself a glass of wine from the carafe in the icebox before he sat down to eat. After the Professor had tasted the wine, he lifted his fork and took a bite of salad. That was Jeff's signal to begin. When Melody was there, it had been her fork he waited for.

They ate without talking. After he had finished, the Professor put on some water to boil and took out the small Chemex pot. Melody had tried to get him not to drink coffee, she had told him all about caffeine and cancer in it, she had even made him taste some of the herb teas she drank; but he wouldn't change. "Coffee's addictive," she had warned him.

"Anything in excess tends to be addictive," the Professor answered. "The point is to avoid excess. Isn't it?"

"I can't talk to you," Melody said. "You already know all the answers." Her voice sounded as if she didn't think what she said was true.

"I never said that," the Professor said.

Melody didn't answer, just sat staring at her cup of tea; but Jeff saw tears come up in her eyes, so he went around to hug her.

But this night she was gone. Jeff cleared the table, then sat down again, watching his father drink his mug of coffee. The bright white light bulb in the kitchen shone on the straight white hair that lay across the top of the Professor's head and reflected off his big, square glasses. Jeff's father looked like a professor, Jeff thought, even though he knew every professor looked different. Jeff's father was tall and broad-shouldered, and he never put on weight no matter how much he ate. He had pale blue eyes and thin lips. His white eyebrows were almost straight, his nose hooked out where it joined his face. He had taken off his tie and his shirt was unbuttoned at the neck. He looked, in his calm face, in his quiet way of sitting or slow way of moving, as if nothing could upset him. Jeff knew that his father would want to say something about Melody, so he waited.

"She's not coming back," the Professor said at last.

"I know."

"We'll rub along all right," the Professor said. "Although there will be a couple of changes."

Jeff felt alarmed. His father didn't like changes, his father couldn't change; Melody said that. "What changes?"

"We'll have to get someone to live in, a student, room and board in exchange for housekeeping and babysitting. We can't afford a maid and there has to be someone while you're so young. I'll move my books upstairs, to the bedroom, that'll give us a room for him." The Professor sipped at his coffee. "I suspect we'll find it doesn't make much difference at all. Most things don't. I'll see if we can't find a boy, they're more reliable."

Jeff relaxed. The Professor always said things didn't make much difference, wouldn't make much difference. He said that when Melody talked about women's rights and signing antiwar petitions or endangered species. "Don't you *care*?" Melody would ask him, her voice ringing, her big gray eyes filled with feeling. She was fifteen years younger than her husband and had long, thick dark hair that she let hang loose down her back, all the way below her waist. "What about nuclear war?"

"That would make a difference," the Professor agreed, without any change of voice or expression. His mild blue eyes looked at his wife.

"Oh my *God*," she would say, turning away impatiently. Her dark hair rippled down her back. Her patchwork skirt whirled around her slender legs. When she was unhappy like this, Jeff didn't know how to comfort her.

Jeff went to the University School, where children of professors could attend without paying, but the children from other families had to be rich. There were sixteen children in his second grade class, six boys and ten girls. One of the girls had a mother who taught math at the university. Two of the other boys, Sean and Jason, had fathers there. Sean's father and mother both taught, physics and English. Jason's father taught history too, only Jason's father taught American History and the Professor taught European. The boys weren't friends, because the parents weren't friends. Jason's father wanted to be chairman of the department, but the Professor had that job because he was older. Jason's father wrote articles that got published in history magazines, and he wrote reviews of history books for the Baltimore paper and sometimes the *Washington Post* too: Jason brought them into school for show-and-tell. Jason's father said the department was a shambles and that was why they didn't attract good students. Jason's father said the curriculum hadn't been changed since 1958, and it was out-of-date. Any man who didn't publish in his field, Jason's father said, could offer no leadership to his department. Melody agreed with Jason's father, but the Professor didn't pay any attention. "It wouldn't make any difference," he said and went back to the work he was doing.

That Melody had gone away didn't make any difference to Jeff at school. His father walked him over in the mornings anyway, and he went home by himself in the afternoons. He wasn't friends with the university children. The town kids never played with the university kids, because the children of professors weren't rich enough to have good toys, and besides, they were the geniuses of the class. Except Jeff, who didn't ask many questions, who did his homework neatly and handed it in on time, who sat quietly at his desk. Jeff was never a favorite with the teacher, or with the student assistants from the Education Department, but the town kids didn't like him even so, because he was a university kid. Jeff sat quiet and did his best to do exactly what the teacher said she wanted them to do. His papers were always perfect.

Sometimes Jeff wondered how everybody knew, right away, what kind of child you were. They all dressed in uniforms, gray flannel pants, white shirts, and blue jackets for the boys, with a red and blue striped tie. The girls wore gray pleated skirts and white blouses and blue sweaters. Everybody looked alike, but just the same, everybody knew the difference.

That spring, after Melody left, the Professor found a student to live with them, a young man named Jackson. Jackson moved into the Professor's old study. For a month he did the shopping, vacuumed the house, saw to the laundry and meals. Jackson was thin, with long hair he tied at the back of his neck like George Washington and terrible pimples on his face that he tried to hide with a wispy blond beard. He almost never went out except to classes. He studied all the time, because he wanted to graduate *summa cum laude* and go right to graduate school without being drafted. At the beginning of May, he told Jeff he had exams and long papers coming up, so Jeff did the vacuuming and shopping and put fewer clothes into the Laundry. Jeff wasn't tall enough to run the machines at the laundromat so Jackson still had to do that, and the cooking. Jackson cooked huge pots of stew that they could eat for two or three days in a row or spaghetti sauce or pot roasts you could warm up. The Professor didn't seem to mind, so neither did Jeff. But after Jackson had gone, the Professor told Jeff they'd have a better selection of possibilities in the fall.

"You could get a girl," Jeff suggested quietly. Girls could cook, probably, at least as well as Melody. He thought a girl would clean the house to brightness.

"They tend to be unreliable," the Professor answered.

During the summer, the Professor concentrated on his research and Jeff amused himself. "Thank God you can amuse yourself," the Professor had often said. Jeff thought probably they wouldn't go to the beach for a week, the way they used to, because Melody wasn't there any more, but they did. They drove over to Ocean City on a Saturday morning and stayed in a one-bedroom apartment a block away from the water. Jeff played on the beach, digging, building castles, watching the people. The waves towered and crashed beyond him. In the mornings, the Professor took him across the highway to the beach and left him there while he went for a walk. "Stay out of the water until I come back," the Professor told Jeff.

"I will," Jeff promised. He watched his father walk away down the beach to think, walking at the water's edge where there were fewer legs to step over. His father wore long khaki pants, even on the beach, and a cotton shirt; but he rolled up the sleeves of his shirt in the heat, and he took off his shoes and socks to go barefoot.

When the Professor walked back, Jeff could tell him from far off, because nobody else wore long pants or walked so slowly along the packed sand down by the water. Jeff always watched for the first glimpse of the Professor, because he always knew he might not return. "He doesn't know anything about being a father," Melody had told him, "so you can't expect very much from him, Jeffie."

They ate sandwiches Jeff had made, then he could play in the water until it was midafternoon and they returned to the apartment to cool off. There, the Professor wrote notes.

They ate dinners in restaurants, crab cakes and crab imperial and steamed crabs, and once, steamed lobsters. They both got sunburned, but not badly. One night, they went down to the boardwalk, and Jeff rode the roller coaster and the rocket—but it wasn't fun anymore, so they came straight back to the apartment. It was different when Melody was sitting beside him, being scared and excited, laughing out loud when the car rolled down an incline, holding him within her arm. Every night Jeff indulged in the pleasures of watching television, because there was a television set that came with the apartment. At the end of the week, they packed up and went back to Baltimore. "It'll be good to get back to work, won't it?" the Professor asked Jeff. Jeff said yes.

* * *

The year Jeff was in third grade, the housekeeper was named Tony and he was a sociology major who liked to have noise around him. He liked to tell the Professor what was wrong with the university when they sat at meals, he liked to listen to his radio while he did housework. And he liked to cook. He taught Jeff to help him and also taught him good recipes. Jeff did his homework after supper that year, because, as Tony said, since they didn't have a TV, there was nothing else for him to do. The Professor worked before dinner and after, as usual.

"I never thought they worked so much," Tony said to Jeff. "I always figured professors had kind of an easy life. Not your old man. But he doesn't publish, does he? I dunno, there must be more to life than this. Where *is* your mother, anyway?"

"I don't know," Jeff said.

"I saw her a couple of times, my sophomore year. At rallies, across a crowded room. She was a good looker. She seemed sincere. Taste that spaghetti sauce and tell me what it needs, will you, kid?"

It was Tony who, by forgetting to take Jeff down to the barber to keep his crewcut short, changed Jeff's way of wearing his hair. Before then, it was cut off short and straight, like a mown field, and it would grow out slowly until it stuck out over his head like a puffball until the Professor would say, "Isn't it about time to cut his hair?" But Tony didn't get around to it, and Jeff's hair grew until it lay long and flat on his head, like the Professor's. But Jeff's hair was dark, almost black, like Melody's.

When Jeff was in fourth grade, a boy named Andrew kept house for them because he had to or he couldn't afford to go to the university. Andrew really wanted to live in a fraternity, he wanted to go to friends' parties, he went to all the football games and basketball games and baseball games. What he did around the house, he did angrily, his face angry above the vacuum cleaner, his hands angry in the dishwater. That year, the Professor started going out every Thursday evening, to have dinner and then play whist afterward. If Andrew had something he wanted to do Thursday night, Jeff was old enough to be left alone. Andrew didn't tell the Professor this, but he told Jeff. Jeff didn't tell the Professor either, because he didn't want to upset the Professor's routine. When he was alone at night in the house, he just went up to his room with a book and sat on his bed reading until he heard someone come in. Then he turned off the light and fell asleep.

The year Jeff was in fifth grade, they had a graduate student from the Physics Department, Ian, who had a thick beard and spent long hours in the lab, working on his thesis. At the beginning of each week, Ian put up a list of when he would be in the house. He took Friday and Saturday nights off and went to see his girlfriend. He was going to be married in June, "Although why anybody gets married these days I don't know. Given the statistics on divorce. What about your old man?" he asked Jeff. He sat with Jeff at the table, doing labs or problems, while Jeff did his homework. Jeff looked up at Ian. If he was teasing, Jeff was ready to show that he got the joke. He didn't seem to be teasing, so Jeff looked serious. "Your father, for example; he's easy to live with. Maybe he was just too old for her. What do you think?"

"I don't know," Jeff said, although he thought he did know, maybe. He knew Melody's complaints, anyway. He didn't know about his father; his father never said anything, one way or the other.

"Don't you wonder?" Ian asked.

Jeff shook his head. As long as the Professor's life suited him, he would probably stay. "He's afraid of changes," Melody used to tell Jeff. "He's a creature of routine. And he doesn't know how hard it is on other people." It wasn't hard on Jeff, however; not nearly as hard as it would be if the Professor decided to leave too. So Jeff didn't wonder, he just made sure that the Professor's life was what the Professor wanted.

The summer before sixth grade, sitting behind his father as they drove back from their week at Ocean City, Jeff asked who was going to housekeep for them that year. "Nobody," the Professor said. "You're old enough now, aren't you?"

Jeff could hear that his father wanted him to be old enough. "Yes," he agreed. He looked at his father. The back of the Professor's neck was sunburned, and so were his hands on the steering wheel. They got caught in two traffic jams, where the road narrowed to bridges to cross rivers.

But the Professor didn't mind. He turned around to Jeff. "It doesn't make any difference what time we get there, does it."

"No," Jeff agreed.

That fall, one of the Professor's whist players became a friend. This friend came to their house to visit and do Greek with the Professor, so Jeff met him. He was a man in his forties, younger than the Professor, who taught theology at the university. He was a Catholic brother, Brother Thomas. "Doubting Thomas," he introduced himself to Jeff, the first night he came to their house. Jeff wondered, without asking, what he meant. The brown eyes studied his face. "It was a joke," Brother Thomas said, so Jeff smiled. "I had no idea you had a son, Horace. Well, I guess gossip said you did, but I'd forgotten."

Jeff shook his hand and looked at the man. He was round and short, his round head was bald except for a fringe of pale hair that ran around the base of his skull. Like the Professor, he wore big, square glasses. He wore a black suit, with the round white collar showing above his black shirt front. "You're old for such a young son, aren't you, Horace?"

"I married late," the Professor answered.

"Ah," Brother Thomas said. He had brought a bottle of wine with him. He insisted that the Professor let Jeff taste it. Jeff sat quiet at the table, working out how they wanted him to behave. He watched their eyes and listened carefully to their conversation. Brother Thomas's eyes often rested on Jeff, but the man didn't ask him questions so he didn't volunteer anything. The Professor paid close attention to what Brother Thomas said, so Jeff deduced that he thought the man was interesting and wanted him to enjoy himself. Jeff took special care over the dinner, so that the brother would like the food, even if it was only hamburgers on rolls. He toasted the rolls and buttered them. He turned the hamburgers frequently, so that they would be cooked but not too thickly crusted. He chopped onions and sliced celery to add to the salad.

"A man with your taste should have a decent set of wine glasses," Brother Thomas said, holding up his glass. They were all sitting around the kitchen table after dinner. The Professor had moved his study back downstairs, and after three years the living room was filled with boxes of books and boxes of papers and boxes of old clothes. There was no place else in the house to sit.

"I can't afford to indulge my tastes," the Professor said.

"You could strike for a raise," Brother Thomas suggested. "Carry placards, deliberately teach untruths. Or how about a sit-down strike?" Jeff had never heard of anyone talk to his father in the easy, off-hand way Brother Thomas did. It looked like the Professor didn't mind.

It was from Brother Thomas that Jeff learned that some people thought the Professor did a good job at the university. "What do you think of your father, putting together the best history department in Baltimore, maybe even Maryland," Brother Thomas said.

"I think that's good," Jeff said. Brother Thomas winked at him.

The Professor, however, denied it. "It's nothing like first-rate."

"Academic reputations take a while to spread; there's a five to ten year lag, you know that—or you should; you're the historian." Brother Thomas sounded very sure. "You watch, Horace, your reputation is catching up with you. The students you've dreamed of are lurking on your horizon."

The Professor opened his mouth as if to say something, but just shook his head. Jeff sipped at the wine. It didn't taste fruity to him, but thick, so that it left a coating across his tongue, and slightly bitter. He kept his face expressionless.

"Look at the sign-ups for your courses," Brother Thomas insisted. "Horace, you can add two and two. Honestly, Jeff, your father," he said, but he said it fondly, as if the Professor amused him.

Jeff looked at his father. He wondered if this was the way the Professor liked to be talked to, but he knew he himself couldn't talk that way.

"Time will tell," was all the Professor said.

"Time is telling," Brother Thomas corrected him. "The other members of your department have even stopped trying to get you fired."

"Have they? That's a blessing," the Professor said.

Brother Thomas chuckled. "I must admit I wondered if you handled their attempts at rebellion the way you did on purpose."

"I didn't handle them at all. I knew it didn't make any difference what they said."

The Professor sounded pleased, though. Jeff could hear that, and he offered Brother Thomas another hamburger.

Jeff waited a couple of weeks before asking his father about Brother Thomas. "Who is he?"

"A monk. A Christian Brother, that's a teaching order," the Professor said. "From the Catholic University; he teaches a Bible course for us."

"That's not in your department. How did you meet him?"

"He played whist with us—then I wanted to study Greek and he wanted to freshen his up."

Jeff sat in surprised silence, wondering why his father needed to learn Greek, wondering how long this friendship had been going on. While he wondered, his father got up from the table and returned to his study. Jeff didn't mind. As long as the Professor was doing what he wanted he would be content with Jeff. The hard thing was trying to figure out what he wanted, because he seldom asked for anything. Jeff washed the dishes, rinsed them, and placed them in a rack to dry. He took out the broom and swept the floor. The Professor liked things neat. All of their extra belongings they packed away into the unused living room, and the rest of the house they kept neat. After four years, Jeff was pretty good at figuring out what the Professor might want, reading his reactions. It was pretty easy, after all, because mostly the Professor didn't think things made any difference. He often said that. And in the same way, so he could give the teachers what they wanted to get, Jeff worked at school, listening carefully not only to instructions, but also to the teachers' reactions.

Occasionally that fall, Brother Thomas would come over to their house for supper. He always brought a bottle of wine with him. Early on, he brought four wine glasses, tall, stemmed crystal glasses, formed from what he called flashed glass, a layer of colored glass on top of a layer of clear. An intricate design had been cut through the outer colored layer, so the glasses shone like jewels. One was red, one blue, one yellow, one green, and the men would say what color they wanted as Jeff set the table. Brother Thomas liked to eat, so Jeff cooked some of the recipes Tony had left for him, like a chicken roasted with two pierced lemons tucked into the cavity so that the meat tasted slightly of lemon, and the juices made a sauce for rice. "The boy has a real hand for it," Brother Thomas said to the Professor. "How did you get so lucky? He certainly didn't get it from you—was his mother a good cook?"

Jeff kept his eyes on his plate and his face still as he listened to what his father would answer.

"No, she hated housework of any kind."

Nobody said anything else. Jeff turned the red glass around in his fingers.

"Let's take our coffee in and get to work," the Professor suggested.

"With pleasure. After I toast the cook." Brother Thomas raised his glass to Jeff and the Professor did the same. Jeff tried to smile at Brother Thomas, but he saw how the man's brown eyes studied him, and he did not know what the man was thinking. He did know, however, that Brother Thomas wouldn't say anything. That much he had figured out, that although Brother Thomas had a lot of ideas, he kept them to himself. Jeff would have liked to hear some of them, but he didn't ask.

In the winter a flu ran through the University School, and Jeff caught it. He spent two days in bed, unable to eat, listening to the sound of his father's typewriter in the silent house. *Tickety-tick. Tickety-tick.* Outside, a gray Baltimore snow fell steadily. Jeff studied the ceiling of his room and kept alert for the first signs of nausea or diarrhea, so that he could be sure to make it to the bathroom. At mealtimes, his father came to the door and asked if he wanted anything. "No, thank you," Jeff said, trying to sound better than he felt, so that the Professor wouldn't be disturbed. He hadn't been really sick for such a long time that he had forgotten how terrible it felt.

On the third day, a Friday, he went back to school, but when he got home in the afternoon and tried to climb the stairs to get to bed, he felt so dizzy he couldn't make his legs move. He rested on the stairs for a while, until he could get to the kitchen and sit in a chair. He was terribly thirsty so he poured himself a glass of ice water, which he guzzled down. For a couple of seconds he felt wonderful. Then he started to cough, deep racking coughs of the kind he had suppressed most of the day. Between the coughing and the dizziness, he threw up in the sink, the water he'd just drunk as well as the little lunch he had eaten. Then he felt better, so he cleaned out the sink.

Jeff made soup for supper and cheese sandwiches toasted in the broiler, and he was careful not to eat much so that he would be able to wash the dishes and get up to his bedroom without his father noticing. He kept his coughing down as much as he could. His ears rang and his body alternated between being too hot and being overrun with chills. He wondered, as he lifted his soupspoon, if his hands were shaking, because it felt as if they were; but, when he looked to check, he could see that they weren't. In bed, he fell asleep without even taking off his clothes.

The next morning he couldn't get out of bed. His teeth chattered and his chest ached and his hair lay cold and wet across his forehead, at his neck, all around his head. He woke himself up, coughing, then drifted off again. Late in the morning, the Professor looked into his room. When he opened the door he awoke Jeff from a shallow sleep. Jeff tried to sit up, but he didn't want to raise his head from the pillow, because then he would feel dizzy, and when he felt dizzy he felt sick.

"I'm going to see Brother Thomas," the Professor said. "I don't know how long we'll be on this passage, the syntax is strange. We're almost out of milk and coffee," he said. Then, about to leave, he asked, "Jeff? You look pale, or is that the light. Is there something wrong?"

Jeff had to say yes.

The Professor came in then and stood looking down at Jeff. He hesitated, then rested a hand on Jeff's forehead. His hand felt cool and dry. "What's your temperature?" the Professor asked. "I thought you were over that flu."

"I'm sorry," Jeff said.

"Where's the thermometer?"

"We don't have one. I'm sorry."

The Professor left the room. The door was open, so Jeff heard him going down the stairs before he slipped back into uneasy sleep.

The next thing he heard was Brother Thomas asking him to wake up. Obediently, he opened his eyes. Brother Thomas put a thermometer into his mouth. The Professor stood tall behind him in a blue cardigan sweater. "Who's his doctor?" Brother Thomas asked. The Professor shook his head helplessly. Jeff had to take the thermometer out of his mouth to cough, but he put it right back in when he was through. The two men listened to him. "What do you mean you don't know?" Brother Thomas asked the Professor. He sounded cross; Jeff hoped he wasn't going to get Brother Thomas angry at the Professor. "Jeff, do you know your doctor's name?" Jeff shook his head.

"When's the last time you saw him?" Jeff shrugged; it was too long ago, he was too tired. "It'll be on the school records," Brother Thomas said. His worried brown eyes were fixed on Jeff.

"Today's Saturday," the Professor said. "The school's closed."

"Who would remember the doctor?"

"His mother might. I guess."

"Can you get in touch with her?"

"I haven't heard from her in four years," the Professor pointed out.

"It's all right," Jeff said. He coughed again, then added, "I had flu this week. Just a relapse. I'm sorry."

Brother Thomas read the thermometer. "One hundred four. And this is still morning, Horace. Have you got any aspirin?"

The Professor looked at Jeff. "In the bathroom," Jeff told him.

"He needs a doctor," Brother Thomas said. "We can give him a couple of aspirin to bring down the fever, but he needs a doctor. His own doctor might make a house call—I don't want to take him outside in this weather."

"I could try calling her family, to see if they know where she is."

"I think you'd better do that," Brother Thomas said. His round face looked sternly at the Professor, and then he hurried out to get the aspirin for Jeff. The Professor put his hand on Jeff's forehead again, before going downstairs. When they had both gone, Jeff rubbed his hands over his chest, because coughing made it hurt. Brother Thomas gave him two aspirins with a glass of water, and he sank back into sleep.

There was a third man in the room when he woke up again, a youngish man. "Do you remember me?" Jeff shook his head. "Well, I wouldn't recognize you either. You've grown." He opened his bag and put a thermometer into Jeff's mouth. He took out a flashlight and looked into Jeff's eyes and ears. He read the thermometer and said, "Hmmmm." He listened to Jeff's chest, front and back, with a stethoscope. He looked down Jeff's throat.

"We gave him two aspirins an hour ago," Brother Thomas said.

The doctor nodded. He took out a pad and wrote something on it, then ripped off the page. He wrote something on the second page and ripped that off too. He handed them both to the Professor. Jeff watched.

"My name's Baker," the doctor said to Jeff. He sat down on the bed, beside Jeff. "You're pretty sick, bronchial pneumonia, and you'll need to stay in this bed for at least three days. No school for a week. Is that going to break your heart?" He smiled at Jeff. Jeff nodded to show he understood. "I want to see you in my office next Friday afternoon. Believe it or not, you're going to feel much better by then. You've got some shots to catch up on, young man."

Jeff nodded. The three men left the room. Dr. Baker started to talk while they were on the stairs, quick and questioning, but Jeff couldn't distinguish the words.

He slept most of that day. Either the Professor or Brother Thomas came into Jeff's room to give him spoonfuls of medicine, every two hours, and ask him if he wanted a cup of tea or some Coke. By Sunday afternoon, he did feel better. In the evening, when the sky beyond Jeff's window was black, Brother Thomas came in with a tray, which he put down on the table beside Jeff. He told Jeff to sit up and then rearranged the pillows behind him. He put the tray across Jeff's thighs and sat down in a chair pulled up beside the bed. It was a chair from the living room, a rocking chair, that the Professor had brought up earlier.

There was clear chicken soup on the tray and a slice of unbuttered toast and a glass of Coke. Jeff tried the soup. He wasn't hungry, but he felt empty.

"It's been a shock for your father, your being sick," Brother Thomas said. His brown eyes watched Jeff. Jeff swallowed quickly so that he could apologize. "It's good for him," Brother Thomas said, "but it is a shock. I never even thought to ask whether he was sending you for checkups. And I'll bet you haven't been to a dentist either."

"I didn't need to," Jeff said. He started to cough again, and Brother Thomas lifted the tray up until he had finished.

Brother Thomas *ttched* as he put the tray back down. "Well, you're a pair of blessed innocents. And you never asked about your mother, did you?"

Jeff shook his head.

"Do you know anything about her? I don't."

"Her name's Melody," Jeff said. "She has long black hair and she's beautiful. She has gray eyes."

"She's living with her family, in South Carolina. I know that much more. Your father wasn't pleased to talk to her." Jeff kept his face empty. "Are they divorced?"

"I don't know," Jeff said.

"You ought to get him to tell you about her," Brother Thomas advised. "It would be good for him; anyone can see that."

But Jeff knew better than that, although he didn't argue.

Jeff stayed in bed for four days, and the Professor or Brother Thomas came to read *Ivanhoe* to him. They brought him books from the library and, when he could go downstairs, Brother Thomas gave him three paperbacks in a set. The Lord of the Rings. "This will keep you busy while you have to stay inside," Brother Thomas said. The long solitary hours did go by quickly as Jeff read the story of unlikely heroes in another world, of magic and love, of battles against unremitting evil, the long, arduous journey, of friendship and betrayal.

On Friday, Dr. Baker gave Jeff a complete checkup, two shots, and asked if his father was with him.

"No sir, he has a class," Jeff answered.

The doctor looked up from the file he was writing in and said, "Well, then, I'll expect you in here for a checkup around your next birthday. That'll be September. You'll be twelve."

"Yes, sir."

"Do you have any questions you want to ask? Anything that's worrying you?"

"No, sir."

"Well, if you think of any. How do you do in school?"

"Okay," Jeff told him. He did not want to say that his grades had been drifting down, that his teachers said he was "lazy" or "dreamy."

The doctor nodded and closed the file. "Don't disappear on me again, all right?" Jeff nodded. "You look like a normal enough kid to me; you're doing fine. No problems. I'll see you next September, unless you need me in between."

"Thank you," Jeff said, leaving.

When he got home, his father was waiting. "Everything okay?" the Professor asked.

Jeff nodded.

"I'm really sorry, Jeff," the Professor said then, his mild eyes apologetic behind their glasses. "I don't know what I was doing, letting that happen."

"It's okay, really. It doesn't make any difference, really. And I liked the books," Jeff told him. If his father started worrying about him that would be a change, and you couldn't tell what would happen when things changed.

"I just didn't know about the checkups," the Professor said. He sounded discouraged. Jeff felt alarmed. He remembered that his father didn't like to apologize, didn't like to feel sorry; he remembered the way the Professor got all shriveled up when he had made Melody unhappy or angry.

"I'm sorry," he had said, "I'm sorry."

"No you're not, you don't even understand what I'm talking about, you don't have any feelings at all," she answered, her eyes spilling over tears.

"I'm sorry," the Professor had said, again.

Jeff tried to reassure his father: "It doesn't make any difference." He hoped that was true. "The doctor says I'm a normal enough kid. That's exactly what he said."

A month later, the whole thing was forgotten. Jeff had caught up the schoolwork, his cough had disappeared, and everything was back to normal, except that Brother Thomas came around more frequently than before, often bringing the ingredients for a dinner which he and Jeff would cook together, as well as the inevitable bottle of wine. As the brief Baltimore spring deepened into the heat of premature summer, the Professor spent an unusual amount of time typing in his study, but that was the only other difference, and like the first, it was no real difference. Jeff relaxed, gradually convinced that his being sick hadn't ruined everything.

But in May his father told him, over their dinner of pork chops and rice, that Melody wanted him to spend the summer with her.

Jeff took a long time answering. "Where?"

"In Charleston, South Carolina," the Professor told him, neatly cutting the meat from the bone of his third pork chop. "Her family is down there," he said.

Jeff tried to think of what he was supposed to say.

"Is that all right with you?" his father asked, salting his rice.

Jeff looked at the Professor's expressionless face. He hoped he was answering the right thing when he said, without expression, "Yes."

CHAPTER 2

Jeff debarked from the plane at Charleston as the sun was going down. The crowd of people from the plane hurried, and he let himself be carried along by them. It was hot, so hot he was not surprised to see palm trees along the cyclone fencing that bordered the runways, hotter because he wore his school uniform to travel in, the gray flannel pants and blue blazer, the white shirt and the striped tie. He moved along with the crowd toward a pink one-story building with a glass tower on top of it, the airport. The sky over this flat countryside was soaked with the colors of the setting sun, and Jeff stepped out of the line of traffic to look at it for a minute.

A hot, reddish gold shone at the horizon and faded out to orange pink about a third of the way up the arc of the sky. The flowerlike heads of the taller palm trees turned into black silhouettes to the west. Wispy stray clouds drifted across the western sky.

Jeff found the baggage claim area without trouble, by following the general drift of traffic. Unlike the Baltimore airport an hour and a half to the north of him, this airport would be hard to get lost in. "Melody will meet you," the Professor had told him as they'd waited for Jeff's plane to be announced. "Just let me know when you're returning and I'll pick you up," he had said. Jeff had the return portion of his ticket—paid for, but the flight unspecified—in the inside pocket of his blazer. He had shaken the Professor's hand and he had not looked back as he walked through the passageway to his plane. He didn't even look back to see if the Professor had waited for him to look back; and once you were on your plane it was impossible to see into the plate glass windows of the observation area if there was someone watching for you or not.

At the luggage claim Jeff picked out his father's battered leather suitcase and went to the waiting area. This was a big room, with two long walls of windows and two short walls of ticket counters. He sat on a plastic chair, his suitcase at his feet.

Outside the window to the runway, the sun went down and the sky turned dark. Outside the opposite window, cars pulled up, their twin headlights unnecessary on the brightly lit unloading area. People moved through the big air-conditioned room, some arriving, some leaving, meeting and parting. A voice overhead announced planes. Jeff waited. He had thirty dollars in his pocket, twenty from his father and ten from Brother Thomas to bring back a bottle of local wine. Jeff kept an eye on his suitcase and on the clock. He wasn't hungry, he wasn't tired. He waited.

And he waited. The room was less crowded now, and the twin headlights drove up less frequently. The air grew quiet, except for an occasional low-toned conversation. Jeff sat motionless, his legs side by side, his hands in his lap, his mind empty; and waited.

A rush of sweet air washed around him, enveloped him; a voice murmured half-laughing, half sad. "Oh Jeffie, Jeffie." He closed his eyes as his cheek came to rest on her shoulder and her flowery scent flowed around him. Her arms wrapped around him and he could feel her hands on his back. He tried to grab at all the sensations at once, the sound of her voice, honey sweet with its lazy vowels ("I'm so sorry to be so late, I was—it doesn't matter, I was just afraid you'd give up on me and go back, and then there was a traffic jam and—Oh, my little boy"), her arms around him holding him close, the perfumed air she carried with her. He remembered.

"But let me look at you. Aren't you going to kiss me? Haven't you missed me? Aren't you going to hug me? Jeffie? Are you angry? Don't be angry at me."

He lifted his head and opened his eyes.

"You're all grown up," she said. One hand stayed on his shoulder; the other touched his cheek, brushed his hair back from his forehead. It was like—the sunshine on the first day of real spring.

"Look at you, grown up. But you look pale. Oh Jeffie, have you been terribly unhappy?" Her eyes filled with tears, which flowed down over her cheeks in a thin line. "I'm so happy to see you," she said, touching his cheek again.

Jeff's heart hurt him, it was so full with the warmth and sweetness. The warmth seemed to run along his bloodstream. He felt his eyes fill with tears. She smiled. "Not so grown up after all, are you. I'm glad." She smiled right into his eyes. Jeff felt his mouth quiver. "But aren't you going to say anything? Haven't you got anything to say?" Her lips brushed his cheek, the palm of her soft hand held his other cheek, and his heart thudded so painfully in his chest that he knew if he had to stand his legs would be too weak to support him. "Say something," she insisted.

Every painful beat of Jeff's heart was saying something—*Mommy*—but he couldn't speak.

"Then at least sit back and let me look at you." She held both of his hands in both of hers and sat staring at him. He stared back. "Well, what do you think of me?" she finally asked.

"Beautiful," Jeff said. His voice croaked a little, so he cleared his throat and said it again, "You're so beautiful." He felt like a man must who has been kept in a dungeon for years and years, and he steps out into the sunlight for the first time. He couldn't possibly have said what he felt. And she was beautiful, too; so beautiful she took his breath away. Her long black hair curved smoothly down along the sides of her face, until it was gathered back to form a gleaming circle at the top of her head. Her eyes—he had forgotten how dark the outer circle of gray in her eyes was and how the lighter gray shone within that circle. Her black eyelashes framed her eyes, and her curved black eyebrows made another circle. Her oval face, her small straight nose, her smiling mouth, the high cheekbones and the tanned skin—"I'd forgotten how beautiful you are," he said softly.

She laughed, a sound like honey, and stood up, still holding on to both of his hands. He stood in front of her, noticing vaguely that she wore a dress and noticing clearly how small her waist was, how long and slender her tanned arms and legs. "Oh, Mommy," he said, and he reached out to hug her, wrapping his arms around her neck, just as he now remembered he had done when he was little, before she went away.

She held him close against her. The top of his head came to her ears. "You're tall," she said.

Jeff shook his head. "I think you're short," he corrected her.

At that she laughed again and stepped back while the sound still sang in his ears. "Get your suitcase, the car's outside and parked where it's illegal. Didn't you have any pictures of me?" Jeff held his suitcase at the end of one arm. She tucked her hand in under his other arm and kept looking at him. "But your father must have a couple, didn't you ask him?"

Jeff shook his head.

"You goose." She smiled at him, like sunlight, again. He had been afraid she would be angry. "You silly, silly goose. We'll have to give you some. And take some of you, for me. I almost didn't recognize you. I had to study you for a minute, you're so different. Then I saw the suitcase. I thought you'd be looking for me," she said.

"I'm sorry," Jeff said. "I was just waiting."

He had hurt her feelings, so he added quickly, "It doesn't matter; I don't care."

"And everything's all right now," she said. "I'm here, and you're here, and we're back together again. I'm so happy," she said, her voice singing the words as they stepped out into the night air.

She made Jeff sit in the backseat of the car, an old four-door sedan. "Children should always sit in the back," she said to him. "And strap yourself in. Children are so light, if there's a wreck they fly around inside the car. The back is the safest place." He did what she asked gladly. He sat in the right hand corner, where he could look across to her as she drove. "I have to make a stop," she said, pulling out onto a highway. "Do you mind?"

"No." Jeff wouldn't mind anything.

"How do you like Charleston?"

"I don't know, I haven't seen any of it."

She laughed again, as if he had said something funny. He thought he ought to ask her a question, so he did. "Is this your car?"

"No, heavens, I don't have enough money to buy a car. A friend of mine lets me use it when he's out of town. I couldn't afford to insure a car, I can barely afford to buy gas, but I don't mind. Detroit doesn't have any of my money, and neither do the fat-cat oil companies—most of the time. And that keeps my personal pollution contribution down."

Jeff was remembering more about her with every minute. He watched her hands on the steering wheel and wondered about the rings she wore; the lights overhead and from passing trucks flashed over her hands, lighting them purple and yellow. She turned off the highway after a few minutes and negotiated a number of turns before stopping in front of a small one-story house, one of a row of similar houses, each with a chain link fence around it. She turned around in her seat to ask, "Do you want to wait in the car or come in?"

"I'll wait," Jeff decided.

"You better come in, we may be a while," she told him. She opened the low gate for them and then took his arm again as they went up the walk to the small porch. A yellow light, covered with the bodies of bugs, shone over the door.

Inside, two women sat at a kitchen table, folding letters into a pile of envelopes. Most of the house was taken up by this kitchen, which had a sofa at the wall farthest away from the stove and sink, with a small TV set on the coffee table. "Mel," the women said, "we were wondering where you were."

"I was meeting someone," Jeff's mother said. "The man in my life; let me introduce him, Jefferson Greene. This is Phoebe."

"Hello," Jeff said, to a young woman whose short, curly dark hair framed her face. Phoebe nodded at him.

"And Willa." Jeff said hello to Willa whose brown hair curled like Phoebe's into fuzzy curls.

"Sit down, Jeffie, my goodness," his mother told him. He sat obediently in one of the two empty chairs at the table. She took the other. "My son," she announced.

Jeff stared at her. She had sounded so proud and glad as she said that. Her big eyes moved from one to the other of the people at the table. A smile teased at her mouth.

"For heaven's sake," Phoebe said. "You never said a word." Both of the women stared at Jeff.

"From the marriage?" Willa said.

"Oh, yes," Melody said. "I had to pick him up at the airport, and I was late and so worried—I can't tell you." She pressed her hand over her heart. "Talk about anxiety."

Melody did not wear a wedding ring, Jeff noticed, but she wore two silver rings with pieces of turquoise set in them, on one hand. On the other hand she wore a big ring with a dark red stone in it and a plain pearl ring. Her fingers were delicate.

"We'd better get going on this, if we want to do a mailing tomorrow. Jeffie will help, won't you? It's women's lib material," she teased.

"Sure," Jeff said. "It doesn't make any difference to me."

Melody's laugh floated over the table. "But it will, Jeffie, it will. You just wait."

They folded the letters into envelopes. This was the second of five mailings, "and we've got all the facts and figures," Melody said, her hands working.

"For all the good it does," Phoebe said. "I don't know, sometimes I think women just don't care."

"What do you expect?" Melody asked, "when we've all been brought up to get married and let a man support us."

"Well, it serves them right," Willa said. "Sometimes I think I'll do just that, it would certainly be easier than—earning the money and keeping the house too. Especially when I think of the men who earn more than I do and don't work as hard. Or as well. It's just what they deserve, some woman hanging like a leech off them. Then they complain about women."

"The trouble with that," Melody said, her voice serious and sad, "is that it's bad for you. Bad for women to do that, bad for themselves, because it just perpetuates things. We have to fight for our self-respect, don't we?"

The other two women nodded in agreement.

"And if we don't do something," Melody went on, "if people like us don't try to do something to change it—then we're contributing to it. If you think about it, we are. Why, I wouldn't take a job working for a man for—all the tea in China."

"Yes, but you've got family to live with," Willa told her.

"And an ex-husband," Phoebe said.

"My goodness, you don't think I'd take a penny from *him,*" Jeff's mother said, angry. "I'm insulted. Yes, insulted that you'd think that and then work with me on this campaign. Why, I have more self-respect than that. And so should you."

They apologized, and after a few minutes Melody's voice resumed its ordinary tones, lazy, full of subdued laughter. Jeff relaxed.

It was late when they left, the streets deserted, most of the little houses dark. They got back onto the expressway and drove for several miles. Melody yawned and asked Jeff how he had liked the two women. He said he had liked them all right. "They're so young," she said, "barely over twenty, both of them. It's good for the young women to learn from the beginning the fight they'll have to make if they're not going to be taken advantage of. It's worse here in the South," she said, "it's much worse."

"I guess so," Jeff agreed.

Sleep hung on his eyelids and pulled at his shoulders. He barely noticed when his mother parked the car in front of a tall house, he noticed only that he stumbled on uneven bricks as they walked to the front door. Inside, she led him up a broad staircase and opened a door for him, with her finger on her lips. "We don't want to wake them up, they sleep lightly," she said. "Oh Jeffie, I'm so happy to have you here with me. Sleep well. Until the morning," she said softly, and kissed him on the forehead.

Jeff peeled off his clothes and stripped back the spread from the bed before lying down on it in just his underpants. He was too tired to look for his pajamas, too tired to see where he should put his clothes away. He turned off the bedside light and lay dazzled and bemused in the darkness before slipping into sleep.

He woke early, but without any sense of strangeness. His room—he sat up in the bed and looked around him—was large and square, airy. All four windows were open, and the gauzy curtains hung still in the motionless air. He heard, beyond the silence of the house around him, an occasional motor, an occasional bird, no human voices. He had to go to the bathroom—badly—but he didn't know where it was. He sat up and curled his legs underneath him.

His bed had four tall posts: four fluted, slender poles, each with an acorn carved at its tip. The walls of the room were white, faded to a kind of pearly color, the high ceiling had cracks running along it, the floor was broad boards of wood. A dresser stood next to one bare wall, with a mirror set on it and a large, dark wood wardrobe beside it. Under the windows on one wall stood a little writing table, with a chair pulled up to it. Jeff's bed was placed between two windows. He saw only one door. He *really* had to go to the bathroom; he hadn't been since he was on the plane.

Jeff got out of bed and unpacked his bag, hanging his trousers and dress shirts up carefully in the wardrobe. He refolded his underpants and T-shirts into the drawers of the dresser and made neat piles of his jeans and shorts. He placed his brush and comb on the dresser top, putting his toothpaste and toothbrush down beside them. He selected the drawer he would use for soiled clothing, dropped yesterday's clothes into it, and dressed in flannels and a shirt. He wondered how early it was and where the bathroom was.

He went to a window and looked out, over little patches of bright flower gardens and bright green lawns to the backs of three other sleeping houses. The air hung moist and cool around him; it came sweet and warm into his lungs. Very early, he guessed. Two of the houses were brick, all of them had a second story veranda, and he wondered if he might push back the screen and pee out the window. Of course he couldn't do that, and he wouldn't, but the idea made him smile.

He forced himself to open the door of his room. His bare feet made no noise on the wooden floor of the half-lit hall. On one long wall, tall lace-curtained windows and two lace-curtained french doors opened onto a veranda. His room was at the far end. The broad staircase they had ascended the night before was at the center, where it turned to mount up another flight. There were two doors on his half of the hall and two on the far half.

One of them had to be a bathroom. Jeff stood, trying to decide which it might be. He thought the second door on his side of the stairs was closer to the staircase than the second door on the far side, which made him guess that was the bathroom. The closeness might mean a smaller room. If he was wrong, if, for instance, it was his mother's bedroom, how would she feel if he opened the door and woke her up? Or, worse, her family's bedroom door, some total stranger. Jeff silently argued with himself that perhaps he didn't have to go to the bathroom after all, but he did, and badly. He opened the door next to his, gently turning the white porcelain handle, gently pushing the heavy door inward. It was—he saw with a rush of relief that brought tears to his eyes and was immediately dominated by intense pressure on his bladder—a bathroom.

While he was there he washed his face in a quiet trickle of water. He would have liked to take a bath in the long tub, but decided he ought not to. He rubbed cold water over his teeth with a forefinger, until they squeaked, because he had forgotten to bring his toothbrush and toothpaste. Then he returned to his own room.

There he put on socks and shoes, brushed his hair, made the bed and sat down on it. Except for the items on the top of the dresser, nobody would know he was there. He hadn't disturbed anything. The light in the room grew brighter as the sun moved up the sky, the sounds outside the window grew louder and more frequent. An odor of bacon rose into his room from somewhere below. He heard footsteps on the stairs. The temperature in his room mounted. He sat with his hands in his lap.

After a while the door of his room burst open. "What are you doing?" Melody asked him. "We've all eaten, why don't you come down?"

Jeff looked at her. She wore her hair in one thick braid down her back, she wore sandals on her feet and a pink sundress. Her eyes looked cross, and her pink mouth was not smiling. "*Just* like your father, come on *down,* Jeffie. Gambo wants to meet you, we've all been waiting. Honestly. You goose." She smiled at him then and held out her hand. Jeff hurried to take it and hold it. "Nobody will eat you." She smiled into his eyes. Her perfume was fresher than the early morning air had been, sweeter.

They descended the broad staircase, and she led him into a dining room where a white-haired woman with liquid brown eyes and loops of pearls over the bodice of her lacy blouse stared at him down the length of the table. On either side of her sat two aged women, who also stared at him. They all had breakfast plates in front of them stained with egg yolk.

Melody pulled Jeff down the length of the table. "Gambo? He was awake and dressed. He didn't know what to do, I guess. This is my little boy, Jefferson Greene. Jeffie, this is Gambo, my grandmother. It's about time you two met," she said, stepping back.

Jeff smiled politely. "Hello," he said. "It's very nice of you to let me come and visit."

She looked up at him, and he was alarmed to see all the sentiment in her eyes. "You may kiss me," she said, and he bent to kiss her cheek. "Sit there"—she waved him to the seat opposite her—"since you're the man of the house. You must be hungry."

Jeff sat. Melody left the room to get him some breakfast. The table was covered with a white linen cloth. A china bowl in which pink camellias floated decorated the center. A long-stemmed glass of ice water was set at Jeff's place and heavy silver utensils. Melody came back in with a plate for him and a glass of orange juice and a miniature rack where two slices of toast seemed to stand at attention. She sat at a fifth chair, beside one of the two aged women, a place where there was no silver or napkin set out. "Gambo is my mother's mother," she told Jeff. "Go ahead and eat, before the eggs get cold. And this"—she indicated the woman beside her, who twittered words Jeff couldn't hear but seemed to be smiling at him—"is Aunt Booty and that"—the woman on the opposite side, who ducked her head in a nervous gesture—"is Aunt Dodo, and that is all the family."

Jeff smiled and nodded and started to eat. Gambo, then, would be his great-grandmother. She didn't look old enough to be a great-grandmother. Her hair was thick and healthy looking, her skin wrinkled but not with the same crepey look that the aunts' faces had, her eyes seemed lively and interested as she stared at him. The other two wore sweaters, even in the warmth of the room, and peered at him through glasses as if even then they couldn't really see him.

He ate two fried eggs, six slices of bacon, and fried potatoes. Melody reached out and took a piece of toast, buttered it, and put it on his plate for him. A white-haired black woman came into the room to pour coffee into three cups. His mother got up and followed her out of the room, to return with her own cup of coffee. Jeff guessed Melody had eaten breakfast in the kitchen.

When he put his fork down on the empty plate, his mother asked him, "Had enough?" She had watched him eat, as if she too were enjoying every mouthful.

"And what are you two children going to do today?" Gambo asked.

"I'd like to show Jeffie Charleston," Melody answered. "And get to know him again."

"That's all right," Gambo said. "We'll talk later then, Jefferson. After all, I have some rights in you too, you're the last of my line, and I expect you know very little of your family. Tell me, is that correct?"

Her voice was soft, low, and slow. Jeff nodded his head.

"I'm very glad to see you here in my house, at last," Gambo said. "Except for—I don't like to say critical things but—and at the breakfast table too, but—a gentleman"—she looked at him seriously down the length of the table—"always lowers the toilet seat. After," she added, coughing gently into her napkin, rising from the table before Jeff had time to answer.

"I'm awfully sorry," he said as she approached him.

"We all make mistakes." She smiled down at him and reached out one hand to touch the top of his head. She wore a thin wedding band and a big diamond on that hand. Her hand was gentle as a bird's wing on Jeff's hair. "I suspect nobody ever taught you any better." She slid her hand under Jeff's chin and lifted his face to study it. "He's a handsome boy, Melody; he has the Boudrault look to him."

"Yes," Jeff's mother said, pride in her voice. The two women looked at each other over the top of Jeff's head. He knew he had done something right, and he was glad for Melody's sake.

"Ready to go outside?" Melody asked him. "Don't you want to see my old hometown?"

Jeff jumped up from his seat, said a general farewell, and followed his mother to the front door, where she awaited him, a broad-brimmed straw hat on her head. The streamers, like the flowers on her sundress, were pink. She took his arm as they stepped outside.

The air was moist and warm, filled with sunlight. Melody led him down a narrow brick path, bounded by Gambo's house on one side and a tall whitewashed wall on the other, and into the street. They turned toward the sun and walked. The street was quiet, the houses—many of them, like Gambo's, set sideways to the street—tall; their lawns were hidden behind walls. But the gates were left open and Jeff caught glimpses of tall trees with broad shiny leaves, hedges of azaleas, beds of rosebushes, and white wrought-iron furniture. His stride matched his mother's, and they moved slowly down the shady sidewalk. The street—with those courtyard-like lawns and narrow alleys leading off unexpectedly, with the houses opulent even when they had fallen into disrepair, with the sun-drenched air—the street seemed foreign to Jeff, ancient and mysterious. He looked up at the shuttered first-floor windows and wondered about the people who lived in those houses.

They walked down to a broad park at the end of a tip of land. This park was ringed with trees, crossed by sidewalks, circled by a four-lane road. They passed a monument to the Civil War dead. "This is Battery Park," Melody told him, "and this whole section is called the Battery; it's the heart of the city. But you'll get more than enough history from Gambo." She laughed and her smile poured into Jeff's eyes. They walked along one end of the park, ran across the road, and climbed a set of cement steps to an elevated walkway that ran along the harbor. "That's the Ashley River coming in," Melody said, "and over there"—she walked in that direction—"is the Cooper. You can see Fort Sumter." She stood still and pointed. Jeff looked obediently to where he could see a brief, dark line on the horizon. They continued walking at a lazy pace, Melody's hand tucked under his forearm. At the end of the walkway they leaned against the railing and looked out over the water. Here, a breeze stirred, blowing down from the land across the river's mouth. "What do you think?" Melody asked Jeff.

He looked at her profile and couldn't find words.

"You must think something," she insisted. Her mouth curved up into a smile.

"Beautiful," Jeff said. He was about to say more when she interrupted him.

"That's Aunt Booty's name, or rather Belle is, but when my mother was little she called her Booty, from *Beauty and the Beast*, and it stuck. It's crazy, isn't it? There is something crazy about the South, you know that, don't you?"

"No," Jeff said.

"The land of lost causes," his mother said. "But what I really wanted was for you to look at the river here."

Jeff looked down and across to where what seemed to be an aircraft carrier was moored, up river. "Is that an aircraft carrier?" he asked.

"Boys." Melody sighed. "Yes, there's a big naval base, carriers and nuclear subs go out of Charleston. I hope you don't want me to take you over the boats; I hope you don't expect that."

"No," Jeff said. He didn't expect anything.

"What I wanted you to see was the water—see how green it is? You know what that means. There are factories, refineries, too, up river, and they've killed the river. Killed it," she repeated. "It used to be you could fish in this river, and it ran brown with mud, and turtles stuck their heads up, so many that they looked like grass. Herons lived in the marshes, crabs and clams. Not any more," she said. "I don't know whether to get angry or just weep. And I'll tell you something else; the Chesapeake Bay is worse." She turned to face him. "Do you know what Captain John Smith said about the Chesapeake Bay? He said it teemed with fish, so all a man had to do was step into its water with his sword out, and fish would leap onto it and he could feast. You've seen it, what do you think?"

Jeff thought about the harbor at Baltimore, where tankers lined up at piers edged by high brick warehouses, and he remembered Sparrow Point, where the air was thick with industrial pollution. "It smells much worse than this," he said.

"Only because the air's right today," Melody told him. "When the wind comes down from the refineries and plants, it stinks—no, it really stinks. But you're right, things are better down here, and do you know why? Because it's a poor country, the South. Poverty may save it—that's ironic, don't you think? The only thing that saves what's left of the ecology down here is because we're too poor to develop. I think, if I didn't know about the victims of that poverty, I'd be grateful for it. But I don't think—in the long run—anything will save us." Her hair hung long and black in the braid down her back, gleaming in sunlight. "Let's sit down in the shade," Melody said.

She led him back down the steps and across the street and across the park to a bench facing the row of houses that faced out over the harbor. These were mansions, with verandas on all three floors, with curved staircases leading up to their broad front doors. They were the kinds of houses that might welcome women in hoop skirts and gentlemen in tall boots. The ancient trees around them were twisted, broad-branched, and hung with Spanish moss.

"We can really *talk*," Melody said. "Are you still at the University School?" She sat close enough beside him to hold onto his hand.

"Yes. I'm going into seventh grade."

"That's the year I was going to take you out, because no girls can enroll—is that still true? No girls after sixth grade?"

Jeff sensed that she wanted him to talk about school, but he was bemused by sensations and couldn't chatter. He felt as if he had been cold, frozen down to his bones and into the marrow, and suddenly now he lay under the warmth of the sun. He could feel himself growing easy, relaxed, under the warmth; he couldn't distract himself from the enjoyment of that. It had something to do with the way his mother held his hand, held to his arm when they walked, touched him with her glance. His sensations were half-remembered, memory growing stronger with every minute he was with her.

"How do you do at school?"

"All right. I get some B's, mostly C's."

"B's without working or B's with working?" she asked.

"With working," he said. The silver and turquoise rings looked wrong on her hand, too big and clumsy for her fingers.

"Oh dear, you must have gotten my brains, not your father's," she said. "Poor Jeffie, is that hard on you?"

"No," he said, "I don't mind."

She laughed. "I never did myself. His brains don't do him much good, do they? I remember when you left for school for your first day, do you remember?" He shook his head. "You were quiet, but you weren't frightened. After all, you'd been in day care for years. I even remember the first time ever I saw you. In the hospital—oh Jeffie, I'd never even suspected what it would be like. Having a baby. They tell you, but you never take it in. I thought I'd died and gone to hell, the *pain*—and the horrible bright lights and sterile box-walls with machines on them, and the nurses who didn't care about what you were going through. I dream about it sometimes."

"I'm sorry," Jeff said.

"Then, when they brought you to me—after I came out of the anesthetic—this little baby, so little and helpless. Your eyes were open but you couldn't see anything really, I knew that. Your fingers were all curled up, and then when I nursed you—" She looked up at him. "Does that embarrass you?"

"No," Jeff lied.

"Then I knew that none of the pain mattered a whit, as long as you were the result of it. It was like ten Christmases all at once. I couldn't breathe properly." Her voice caressed the memory. "I didn't mind that or the bleeding. None of it could make even a dent in my happiness. Sometimes I think that was the happiest time of my life. And we were always together, for as long as I could, we'd go everywhere together. You'd look at me with your big eyes, you'd only look at me, always—Your eyes have changed," she observed.

Jeff didn't know what to say.

"I'm so glad to see you again," Melody declared. "You don't know how I've missed you. Have you missed me? Was it very terrible for you? Is it still? No, I don't think I really want to hear about that, it'll just make me feel more guilty. And besides, it's all behind us now, isn't it?"

"Yes," was all Jeff could say.

"Come on, why are we sitting here? I want to show you my city. You can walk for hours and never see it all. Come on, Jeffie."

They ambled up streets and down alleys, through a church graveyard, and along a business street where they peered into the windows of antique shops. She showed him the oldest part of the city, where houses built in Revolutionary times were being renovated. At last they stopped at a small restaurant for something to drink.

Melody wanted to sit outside. The glass-topped tables were small, the chairs set on uneven bricks, the area roofed over by a rough wooden trellis over which grapevines had been trained. They sat in dappled sunlight. Their table had a little vase of fresh daisies on it, the napkins were linen, brick walls enclosed the garden. Melody studied the handwritten menu, Jeff studied her. She looked at him mischievously over the top and asked if he wasn't hungry, because she was. They ordered sandwiches and iced tea, which Melody said was very good here. "Do you like it?" Melody asked him, as he ate his sandwich.

"It's good."

"No, you silly goose, the restaurant. It's my absolute favorite for lunch; I'd eat here every day if I could afford it. *Do* you?"

"Very much."

"Why?" she asked him. Her gray eyes were teasing. "Well, Jeffie, you don't say very much and I really do want to hear what you have to say. I don't want to pry into your secret thoughts, so I thought—if he'll talk to me about the scenery, then I can hear what he has to say."

Jeff, who felt by this time as if all the hard frozen places within him had melted away, smiled happily back at her. "I like it—the way I like Gambo's house, and everything we've seen today—because . . . it looks as if somebody has taken the trouble to make it pretty. And it's lasted such a long time. It makes my eyes feel good, because—it's the same way you look."

"A compliment? Then you're not disappointed in me?"

Jeff just shook his head.

"But don't you have any questions? There should be so many questions you want to ask me and you haven't asked me any. Not one."

As if she had summoned them up, Jeff realized that he did have questions, answers he badly wanted to hear. "Yes," he said.

"Then ask them, for heaven's sake—what do you think I'm here for?"

"How old are you?" he asked.

"Oh dear, the worst first." She smiled across the table at him. "I'm thirty-two. What do you think of that?"

"Then you were twenty when I was born. Isn't that young?"

She leaned her chin on her hands and nodded her head. He had the feeling she wanted to laugh at him, but if she did, her laughter would be friendly.

"How tall are you?"

"Five-six and a half."

"Where did you go?"

"Home. Here. I came right here, and I've been here ever since. I grew up here, Gambo raised me, well, from the time I was nine. This is my real home."

"What about your parents?"

"My daddy was killed in the Second World War, and after a few years my mother remarried. He was a nice enough man, I guess, but—they moved up to Minnesota, we all did, and he didn't have any luck. One summer, when I was eight, I visited Gambo—and I was so happy. There wasn't all the worry about money and keeping jobs and to make it worse my mother had had a couple of children in the meantime—I don't know. It was what you said, as if somebody had taken so much trouble to make things look nice. So I asked Gambo if I could live with her. It didn't matter how much it cost because she's rich. And we got along so well, she sort of adopted me. I'm the only young person in her family, so it'll all come to me someday anyway."

"I thought you said your mother was her daughter."

"She is. Otherwise how could Gambo be my grandmother?"

"But didn't you say there were other children? So you have brothers and sisters or something," Jeff said.

Melody shrugged. "Maybe, I don't know; they don't keep in touch—and they're not the same kind of people at all. Gambo's never even seen them."

"Why not?"

"My mother never brought them here. Well, she couldn't afford the journey, not on what he makes, so as far as Gambo's concerned I'm the only one. More questions?"

"How old were you when you married the Professor?"

"Nineteen—I dropped out of school. He was my teacher in the World History survey course. *That* takes me back, it really takes me back."

"Why did you go away?" Jeff finally asked.

"Oh, Jeffie." She reached across to put the palm of her hand against his cheek. "There were so many reasons. What does the Professor tell you?"

Jeff couldn't answer. That irritated her, so he said quickly, "I never asked him. We never talk about you."

At that she laughed again and clapped her hands together. "Isn't that like him? Just like him, just exactly like him. I thought I could save him, I thought I could wake him up, but I never could. Nobody ever could, that's what I think now. Look," she suggested, "you just got here, and you don't know me, you ought to get to know me and then see what you think. Whether I could have been happy with him. Okay?"

"Okay."

"Is that all the questions? After all this time?"

"Well—what are those rings?"

She held her right hand out. "These"—she touched the turquoises with a fingertip—"were given to me by a man I'm dating. You'll like him. I hope you'll like him. It's his car. And this one"—the old-fashioned looking ring, with the reddish stone—"I found in an antique store. I thought it might be worth something, if the stone was a ruby, and the dealer didn't have any idea of what she had—she was just some old lady who didn't know anything; she had no business being in business, I felt so sorry for her—So I bought it, on speculation. But when I had it valued . . ." She threw her hands up, empty. "But it's a hundred dollar ring I got for three dollars."

"And that one?"

She spread her hands out on the tabletop. "The pearl Gambo gave me for my sixteenth birthday. It was one of hers."

Jeff looked at her hands, the fingernails glistening with clear polish, the nails shaped, the delicate bones at her wrists. He reached across and put his own hand over hers, surprised at himself for doing it. "You have beautiful hands," he said to her.

She understood what he was feeling, what he really wanted to say to her. "I love you too," she answered him.

Melody had left her purse behind, so Jeff paid for the lunch out of the twenty dollars of his own money. The bill came to twelve dollars, to which Melody insisted that he add a three dollar tip. "Do you know what waitresses get paid in places like this? A dollar fifty an hour, and the owners get away with it because it's not a big enough business to require minimum wage. So they depend on tips."

Jeff took the change he had just been given out of his wallet. "Were you a waitress?"

"No, but I know some people who were. And part of it is because they're women, they get away with paying women less and the poor women just . . . take it. I don't want you to be like that, Jeffie."

Jeff nodded his agreement. He would try. He felt guilty that he had never thought of it before.

Back at Gambo's house, Melody took him into the kitchen and introduced him to the black woman who was working out there, Miss Opal. The kitchen, back behind the house and attached to it by a short hallway, was a low-ceilinged, dark room, its temperature even higher than that outside because of the heat from the big range. Miss Opal had set out two trays, for the old ladies, she said. They wanted afternoon tea in their rooms, so they would be rested up for the celebration dinner in young Jefferson's honor. Miss Melody, she said, had had several phone calls, the messages were written down. Melody told Jeff that her friends didn't believe she had a son, they didn't believe she was taking some days off just to be with him, she guessed she wouldn't bother returning those calls too quickly because she had told them and told them she wouldn't be available to help out. She told him to wait there, she would go up and get her guitar then they would sit outdoors. "I'll serenade you."

When they were settled outdoors, Jeff said, "I didn't know

you played the guitar," as he watched her tune the strings.

"I just started," she told him. She sat cross-legged, her feet tucked up under her bright skirt, her hat set beside her on the grass. Jeff lay on his stomach, resting his chin on his folded arms so he could look at her. She watched her own hands as she played and sang. "What kind of songs do you like?" she asked him.

Jeff couldn't tell her any. She forgave him that and simply played what she wanted. Her songs were mostly sad. "Where have all the flowers gone?" one asked, then, "Where have all the young men gone?" They had all gone to war and been destroyed so the song asked, "When will they ever learn?" She sang a song about a calf being taken to market, a song with a refrain in the voice of the uncaring winds: "Calves are easily bound and slaughtered, never knowing the reason why," she sang; "But whoever treasures freedom, like the swallow must learn to fly." She sang a song he rather liked, about a mine caving in, in Nova Scotia. She played the same thin strum on the guitar for that one that she had played for the others, but Jeff could hear in the song itself how the guitar might sound behind the melody line, how it should sound, strong and rhythmic: "For all their lives they dug a grave, two miles of earth for a marking stone, two miles of earth for a marking stone."

The guitar didn't sound so good, but Melody's voice—low and sweet, holding onto the notes—poured over him. She sang as if she believed each and every word. Her eyes shone with sincerity and she curved over the instrument like a flower bending in the wind.

Jeff watched and listened, basking in his own feelings: of being with his own mother, who wrapped her love around him; of being—strange as it seemed—home, where he was welcome; of waking up to a world where his help was needed to right what was wrong; of lying on soft grass under trees hundreds of years old beside walls that his ancestors had built; of being logy with the perfumed heat of the day.

Melody had to go out to a party that night. She piled her hair on top of her head, put on a lacy blouse and a long patchwork skirt, and kissed Jeff good night. "I have to go," she said. He didn't mind and said so. "See you in the morning," she said, her hand lingering on the top of his head just as his eyes lingered on the place where she had been standing, long after she had gone out the door.

He sat with Gambo and the two aunts in a living room dominated by a big color television set. Gambo held the remote control box in her hand, and she turned the sound down so that she could talk with Jeff, who sat beside her on a satin-covered love seat. The two aunts had straight-backed chairs drawn up close to the television screen.

"You're a Boudrault and you don't even know what that means," Gambo said. "There's so much to tell you." Jeff looked alert and concentrated on not being distracted by the moving figures on the screen at the corner of his vision. Gambo folded her hands on her lap. The large diamond ring she wore on her left hand glittered. On her right hand, a ring of small diamonds surrounded a flat green stone. Her eyes followed Jeff's glance.

"An heirloom." She held out her right hand for Jeff to look more closely at the ring. "My great-grandmother's engagement ring, made to order here in Charleston. She loved jade. Her collection of jade figurines is in the bank now—the cost of insuring it is prohibitive, over sixty pieces, each exquisite. The goldsmith worked her initial into the setting, but you can only see that under a magnifying glass, the letter D. They say the goldsmith was in love with her. Of course, everybody was: she was a great beauty in her day. We had a portrait, but like so much else it has been lost to us. I never saw her. She died young, in childbirth, but this ring my grandmother left to my mother, my mother to me. Dolores, her name was Dolores. This other"—she held up her left hand—"was my engagement ring and I always wear it. But the jade is dearer to me as the years go on. He was killed, you know, in the First War, and I was left with my memories and the one child. Just as Melody's poor father was killed in the Second War. The Boudrault women have married young. They have not been fortunate in their marriages, not fortunate at all." Her voice was dry, cracked like fine china after years of wear. She went on and on, until Jeff had a sense of family spreading out around them endlessly, and only an hour later, when she was lost in reminiscences, did he understand that the names she mentioned, the people she spoke of, were most of them long ago dead. The family spread not out and around, but back, back into time. At last, she looked at him and said, "I feel—as if I can pour myself into you, everything I've learned, everything I know, and you will take it on into your life." Then she rose and withdrew from the room. The aunts—only they weren't aunts, Jeff remembered, but cousins from different branches of the family—remained where they were, staring into the television, chattering like birds to themselves. Jeff too went upstairs to bed.

In his room, he changed to pajamas, folding his clothes neatly into the drawers, putting soiled socks and underwear away. He went down to the bathroom, peed, lowered the toilet seat, brushed his teeth, then washed his face so that he could have the pleasure of drying it on the thick, soft towel. The night was too warm for even a sheet.

There was something about the house and the women in it that made him feel contented, as if to be contented was something you actually did. He thought lazily that he would figure out what it was and lay back on the softness of the bed, under the dark air. But he fell asleep.

After the first couple of days, Jeff didn't see so much of his mother, unless she took him with her to a meeting or to help with stuffing envelopes or distributing posters. But her presence marked the day for him. She knew, somehow, what he wanted her to do, or say, as if she could read his mind and know how he was feeling. It wasn't that Melody did exactly what he wanted to do, but that everything she did made him feel good, feel loved. It was as if she could see what he saw the way he saw it; as if they were close, even when they weren't actually together. Whenever they were together her eyes shone with affection and pride. He knew he was doing the right things for her, learning about discrimination and pollution, being no trouble to Miss Opal, who praised him for his personal neatness, good appetite, and gentlemanly manners. Gambo talked to him and talked to him, until Jeff had pieced together the names and events so that he could follow her conversation and ask her the questions she wanted to answer. The aunts seldom spoke, but he was conscious of their admiring and approving eyes. During the days he wandered around the historic parts of the city, or traveled by bus to scenic spots beyond its industrialized outer ring, to see plantations and gardens. He had, in the first days with Melody, spent all of his money, even the four dollars left from Brother Thomas's ten dollars when she had bought the most expensive possible bottle of local wine for him. However, he found that Gambo was more than happy to finance an expedition. If he told her at breakfast how much he needed, she would take out her black change purse and give him the dollars he asked for.

Jeff learned the songs Melody liked, until he could sing with her, and in the late afternoons or on evenings when she was at home, they sang together. She started to teach him how to play the guitar, then didn't have time, so gave him the books she had used. He spent long hours with the instrument, conscious as he held it that she, too, had so held it. He placed his hands where she had placed hers and could almost feel the imprint her hands had left, warm beneath his own. His sense of contentment continued and became the tone of every day. He listened and learned.

Even Miss Opal had stories to tell him of growing up in the old city and the life of the black communities on the nearby islands. Miss Opal lived now in a public housing apartment with her grandson, Willum, whom she had raised since he was five, when his parents both moved up north to take better jobs. Willum was in high school and gave his grandmother a deal of trouble. Miss Opal didn't complain about Willum. This was the way men were, she seemed to say; you had to give a young man plenty of freedom. When the devil got into Willum, she prayed for him, and chuckled over the scrapes he got into and saw to it that he was punished too.

Miss Opal called him Jefferson, as did Gambo and the aunts. His mother called him Jeffie. He had asked her what he should call her, and she told him Melody, "because I'm your mother but I really want to be your friend." Her name, Melody, sang within him, like the music he could sometimes win out of her guitar. The slow days passed. Jeff passed through them, a Boudrault in his own country. Their general history was his own history, too, the story of his own family was part of the history. His ancestors, all the Boudrault men, had stepped in their long boots where he stepped now or riding tall horses.

Jeff knew, when July turned to August and the long August

weeks went by, that he would soon be going back to Baltimore, but even as the day of his return grew closer he could not imagine it. In his final week, he took to traveling farther out from the city. He rode the bus down around John's Island, then once all the way to the end of the southern line. The bus stopped at a crossroads, by a general store. Jeff got off and walked, heading away from the city, passing rickety houses up on cinder blocks, where clothes blew in a steady breeze, crossing between long fields of vegetables, walking under a tunnel of live oaks that arched over the roadway, where Spanish moss hung down like furry icicles. The trees were not tall and straight like the great northern oaks, but bent and convoluted. Their leaves grew small and thick. The hanging moss draped down from them, melancholy but not heavy.

Jeff walked on and on. He came at last to a broad marsh, through which a narrow creek cut. Beyond it, a line of low trees, palms and pines, marked one of the sea islands.

If he had a boat, Jeff thought, he would like to go over and explore the island. It stretched as far as he could see beyond the marsh. It looked like a different world; it looked tropical.

It was late in the afternoon when he returned that day, but nobody questioned him, nobody criticized his dusty legs or long, unexplained absence. Melody had gone out to a cocktail party and would not be back until much later in the evening; he was in time for dinner, so Gambo and the aunts had not been disturbed. They did not even ask him where he had been, what he had been doing, as if whatever he had done, wherever, must—because he was himself—be as it should.

The next day Melody took him to the bus. She had exchanged his airline ticket for a bus ticket, saying that the Professor had no sense of money, that there were better uses for the extra dollars.

Jeff's bus, which left Charleston at five in the evening, would take sixteen hours to make the journey to Baltimore. They stood beside the big Greyhound saying good-bye. With his eyes, Jeff drank in his mother's face. She held both of his hands in hers, and her beautiful gray eyes filled with tears. "You never met Max, and he wanted to meet you," she said. Jeff didn't know what to say. "I've been so proud of you, Jeffie. And you've been happy, haven't you?"

Jeff agreed, although happy wasn't the word he would have chosen to express the wonder of the summer. The driver leaned down and urged Jeff into the bus. Melody wrapped her arms around him and kissed his hair. "You have money?" she asked him.

Jeff shook his head.

"And I don't have any with me," she wailed. "Oh, Jeffie, what a bad mother I've been."

Jeff smiled at her. "No, you aren't, Melody," he said. "It doesn't make any difference, I won't starve to death in a few hours."

He had to climb onto the bus, then, and find a seat. By the time he was settled by a window she was gone.

Jeff sat alone, toward the back of the bus, beside the window. Few other people rode on it. The bus went west on the highway out of Charleston. Once they had left the city, they were traveling through a scrub pine forest and then, as they turned to head north, over flat land—flat fields, flat marshes, little flat ponds up against the highway. Slowly, the late afternoon light faded into the golden shades of sunset.

Going from Charleston, which lay behind him, to Baltimore, which waited ahead, Jeff felt not so much that he was traveling as that he occupied one single place, which rested between the other two. He looked out the window.

It was not simply going from a warm to a colder climate, or from his mother to his father. It was also going from one self to another. In Charleston, he was Jeffie, Jefferson, Melody's son, the last in a long line of Boudrault men. In Baltimore, he was Jeff Greene, self-sufficient and reticent, no trouble at all, occupying his corner of the world. But he knew now how it felt to be loved, to be happy.

The bus rumbled on.

One of the small ponds came up into view. A solitary blue heron stood at its edge, half-hidden in the pale marsh grass. The heron's legs were like stilts under its clumsy body. Its dusky feathers hung shaggy, ungroomed. It was perfectly motionless. Its long beak pointed down from a head both unnoble and unbeautiful. Its beak aimed down into the still, dark water. The heron occupied its own insignificant corner of the landscape in a timeless, long-legged solitude.

The bus swept past the pond. After a while, the sun completed its setting and darkness came up beyond the windows, a darkness lit by the occasional farmhouse window, the occasional crossroads, the occasional sign, the occasional town.

Jeff sang Melody's songs to himself, under his breath, under the rumble of the motor. He thought that someday, maybe, he would have to choose between his parents, the two of them. At the thought, his heart beat painfully in anticipation: he knew who he would choose, he knew why, and he said her name.

CHAPTER 3

Jeff climbed down the steps of the bus. He didn't see the Professor. He had picked up his suitcase and stood looking dazedly around—before he caught the eye of a short, round man in a black suit, who was waving to attract his attention. A clerical collar shone white around the man's neck. Brother Thomas. Jeff's suitcase felt heavy.

"Welcome back, welcome home," Brother Thomas said. "Your father asked me to meet you. You look taller than I remember; have you grown? And tan too; did you have a good time? The car's right outside, unless somebody's slashed the tires or removed the engine. Whatever made you take the bus back? How was the trip?"

Jeff tried to put an answering expression on his face. He followed the short figure through the waiting room and out to the street. He walked into a wall of heat, hesitated, then forced himself on. Brother Thomas put Jeff's suitcase in the trunk; Jeff collapsed weakly into the front seat. He had stopped being actively hungry some time in the middle of the night, but ever since then he had felt as if he was getting paler and paler. He knew he only had to wait until they got to the house to eat, but the closer that time came, the less he felt the strength to hold on that long. He leaned his head back against the car seat. He closed his eyes. He was thirsty, too, so thirsty his tongue felt twice as thick as usual.

"I can't sleep on buses either." Brother Thomas spoke beside him. Jeff opened his eyes, turned his head. "Planes, I can, and trains and cars. But not buses. I don't know what it is. Do you feel all right?"

"Just hungry," Jeff said.

"Didn't you get enough breakfast?"

Jeff smiled at that and shook his head.

"Did you get any breakfast?" Jeff shook his head. "Why not? But what about dinner last night, did you have dinner?" Jeff shook his head. "The bus must have stopped, they always do; why didn't you get out and eat something?"

"I didn't have any money."

Brother Thomas opened his mouth, then closed it. He pulled the little car out into traffic. Jeff closed his eyes again. The air steamed and smelled thick with exhaust fumes. The noise of traffic rang in his ears.

Brother Thomas pulled the car to a stop and Jeff opened his eyes. They were in the parking lot beside a small stucco building. Jeff wanted to protest that he really wanted to get home and eat, but he didn't have the strength. "Come on," Brother Thomas urged him. Jeff obeyed.

Brother Thomas led him into a restaurant, where they sat at the counter to order eggs, sausages, fried potatoes, toast, juice and milk for Jeff, and a cup of coffee for Brother Thomas. Jeff gulped down a glass of water, then another. When the food came, he ate unhurriedly but with full attention. When he had finished, he could feel the energy being carried around his bloodstream. He turned to his host, whom he discovered staring at him. "Thanks," Jeff said. "Really. I was hungrier than I thought." He picked up his water glass and emptied it again.

"I wish I could eat like that and not put on weight," Brother

Thomas said. "You do look better. Less like a cooked noodle. Did you have a good time?"

"Yes. I've got a bottle of wine for you. In my suitcase. My mother"—his heart lifted at the word and at the memory—"helped me pick it out."

"Ready to go?" Brother Thomas put a five dollar bill down on top of the check.

"I'll ask the Professor to pay you back. I'm sorry," Jeff said.

"Nothing to be sorry about," Brother Thomas said. They went back to the car. "He really wanted to meet you, your father. In fact, we were going to have dinner at the airport tonight, when your plane came in, all of us. There's a pretty good restaurant out at the airport. But he had a faculty meeting this morning." Jeff shrugged. Brother Thomas, his face blotched by the heat, beads of moisture on the bald top of his head, didn't say anything else about it. "Was your mother as beautiful as ever?"

"She really is," Jeff said. His words were caught up in a terrific yawn.

"You can tell us all about it, tonight," Brother Thomas promised him. He made sure Jeff got into the unlocked house then drove off, waving aside Jeff's thanks.

In the narrow hallway, then in his own small room, unpacking his bag, Jeff had a strange sense of disappointment. It wasn't because the Professor hadn't been there to meet him; maybe it was because summer was over, or because the house was so—dark and small. Jeff fell onto the bed in his underwear and fell asleep. Heat lay over him like a wet woolen blanket.

When he awoke, it was late afternoon and his body was bathed in sweat. For a long moment, he did not quite know where he was. Then he opened his eyes. The cracked and yellowed paint on the ceiling, the cramped room, the window framed by limp curtains and itself framing a view over rooftops to the flat surfaces of distant buildings, the sulfurous sky—he sat up in bed. Everything looked dingy, although it looked also as if it had been recently cleaned. Jeff felt the little house pressing close around him.

He went to take a shower. From downstairs, he heard noises. In the shower, which he ran cool, he concentrated on folding close in around himself the remembered contentment of the summer, like armor against—he couldn't name it, but it threatened him. He summoned up Melody's image, he summoned up her voice; to himself he sang her song about the calf being taken to market and the swallow soaring above.

Jeff dried off, stepped back into his underpants, and went to put on a shirt and a pair of shorts. He combed his hair in front of the mirror. Glancing into the glass, he caught his own eyes: gray, a smoky gray circle rimmed with darker gray at the outside, faint darker gray lines radiating out from the pupil; the eyes were circled by thick dark eyelashes; they were large eyes, a rounded almond shape. He stared at them, his glance going from one to the other mirrored eye, surprised.

These were his mother's eyes. His eyebrows did not arch over them, as his mother's did, but were straight. His hair lay flat on his head; his mouth was broader, thinner than Melody's. But the shape of the face—he almost traced it in the mirror with his finger—the straight, narrow nose, the chin, was very like hers. He looked back into his own eyes, a gray so deep that it did not ever change colors. They were like hers, they were hers. He felt almost as if he could convince himself that he was looking at Melody, that she was with him now. He hugged the idea to himself and went downstairs.

The Professor sat in the kitchen, and Brother Thomas stood

at the sink, peeling potatoes. The back door stood open. Both windows were open. They were trying to relieve some of the heat that poured out of the oven. Jeff smelled roasting beef.

The Professor studied him for a moment with mild blue eyes behind big glasses. Jeff studied his father. Finally Jeff said, "It's hot."

"That it is," the Professor agreed. His face was flushed and not tanned. "Did you enjoy your summer?"

"Yes," Jeff answered. "Did you?"

"Yes," the Professor said. Jeff sat down. Brother Thomas continued peeling potatoes, then he put them in a saucepan to parboil. He turned around to face the two at the table.

"Is that all you have to say?" he asked them. "Well, I've got questions. You two may be incurious by nature, but I'm not. Shall we open Jeff's wine?"

When they each had a tall glass of wine, Brother Thomas proposed a toast, "To Jeff on his return." He tasted the wine solemnly. "Your father had a quiet summer," he told Jeff. "Work, work, work. Drone, drone, drone. Buzz, buzz, buzz." He looked at the Professor as he said this, his expression friendly.

Jeff's father didn't seem to mind the teasing. "And Jack is a dull boy," he said.

Brother Thomas smiled. "Well, you didn't say anything. 'Did you have a nice time? Yes, how about you? Yes.'" His voice as he mimicked them was flat, monotonous. "For all he knows you spent the summer in and out of jail."

"On what charges?" the Professor asked.

"I don't know, Horace, inciting to riot, being a public nuisance, you know, your everyday criminal charges. Murder and mayhem."

Jeff looked at the two men, surprised, amused. They had

always talked like this but he had never heard the undercurrent of joking before. He had changed, he thought, Melody had changed him. His hearing the joking was because of her, his enjoyment of their conversation was because of her.

"Moral turpitude," the Professor suggested. "I always liked that, that and breach of fiduciary trust."

Jeff tasted his wine and remembered something. "I spent the change. But I'll pay you back," he told Brother Thomas.

"Don't worry. What did you spend it on? Or, how did you like the South?"

"I liked it fine," Jeff said. "Gambo's house is—old and big." He looked around his own kitchen, seeing the smallness of it, the black places where white porcelain on the stove and sink had chipped away, the yellowed paint on the walls and cupboards, the musty brown linoleum floor. He thought, looking at the Formica table and the slightly rusted stainless steel tubing of the chairs they sat on, of Gambo's dining room, with its long, polished table, its high windows, the china and silver set out on lacy mats.

"You look like sleeping beauty, waking up," Brother Thomas said.

Jeff flushed, and smiled. He didn't look at his father. "It's all so old and beautiful. Even though it's hot, it's not hot in the same way, because of the trees and grass and the bricks and the breezes off the harbor." He couldn't explain how the large airy rooms made him feel.

"And who is Gambo?" Brother Thomas asked. "No, first, why did you take it into your head to come back by bus? I gather"—he turned to look at the Professor, who nodded agreement—"that you refused to fly."

Jeff didn't know what to say. "It doesn't cost as much," he

explained to his father. The pale blue eyes behind glasses showed no expression. "And we could walk to the bus station. She doesn't have any money, not very much, I think." The eyes flickered, then returned to expressionlessness.

An uncomfortable silence occupied them. Jeff looked at Brother Thomas, who was staring at the Professor, and the man's brown eyes looked surprised, but he didn't say anything. Jeff knew he had said something wrong; he'd forgotten the rules for this house. He couldn't be sure what was wrong about it, except that something was. But he wasn't going to tell on Melody.

"Gambo's my great-grandmother," he said, to change the subject. "She's a Boudrault, that's an old family; she knows all about her ancestors. She told me about them. It's her house, down on the Battery—that's the old part of the city. I guess"—he decided to say the words boldly—"my mother lived there when she was growing up." He looked at his father.

"I never met Gambo," the Professor told Brother Thomas. "Melody"—he looked at Jeff as he said her name—"used to go down in the summers for a long visit, but I never went. I gathered that Gambo's always lived in Charleston, a rather wealthy family, something of a southern belle. She must be pretty old now, although I think she was married young—not that old really, if her husband died in 1918, not at all old for a great-grandmother. In her seventies? Jeff, do you know?" Jeff shook his head.

"She doesn't look as old as the aunts," he offered.

"The aunts? What aunts?" Brother Thomas asked.

Jeff tried to explain about the aunts who were really cousins, and then about the mornings and how the air was sweet and fresh. He talked about the shaded streets of the city and the outlying plantations, restored so you could see what life had been like. They ate roast beef and oven-roasted potatoes, and the two men finished the bottle of wine. Brother Thomas asked Jeff questions and Jeff answered them.

"What did you do all day?" Brother Thomas asked. Jeff told him. "What did you like best?" Brother Thomas asked. "I liked it being so beautiful," Jeff answered. "I like playing the guitar." He didn't mention other things he had liked, the fluttering attentions of the aunts, his great-grandmother's way of telling him and telling him that he was a Boudrault of Charleston, Melody kissing him good night.

"Are you going back next summer?" Brother Thomas asked.

Yes, Jeff wanted to answer, wanted to be able to answer with confidence. But "I don't know," he said.

"You never can tell with Melody," the Professor told Brother Thomas, his eyes on Jeff.

Jeff didn't argue, but he knew what he knew.

Jeff wrote his thank-you note to Gambo right away, and after a week, when school had opened and he had something he could write about, he wrote a letter to Melody. He made it as interesting as he could—telling her about his classes and teachers, especially that there were no women teachers because he thought that would interest her. He thought he might get an answer after a week, and for the last two weeks of September he waited impatiently every day to get home and look at the mail. The Professor usually got home first, because he had scheduled all of his classes in the morning that year, to clear away the afternoon and evenings for work, he said. But in the pile of magazines and advertising on the kitchen table there was never a letter for Jeff.

Jeff thought maybe his letter had gotten lost. "Do letters get lost?" he asked his father.

"Sometimes," the Professor said. "Not usually."

So Jeff wrote again. He spent a long time planning what he would say, several days, to gather the most interesting topics. That way he could always be thinking about Melody. He sang to himself, sang the songs she had sung to him, and that also kept her close. "I wrote you before," he wrote, "did you get the letter?"

While he waited for her answers, he started reading about the South. He found books in the library about the Civil War, first, about Lee and Beauregard, Manassas, the burning of Atlanta. He read *Gone with the Wind.* Then he found books about colonial days and the South during the Revolutionary War, Marion the Swamp Fox, the Oglebys of Georgia. He hurried through his homework so that he could read. During the school day, he thought about the South and himself as a Boudrault, because that also was thinking about Melody. His grades went down further, and the teachers said he was daydreaming during class. The other boys formed themselves into friendships and ignored Jeff. He played soccer, if they needed someone, but always ate lunch alone.

But his mind was on Melody, remembering, holding her close. He knew that if he didn't hold the memories close they would drift away, and she would drift away. The Professor gave him five dollars a week for allowance, and Brother Thomas gave him ten dollars for his twelfth birthday present, so after a few weeks Jeff had enough money to go to a pawnshop and buy himself a guitar. It was a heavy old steel string guitar, a Stella. At first, when he played it for too long a time, his fingertips would throb with pain and sometimes the tips would bleed. Then he learned how to use a flat pick and developed callouses on the tips of his left hand. After a while he could play for as long as he wanted.

And still Melody did not write him a letter. Jeff didn't think about that. He thought instead about love, and if you loved someone—well you just loved them, you didn't love them just if they did what you wanted, like write you letters. You either loved them or you didn't. He wrote her another letter at the beginning of November, this time with news of his guitar. He told her that when he played it he thought about her and that was why he liked it so much: that was the truth. One rainy November day, during Civics, he had an idea. "What if you write letters and the person has moved or gone away?" he asked the Professor that evening.

"Then the letters are returned to you," the Professor said.

"So if they don't come back they've been delivered."

The Professor nodded. "Why are you asking? Are you considering a career in the postal service?"

Jeff didn't know what to say, so he didn't say anything. Melody had gotten his letters and she didn't want to answer, or she was too busy. Probably she was too busy, she did have a busy life, he'd been there and seen that. He felt his father's eyes on him and wondered if his father knew why he was asking; but he didn't say anything because he wouldn't criticize her. He would be Melody's knight, here in their scruffy little house, like old-fashioned knights who loved their ladies—sometimes without seeing them for years. But the knights were always faithful, no matter what. Jeff liked that idea, and he felt a little smile form itself on his face. Knights wore tokens, scarves usually, that their ladies had given them; and he had a guitar. He would, he decided, write to Melody every month, at the beginning, so she would know about him, about how he was faithful. If he made his letters interesting enough, she might answer. If she didn't answer, that didn't mean she had forgotten him. If she forgot him that was just because he was easy to forget. So he didn't have any right to have hurt feelings.

"Jeff?" the Professor asked, breaking in on his thoughts. "What are you thinking about?"

"Melody," Jeff answered, looking him straight in the eye, like throwing his metal gauntlet down on the table in challenge.

But the Professor just nodded his head, as if he understood, and went back to his hamburger. He changed the subject: "That guitar of yours—it isn't as pretty as some I've seen around campus. Does that mean anything about its quality?"

"It's not a very good one. But I'm not very good at playing it."

"Are there good ones?"

Jeff had spent a couple of Saturday afternoons hanging around instrument shops. But he didn't know his father was interested, so he hadn't said anything. "There are Gibsons, some of the old Gibsons are pretty good." His father still paid attention. "And the Martins, they're terrific, if you know how to play. I've never played on one, but I heard some people in a store. The wood on those is beautiful."

The Professor's eyes grew vague, and Jeff dropped the subject. Then the Professor said, surprising Jeff, "There's a man named Bream. Brother Thomas has tickets to a concert he's giving over the Christmas holidays. He thought we'd like to go."

"Okay," Jeff said. It didn't interest him very much, he'd never heard of the guy. His guitar was his link to Melody, his token; that was its value for him. "Is he a guitarist?" he asked, to be polite, because it was something his father seemed to want him to be interested in.

"He plays the guitar and the lute, I think. This is a lute concert. We thought you might like to hear him."

"Okay," Jeff said again.

"We wondered if maybe you'd like to take lessons."

"I don't think so," Jeff answered quickly. He knew how the guitar worked for him, just like looking into his own eyes in the mirror worked, to bring her close. He didn't want to risk any change. "Thanks anyway," he added.

The concert surprised Jeff, caught him unaware. It was given at the Peabody Institute, in a narrow auditorium room that was crowded with people. Julian Bream came onto the stage carrying his own chair to sit on, and the audience clapped for just a little bit, then stopped, rustling into an eager silence. Jeff couldn't see the musician clearly, just a figure on a chair on the stage, holding what looked like a misshapen guitar. But when he started to play and the music filled the air of the room, winding and weaving until it lay over Jeff like a net, Jeff almost forgot to breathe. It was like guitar music, the plucking on strings, the tones reverberated out from the belly of the instrument, the one hand on the neck, the other on the strings; but it rang like church bells, quiet church bells. Melodic lines, chords, harmonies—how the almost motionless figure could make such complicated music Jeff did not know. He felt the music enter his body and flow along with his blood.

Some of the pieces were slow, some in quicker rhythm, some were one simple clear line and others were dense progressions of chords. For a long time, Jeff gave himself over to the music.

Until he realized what he was doing and then he tried to stop. He resisted the notes as they called out to him, because he could hear how weak and thin Melody's songs were in comparison to this man's mastery. The concert was wonderful, but he wouldn't let it capture him. When he found himself sitting forward in his seat, he made himself lean back. He forced his eyes to wander over the rest of the audience rather than staying riveted to the figure on the stage. If he was Melody's knight, he could admit no imperfection in his service to her, no disloyalty.

"How'd you like it?" Brother Thomas asked him as they made their slow way out of the auditorium. "Isn't he something?"

Jeff nodded agreement and added, in honesty, "I've never heard anything like it. Thank you." Music with song was one of his links to Melody, and nothing would come before that; but he couldn't deny the truth, so he said, "It was wonderful."

CHAPTER 4

Jeff had sent Melody a scarf for Christmas, a green silk scarf painted over with pinks and golds and oranges, like a garden. She would have to write him a thank-you note for that, he thought, but that wasn't why he'd sent it. He sent it so that he would be perfect in his love.

They didn't celebrate Christmas at their house, not with a tree or stockings or lots of presents. They never had, Jeff guessed, since he couldn't remember any Christmases, even from when he was young. Usually, the Professor got him a present, a book—he'd gotten a fire engine one year, he remembered, with a ladder that went up and down. Since they'd been alone together, Jeff always got a present for his father, too, a book about wines, or a new and fancy corkscrew, or a keycase. This year, he'd gotten his father a belt, because the Professor's old one was cracked and worn where the leather had been too often rubbed. Jeff couldn't remember what he'd given his father last year, or what he'd been given. But the present for Melody felt to him like no other present he'd ever given, or gotten. He knew it was perfect, and perfectly beautiful. He thought about how much she would like it. When he thought like that, happiness swelled up warm within him.

On Christmas morning, Jeff brought down the box for his father when he came to make breakfast. Usually on vacation days they ate breakfast and lunch whenever they felt like it, because the Professor often worked late and slept late; but on Christmas Day they ate all three meals together. Jeff put his box, gift-wrapped by the store, at his father's place. When he heard the Professor stir upstairs, going into the bathroom for his morning shower, Jeff started to cook sausage links and broke eggs into a bowl. When everything was ready, he called up.

The Professor, dressed, his white hair damp on his head, came to the table empty-handed. He unwrapped his present silently and thanked Jeff, then ate his breakfast slowly. Jeff didn't mind not getting a present, but he was worried that his father might mind having forgotten. He wondered if he should say something to the Professor, to reassure him; he wondered if he could remember next year that they weren't exchanging presents any more. He ate as slowly as the Professor and wondered if Melody had opened her scarf yet.

The Professor cleared their plates from the table and poured himself a second cup of coffee. "Well," he said. "Merry Christmas." He sounded uncomfortable, and he stood uncomfortably beside the stove, holding his coffee mug awkwardly. Jeff tried to think of how to say to the Professor that he didn't care about getting a present, when his father abruptly left the room. Before Jeff had time to figure out—listening to the footsteps in the hall going down to the study—if his father was angry, or what, the Professor returned, carrying a large, flat box across his arms. He had wrapped the box around with red tissue paper.

"Merry Christmas," he said again, still uncomfortable. He put the box on Jeff's lap. He took his mug and sat down to watch Jeff.

Jeff looked at the flat box and then at his father. His father's discomfort was catching. "Thank you," he said. "It's not a book," he observed.

The Professor leaned his elbows on the table. As uneasy smile moved at his mouth, just a little. "Open it."

Puzzled by his father's strange mood, Jeff did. He took the paper off carefully, then pried up one end of the cardboard box. As soon as he saw the smooth curved strip of wood, he knew it was a guitar. He pulled it gently out of the box.

A Martin.

And one of the old ones.

He put it across his lap and laid his hands on it, touching it. The six steel strings stretched taut up over the belly and along the fretted neck. The frets and tuners glowed, their metal worn to a deep shine by age and by use.

Jeff ran his fingers all around its outlines, its deep curves, its straight lines. He plucked at low E and heard the mellow, clear reverberation of a perfect note. He looked up at his father, across the table. "It's an old one," he said. Then his voice choked and he swallowed. "May I be excused?" he asked quickly. He didn't wait for an answer because he could feel tears swelling up behind his eyes. He left the kitchen hastily. Halfway up the stairs, he remembered and turned back. He put his face just through the doorway. His father had been staring into the mug of coffee, his face expressionless. "Thank you," Jeff said. "Thank you," he said again. His voice sounded steady, but emotions pushed up behind his eyes as he repeated his thanks, and he rushed down the hall. The Professor didn't like tears and emotions—and it would be a rotten way to show how much he liked the guitar to throw all that emotion at the Professor, to show how he was feeling.

And he was feeling—Jeff sat on his bed just hugging himself—

he didn't know what he was feeling; it wasn't just happiness because it hurt him. It didn't hurt anywhere particular, but as if he wasn't large enough to hold the feeling and still he had to hold it. It was as if something he wanted so badly he didn't even dare to notice how he wanted it, because he couldn't ever have it, had come to him—just fallen out of the sky. He didn't deserve it. He couldn't understand how it happened now to be his. He couldn't even think, he could just feel.

Jeff got a pick and sat down again, holding the Martin. He put his fingers on the strings and started to play. He played a simple progression, A-D-E, and the perfect sound brought tears to his eyes again. He waited, then played again, the song that reminded him most of Melody. "On a wagon, bound for market, sits a calf with a mournful eye." After a few minutes he found his voice to sing it.

He played and sang the few songs he knew over and over. At last he realized how hungry he was and went downstairs, where he discovered it was well past lunchtime. The Professor emerged from his study to stand in the kitchen doorway while Jeff hurriedly ate a peanut butter sandwich and gulped a glass of milk, impatient to get back to the Martin. The Professor looked like he wanted to say something, so Jeff waited. Music rang inside his head.

"If you'd rather have a new one," the Professor said, "there's no trouble. I'd rather you have what you want."

Jeff felt laughter rising in him, and he let it ride through him. The last thing he wanted was a new Martin, not with this solid gold old one, made in better days by better craftsmen. His father's ignorance in suggesting that made him laugh; a clear bubble of happiness made him laugh.

The Professor's eyes flickered once, and his face didn't

change. He nodded, once, briefly, and walked away. Jeff heard the study door close behind him. Shaking his head, smiling to himself, he swallowed down the rest of the milk. He rinsed out the glass, then washed it and set it upside down on the rack to dry. He capped the peanut butter jar and put it away. He washed the knife he had used. But the flicker in his father's eyes had looked like hurt feelings.

Jeff stopped smiling. But that was ridiculous, the Professor didn't fool around with feelings, they weren't a part of his life. But what if—?

What if Jeff had gotten the greatest present anyone could have given him and the Professor thought he didn't like it. But he'd said thank you. Melody would have understood, he thought impatiently. But what if the Professor didn't.

Jeff moved thoughtfully down the hallway and stood before the closed door. He shouldn't, he knew, interrupt his father at work. But he *really* didn't want the man to misunderstand; because, after all, the Professor knew nothing about guitars. Jeff knocked on the door.

"Yes?"

So Jeff opened it and went in.

The Professor sat at his desk, in the middle of the room facing the door, working on a pile of papers.

"I'm sorry," Jeff said. He stepped into the room, one step, then stopped.

"Don't worry about it, it doesn't make any difference. We can go back tomorrow so you can pick out the right one," the Professor said.

"You really don't understand. Because it's the best present anyone could give me." Jeff hurried the words out because his throat was choking up again. "The old Martins are—they're wonderful, the way they sound. Much better than the new ones. I didn't expect—anything like that." To his horror, tears were in his eyes.

"I'm sorry," he apologized again. "I don't mean to be—emotional at you—I just—I just like it so much."

His father looked at him. "Thank you for taking the trouble to make that clear."

Jeff heard the humor in that and a little laugh came up through his choked throat. "Yes, sir," he said, smiling back, leaving the room, returning to his Martin.

By the end of the afternoon, calloused as they were, his fingertips throbbed. He had learned, among other things, that he was much more limited than his instrument. He wanted to learn more chords, more songs, more strums—he wished the stores were open so he could rush out and buy a couple of instructional books.

For Christmas dinner, Jeff roasted a chicken, made stuffing from a mix, cooked a package of frozen peas. He poured out a glass of white wine from the carafe in the refrigerator and called his father to dinner. They sat down in silence, and Jeff carved. The Professor couldn't carve a chicken without hacking it into unrecognizable, unappetizing slabs; when the Professor carved, the chicken looked as if it had been torn apart by some inner explosion.

"Not much of a Christmas dinner, is it," the Professor said.

Jeff was surprised. It had been years since he had thought about that. "We never do much for Christmas," he reminded his father. "We never did."

"That's true. But I wonder if we should have."

"I don't see why," Jeff told him. "It doesn't make any difference."

"You know," the Professor said, lifting a bit of breast meat to his mouth, "I don't think I ever realized that there's a lot of your mother in you."

Jeff didn't know what to say. "I'm sorry," he said, apologizing for the tears yet again.

"When she first loved me," the Professor said, thoughtfully, without expression, "when she loved me, I felt as if—I had swallowed sunlight. Like the sun was rising inside me."

Jeff just stared at his father.

"I've never felt so helpless, before or since. Happy, too."

"Then why did you get divorced?" Jeff asked.

"We're not divorced," the Professor told him. "But what I mean to communicate to you—however clumsily—is that you should not be sorry to be like her. She had a way of knowing how I was feeling; I don't know how she did that." He returned his attention to his plate. Jeff watched him for a minute before lifting his own fork again.

"You know, I never call you anything." He didn't look up.

The calm voice answered: "Thomas noticed that, years ago. I'm not the Daddy type, or Pop—I can understand your difficulty."

Jeff looked up.

"When you think of me, do you call me anything? More than just *he*."

"Yeah. Professor," Jeff answered, with a grin.

His father chewed. "Yes. That would do."

Jeff thought it might. "Yes, sir," he said, then tried it out, "Yes, Professor." Yes, that would do fine. "And Professor," he said; his father lifted his eyes again, chewed without speaking, "the Martin is perfect. I can't ever thank you enough."

"Good," the Professor said. "That's what I hoped. That it would be perfect, that is. Not that you would feel bound by everlasting gratitude."

* * *

Brother Thomas never came to see them on Christmas Day, because it was a holy day; instead, they had a special dinner on the day after Christmas. This year, he made them veal marengo, "A ragout, not a stew," he told Jeff as he cut a veal roast up into chunks. "With mushrooms and tomatoes, a little wine and the peel of an orange. Why don't you bring down that famous guitar of yours and give me a little musical background while I labor here?"

Jeff hesitated. He'd never played for anybody. "I'm not very good," he said.

"I don't mind, do you?"

"Well," Jeff said.

"Do you want to be better? Do you plan to be?"

"Sure."

"Then what's the harm?"

So Jeff brought the Martin down and played on it. Brother Thomas seemed to be listening at most with only half his attention, so Jeff forgot he had an audience. When it was time to set the table, Brother Thomas made his assessment: "You're not very good now, but I'll be surprised if you don't turn out to be quite good. Do you want to call the Professor?"

Jeff was pleasantly surprised. It turned out to be an evening of surprises, because Brother Thomas told them, as they sat full over empty plates, that he was going to England for a year to study at Oxford. He beamed at them, "Can you imagine it? The dreaming spires and me. Me and the dreaming spires."

"I'm very happy for you," the Professor said. "You must be pleased to have won the grant."

"Pleased—that's an understatement. This is Tommy Richardson from Peoria, whose father worked in an assembly line—the unsuccessful son, not the black sheep among the children, but certainly the maverick—you've been there, Horace, but I never thought I ever would."

Jeff looked up; his father had been to Oxford? Brother Thomas had been a kid named Tommy, whose brothers and sisters did better than he did?

"When do you leave?" the Professor asked.

"In a couple of weeks, which means I have to ask a favor."

"What's that?"

"Could you two give a home to my stereo while I'm away? The books and pictures I'll box, but the stereo—I'd like it to be used, it's better if it's in use."

"We could keep it in the living room."

"You could play it," Brother Thomas said. "There's room at the back of the kitchen, there, just as long as you keep the cover on when you're cooking—it's about the only room in the house with any space. Anyway, thanks. And then, if you'd come over during the summer . . . ?"

Jeff looked at the Professor. He didn't want to make any plans for the summer. His father smiled, shaking his head. "We can't possibly afford it, you know that. We can barely afford to live the way we do."

"Don't be such a stick-in-the-mud, Horace," Brother Thomas insisted. "Your salary isn't that bad, your expenses can't be that much. What've you got, a mortgage at least ten years old so the rates aren't high—"

"But I had to borrow the down payment too, from the University. I'm still paying that off, as well. With interest. And then, there were bills Melody had run up, and she'd borrowed some money so she could make donations big enough to do some good. She wanted to. I've pretty near cleared those away now, but there's the school, too, and living expenses. We don't have any savings,

Thomas. I'm really sorry, we just don't have the money."

"I thought you didn't have to pay for me," Jeff asked.

"That went out when you were in fourth grade."

"I'm sorry," Jeff said.

"It didn't make any real difference," the Professor said.

It wasn't just the tuition, it was also uniforms, books, supplies, lab fees, Jeff knew. He felt bad, because his father's money was being wasted. He wasn't doing very well in school, C's at the best; and somehow, over that first seventh grade semester, he had become a real nobody. He had gone from being nobody much to somebody nobody liked. He wasn't disliked, exactly, he was just in the way. It used to be that he was sort of there, on the playground for a soccer game, or at his desk in the classroom. Nobody minded him being there, but nobody actually wanted him there. Now, they would just as soon not have him there; not because he was disliked, but because he was in the way. Like a fly in the room. You didn't really mind the fly, you just waved it away. You didn't notice when it had gone. Jeff didn't think about school, except to dislike the careless tone of voice in which he was told to change his seat or that he wasn't welcome in some game. "Move it, Greene," one of the boys would say. Jeff never even bothered looking to see what boy it was. In classes, except that he seldom spoke because he heard faint sighs whenever the teacher called on him, it didn't make any difference to him. It didn't make any difference to him away from school. He had the guitar and now the Martin, he had his memory of Melody, and nothing could touch him.

Jeff wrote to his mother at the first of the month, January, February, March, April, May, and June. He gave up hoping for a response. He did get postcards from Brother Thomas occasionally, pictures of castles, or the pages of illustrated manuscripts, with an informative message and the signature scrawled at the bottom, *BroT*. But from Melody, nothing, not even after Christmas. Jeff didn't let himself think about that. The stereo sat at the back of their kitchen and often poured out music, because Brother Thomas had also left his records for them to take care of. Jeff became familiar with names like Mozart and Handel, Bach, Brahms and Beethoven, Shostakovitch, with their music, in which melody—song—was only a part of it. Out of his allowance he bought himself a couple of records of people who played guitar and sang: Joan Baez who reminded him of Melody; Pete Seeger, many of whose songs were familiar to him; Judy Collins. By listening, he learned to mimic some of what they did on the guitar; the Martin could do anything he asked of it. It could do, he knew, more than he asked of it, more than he could yet ask.

One day in May, Jeff finally asked his father whether he had any photographs of Melody.

"No, I don't," the Professor said. "I never needed them—I never had any trouble remembering her."

Jeff waited, but he didn't add anything to that. Jeff wondered why Melody had said so confidently that the Professor would have pictures, but he didn't ask.

Melody's name came up again at the end of the month, again over dinner, but this time because Gambo wrote a letter to the Professor saying, yes, of course they would have Jeff for the summer, asking when he would arrive. The Professor showed Jeff the letter, which was about two lines long and signed with an unfamiliar name, Mrs. Boudrault Melville. The handwriting looked old, thin and wobbly. It looked much older than Gambo did, and weak—as if she didn't have the strength to close her

O's or lift the pen cleanly off the page to start a new word.

"That can't be her name," Jeff said.

"Her husband's, she's a widow. I believe her name is Eulalie. Melody called her 'Gambo,' and I never met her. Do you want to go?"

"Yes. If it's all right with you. Did you write and ask her?"

"Well, I thought you'd want to, and I thought I'd waited long enough for them to contact us. I'll get the plane tickets. Unless you want to take the bus?"

"No," Jeff said quickly. Then he thought. "Unless—it's a lot cheaper, isn't it?"

"Not enough money to make any difference. I think, this time, I'll ask the airline counter to hold the return ticket for you to pick up. Unless you mind that?"

"Why should I? But Professor, how come you never met Gambo?"

The Professor shrugged. Then he decided to answer, but kept his eyes on the bites of rice he lifted on his fork, kept his face expressionless. "We had a quiet wedding, so she didn't come up for it. Then, Melody, when she visited her home, stayed for weeks and . . . somehow they were always inconvenient weeks. I taught summer courses in those days, we needed the money, and there was you to take care of. Gambo wasn't used to children, not little children. And then . . ." His voice drifted away, and he picked up his knife to cut meat off his piece of chicken.

"Professor, why did you two—separate? If it's any of my business," Jeff asked.

"I guess it is," the Professor said. Jeff knew he hadn't offended his father. "But I don't know how to explain it. Do you know what Tolstoy says?"

Jeff just waited. The Professor knew perfectly well he had no idea what Tolstoy said.

"Happy families are all alike; every unhappy family is unhappy in its own way," the Professor told him.

"That's an answer?"

The Professor chuckled. "I must admit," he said.

It was all right, Jeff knew. He knew he shared a sense of humor with his father. He hadn't always known that, but he had learned it. And he was going to spend the summer with Melody.

"I think," the Professor said, arranging his utensils side by side on the plate, "that I was a continual disappointment to your mother. From the beginning. At the beginning, she wanted a particular engagement ring—something like what her grandmother has. I never saw it, but it sounds impressive."

"It is."

"I couldn't afford that, of course, not with the down payment on this house, and she wanted a house, of course—and she didn't want a small diamond. I explained it to her, and she said she understood. But she didn't understand. And she understood less as time went on; she minded it, she was always disappointed. That's the kind of disappointment I mean. And this house wasn't what she wanted either."

Jeff heard that the Professor didn't want to say any more about it, and since he didn't want to make his father uncomfortable he didn't ask any questions.

"When do you think I can go down there?" he asked instead.

"A couple of days after school lets out?"

"Can I take the Martin?"

And he was thinking *Melody*.

CHAPTER 5

Jeff waited patiently at the Charleston airport. He didn't even mind the waiting, because it prolonged the pleasure of anticipation. He felt warm and eager, inside himself. He felt his own face smiling, and he couldn't have stopped it if he'd wanted to. He hadn't brought the Martin because it would have had to have its own seat and that was too expensive. But if that was all he had to give up for a summer with Melody, he didn't mind.

He couldn't sit still. He walked around the waiting room. This time he had arrived during the evening commuter rush and the big room thronged with people. Jeff stood by the windows overlooking the field, looking out to the hot sky, looking back across the crowded room to the doors. He wanted to hug himself.

It was almost two hours later and Jeff stood dreaming by the tall windows, half watching a jet taking off into a blood red sunset, the air shimmering behind the turbines, when he heard his name called. "Jeffie? Jeffie?" His heart beat fast. The sunlight within him seemed to explode. He turned around.

She stood back from him and had a camera with which she took two quick pictures. Then she lowered it and smiled at him. "Oh Jeffie," she said softly, and she hugged him tight. The camera hurt his breastbone, but he didn't mind that.

"Melody." He said her name, breathing in her perfume at the same time. She was smaller than he remembered, more delicate.

"You're growing." She smiled at him. Her eyes were just as he remembered, deep, steady gray, the dark eyelashes framing them, beautiful. But her hair—

"Your hair," he said.

"Do you like it?"

It was curled into a frizzy profusion, cut shorter so that it came just to her shoulders, and a layer of curly bangs covered her forehead. She stepped away and pirouetted around, so that he could see it from all sides. It rested around her head like a dark cloud. "Do you?" she asked, smiling into his eyes.

"You're beautiful," he said. Her laugh flowed over him, in the remembered way.

"Are you glad to be back? But we have to hurry, Max is waiting and he hates to wait; you remember Max—it's his car, but you never got to meet him, did you? We're already late—I guess you know by now I'm always late. Do you mind terribly? Where's your suitcase?"

Jeff followed her out the door. She wore a sundress, blue this evening, gathered in at her slender waist, and she was tanned. But she wore sandals with heels this time, and when she walked there was a delicate clicking noise to mark every step. She tucked one hand under his arm and led him to the car. He opened the back door and put in his suitcase, then followed it. He had barely closed the door when the car started off.

The man behind the wheel had mousy brown hair that hung around his collar. He had a long, skinny neck and his nose, in profile, bent sharply at the middle, as if it had changed its mind about which way it wanted to point. "Jeffie," Melody said, turning sideways so she could see both of them, "this is Max, the man in my life."

Intense blue eyes studied Jeff in the rearview mirror.

"How do you do," Jeff said.

"Don't you see now, he *could* come with us," Melody said to Max. She explained to Jeff, "There's a party over on Mt. Pleasant. Max? He's perfectly presentable."

"I told you, babe. We've had this all out; you aren't going to try it on me again, are you? You don't have to come with me, but I'll need your camera if you don't. It's no skin off my teeth."

"All right," Melody said, disappointed. "But we can stop and get Jeffie a hamburger, can't we? So I can at least have a little time with him?"

"I guess so."

"I'm really sorry, Jeffie, but—and Max is hopeless with a camera, I *have* to go."

"That's okay," Jeff said. "I didn't know you took pictures."

"I just started six months ago, or so. Max did an article on industrial pollution, and we wanted some pictures—so I got a camera. And then, it was so successful that I kept on with it. I even have a darkroom, down in the cellar; you'll see. You'll be proud of your old mother." Melody smiled.

"You're not old," Jeff said. He wondered if she was in love with Max, and he thought from the expression on her face when she looked at him that she was.

They sat at a booth in a diner, Melody beside Max, the camera placed carefully on the seat beside Jeff, who faced them. Max had a long, narrow face, out of which his blue eyes shone. His eyes were sky blue and intense, as if some fire burned behind them. Jeff could feel a kind of power coming at him out of those eyes. He wasn't comfortable.

Melody went to the bathroom. Jeff watched her walk away and then turned his eyes back to those blue ones—they were like the eyes of an Old Testament prophet, he thought, somebody who had lived in the desert and gone a little bit crazy from talking with God.

"How long you staying?" Max asked him.

"The summer, I guess."

"I was out of town most of last summer," Max said. It sounded like he was warning Jeff.

Jeff didn't know what he was supposed to say to that. "What business are you in?" he asked. He heard his voice cracking on the question.

"'What business are you in?'" Max's voice mocked him. "I'm a journalist, when anybody has the courage to print what I write. Freelance. When they won't, I'm a pretty good carpenter-handyman, or I do PR for people, lawn work, just about anything. Tonight I'm a society photographer for some dumb chick's engagement party. And what's your business?"

Jeff felt the man's hostility. He shrugged his shoulders, kids didn't have business.

"No, seriously, what's your name, Jeffrey? Jeffie's no name for a kid of—what are you, thirteen?"

"Almost."

"I don't know why anybody has kids, in this world. But then I guess she wasn't planning it, she just got pregnant so she had to get married. It wasn't as if she wanted to have a kid, or get married. But abortions were illegal then and she was such a straight chick—that's what she says anyway. I never believe half of what she tells me."

Jeff held the gaze of the probing blue eyes, but he couldn't speak. He didn't think his face was giving away what he was thinking.

"As chicks go she's not too bad. We've been together, off and on, for more than three years."

A waitress brought two cups of coffee and Jeff's supper. He didn't want to eat, but he made himself. Melody came back and slid in beside Max. "Are you two getting to know each other?" she asked, but her eyes watched Max's face for his response.

"Don't be any dumber than you can help," Max said. Melody looked across the table to Jeff and smiled apologetically.

"He's terrible, isn't he?" she asked. Jeff almost grinned in answer, but stopped himself by jamming hamburger into his mouth. "Jeffie, Gambo had a stroke in March, and she's weak. So it won't be quite the same. She stays in her room a lot of the time; they have a nurse on nights when Miss Opal isn't there. Her mind's all right, but her heart—I guess it was always weak. You'll be careful with her, won't you?"

"Of course. I didn't know."

"She was in the hospital for a long time—well, she's old and it's to be expected. Are you finished? We have to go. Max'll get two hundred dollars for this job, and we can't be late. We have to catch the guests arriving. Do you have any money to pay?"

Jeff did, his father had given him twenty dollars again.

"If I'd known it was the kid's treat I'd have ordered myself something," Max said.

"Don't be awful Max," Melody said. She put her slender tan hand over his on the table, the hand with the silver and turquoise rings. Then they slid out of the booth. Max wore a shirt and tie and blue jeans that rode just at his hips. He moved smoothly, like an athlete. He put his arm over Melody's shoulders; she smiled up into his eyes. Jeff passed her the camera and she slung it over her shoulder. "Let's get going. We have to drop Jeffie off, but that won't take long. I'm sorry Max, his father just wrote to say when he was arriving, he didn't ask if it was convenient."

"What the hell," Max said. Jeff followed them out of the diner.

They dropped him off on Broad, because the ten minutes taken negotiating the one-way streets to get to Gambo's house and then back again would be ten minutes too many, Max said. Jeff watched the car drive away, its two bright red lights at the rear, the two heads inside moving close together, as Melody shifted over to sit next to Max. She had said she would be very late and she'd see him in the morning. She had said he should go in quietly, so as not to disturb Gambo. "Miss Opal is waiting for you. See you in the morning, Jeffie." She reached back to lay one of her soft hands against his cheek.

She did love him, Jeff believed that; she wanted him to go to the party with her. They had the whole summer, after all. He picked up his suitcase and walked to Gambo's house. The dark air smelled of flowers, and the houses showed lighted windows above the high fences. He passed people walking toward the busier streets, he overheard soft voices in conversations that floated down from the second-story verandas. He entered Gambo's house by the kitchen door.

Miss Opal sat at the table, drinking a glass of iced tea, thumbing through a magazine. "You're late," she said, at the same time Jeff said, "I'm here." They greeted each other. He told her he wasn't hungry. He apologized for being late, keeping her late at the house.

"Oh, I sleep over here now, this is my home now," she said. "But you'll want to see Mrs. Melville."

"Is she feeling all right?" Jeff asked. "I didn't know she'd had a stroke."

Miss Opal nodded her head slowly. "She's mending. It'll take more than a stroke to kill off your great-grandmother. Your momma treats her like spun glass, but that's wishful thinking, if you ask me. Let's go let her know you've arrived. She's not what she used to be, though. You'll see that."

Jeff followed her down the passageway to the dining room. He set his suitcase by the staircase. The size, the symmetry, and the beauty of the rooms opened around him. He took deep breaths, to swallow it all at once.

Gambo sat with the aunts in front of the television. She held a cane in one hand and the remote control in the other. She looked older, about a hundred years older. She was dressed in silk and jewels, the diamond flashing on her left hand, the little jade adorning her right. Her hair was perfectly arranged. But her face looked bony, and her fingers moved nervously along the top of the cane, and her dress was loose, bunched in at the waist. Her skin was pale, and her eyes riveted to the TV screen. She lifted her cheek to his kiss. "You go on to bed now," she told Miss Opal. "There was no call for you to wait up for him, and you're tired. He's a Boudrault, we find our way home."

Her voice, too, had changed: it creaked, and she took deep breaths between sentences.

Jeff sat down beside her. "Hello, Gambo, you look fine," he said, even though she didn't. But the more closely he looked at her, the more she looked about the same, essentially the same. He felt as if he had never been away.

The aunts turned to him with twittering voices. "The boy's back," they said. Jeff got up and greeted them. They said hello, hello, and then their eyes flicked back to the television screen.

"Oh look, it's that new Japanese car."

"I saw one, last week, parked all afternoon, right out front."

"You didn't, you're making that up."

Jeff returned to Gambo. "They just get worse," she told him. "Someday, they'll have to go into a home, but not while I'm alive," she said. She read the expression on his face. "They'll live forever, not that I envy them, and they'll be taken care of. How did your mother look to you?"

"The same," Jeff said.

"Even with that hairdo?"

"Well," Jeff admitted. "I liked it better long."

"At least your taste is sound," Gambo said. "I don't know why she can't resist fads and fashions. It's that man, of course—with Melody it's always some man—and that one just doesn't go away. I wanted to meet your father, but Melody never would bring him down here. She said he wouldn't be comfortable in this setting, she said it was too rich for him, as if we were a chocolate mousse. I always thought she was afraid I'd win him away from her. I always did have a way with men. And Melody has a jealous streak—I've always suspected that."

Jeff didn't know what to think. "She's always beautiful."

"Beautiful," Gambo said. "Since it all comes to the same end, I'm beginning to wonder myself what even that's worth. In another five years I'll be just as brainless as they are." She indicated the aunts with a gesture of her hand that made her diamond catch the light and glitter. But her fingers trembled, and she caught hold of the cane again. "I told him it was too big, flashy, but he wouldn't have it," she said. "And in another sixty or so you'll be just like us. I don't know why we bother."

Jeff didn't say anything.

"Go away, Jefferson. You make me tired," Gambo said. She leaned her head back against the sofa and closed her eyes.

Jeff went upstairs to his own room. He unpacked his suitcase into the drawers. He changed into his pajamas and folded back the bedsheets. Then he turned off his light and sat by the window, looking out over the backyard to the familiar lighted windows, savoring the remembered sounds and smells. But he'd thought Gambo liked him, he'd thought he was welcome, he'd thought this was his real home. The disappointment tasted bitter, but he swallowed it quickly, because what Gambo and the aunts thought didn't make any difference. It was Melody, only Melody who mattered.

After a long time, he went to bed. He hadn't heard her come in, and he thought he would wait up until she was home safe, keeping watch over her even though she'd never know. But he fell asleep.

When Jeff went down to breakfast, Melody was not yet awake. Gambo had eaten and was drinking a cup of coffee, taking pills that she selected out of a tiny gold box set by her place. He said good morning to everyone, first Gambo, then the aunts. Gambo rang for Miss Opal to come and ask what Jeff wanted for breakfast. "You're going to have to amuse yourself, I don't know what you're going to do with yourself," Gambo said to Jeff. Her eyes were not friendly.

"I don't mind," Jeff said.

"Very generous of you."

"I'm really grateful to be here. I'm very glad you asked me," Jeff said. He didn't understand what he had done wrong, so he didn't know how to undo it.

"I didn't ask you, you asked yourself."

Jeff didn't know what to say. "I'm sorry," he said.

"As long as you understand that."

"I'm sorry you're feeling tired."

"Not tired, old. Young people don't understand so I can't expect you to." She breathed raspingly twice before continuing,

"I must admit I thought your father would know better."

Jeff thought she shouldn't talk, and he looked around at the long windows with their folded drapes, at the smooth, creamy walls and the portraits hung on them. He smiled at the aunts, who chattered with their heads together, casting sidelong glances at him. He heard Melody's footsteps on the stairs and he looked to where she would appear.

She stood in the doorway for a minute, slim and smiling, her eyes seeking Jeff's before she went to kiss her grandmother good morning. Miss Opal set a plate down before Jeff and he picked up his fork. Melody wore a flowered sundress and sandals and she moved as gracefully as wind over a garden of flowers.

"I'll never understand why you did that to your hair," Gambo said.

"I like it," Melody said. "I like the way it looks."

"It looks common."

"If you want me to, I'll grow it out again," Melody offered, her hand on the back of Gambo's chair.

"I've given up trying," Gambo said. She reached for the little bell again.

"You know, I'm going to eat in the kitchen," Melody said.

"Take the boy with you," Gambo said.

Jeff got up happily, carrying his plate and juice glass. He ate at the kitchen table, watching his mother ask Miss Opal for scrambled eggs, then sit down across from him while Miss Opal set the table with a fork and coffee cup, with a little bowl of jelly and a glass of juice. Melody didn't think there should be servants, so she always ate breakfast out in the kitchen, because she didn't think Miss Opal or anyone else should have to wait on her; Gambo didn't approve but Melody stuck to her principles.

"She's crotchety this morning," Melody said.

"What can you expect?" Miss Opal asked, beating eggs in a little bowl. "She never likes it when you're out with that young man."

"He doesn't come here," Melody said, "and she can't ask anything more than that."

"Oh well," Miss Opal said, "once she faces up to things, she'll be herself again. Facing up is the hard part."

"Well, I wish she'd hurry up," Melody said. "I don't know what she's got to complain about."

Miss Opal poured the eggs into a pan and stood with her back to them. "Just the usual things, and they're enough," she finally said.

"Jeffie, Jeffie. What would you like to do today?" Melody reached over to take his hand, which he reached out to have taken. "I've got to work in the darkroom for a couple of hours, developing, and then I'll have to run off prints this afternoon—how would you like to take your old mother out to lunch? Would you like that? It'll give me something to look forward to."

"Yes," Jeff said. "Yes, please."

"Can you amuse yourself this morning?"

"Sure. Can I borrow your guitar?"

"I sold it last fall. But I thought you had one of your own."

"I didn't bring it. That's okay. How come you sold yours?"

"You know, I can't remember. Miss Opal, can you remember?"

Miss Opal set a plate of eggs down in front of Melody, flanked with strips of bacon and slices of buttered toast. "You said you needed the money, that's all I remember."

"Well, there must have been some reason," Melody said. She ate hurriedly.

"I could come down and help you out in the darkroom."

"Oh no. No. Not today anyway. Are you interested?"

"Sure."

"Then I'll teach you, I promise, first thing. It'll be our project for the summer, okay? I'll meet you up here, about noon; that should give me enough time. I'd steer clear of Gambo if I were you. She's having a bad day. Why don't you take a walk?"

So Jeff did that, because he wanted to do what Melody wanted him to do. When he was doing what she wanted, they were connected—in a way—they were touching, even if they weren't really.

He wandered for a while, and then walked uptown, to one of the cemeteries beside one of the old churches, where he strolled along the stone paths, reading inscriptions. The high walls made it seem like an overgrown garden, and muffled the city noises just beyond. The air grew hotter so that even in the shade of live oaks and glossy magnolias it was uncomfortable. Jeff sat beneath one of the oaks and waited through the ringing of the church clock, which marked off the quarter hours as the morning passed on toward noon. The thick silence of the graveyard was broken only by the chiming of the clock, 9:30, 9:45, 10, as he waited; 11, 11:15.

He was a little early getting back to Gambo's. He could hear lunch being served in the dining room. He sat on the bottom step of the stairs and waited for Melody. By the time she finally appeared, the women had finished their meal and gone back into the living room, to watch the afternoon soap operas. Melody ran up the stairs past him, "I've got to wash my hands and get my purse, I'll be about two seconds. Are you terribly hungry?" She stopped halfway up, came back down to where he stood and put her arms around him, then kissed his head, just above the ear. "It's so good to have you back," she said, then ran up the stairs.

When they had ordered their lunches, after conferring about how much money Jeff had, she leaned across the table to smile into his eyes. Happiness welled up in Jeff so that there was nothing left of him but the beating of his heart and the gray of his mother's eyes. "What did you do this morning?" she asked.

It took him a minute to collect his thoughts. She laughed as if she knew the effect she had on him. "I went up to see the cemetery," he said.

"I missed you terribly, all the time," she said.

"Me too."

"You've gotten taller."

"Not much, only an inch or so."

"Did you like Max? Isn't he wonderful? I'm so glad you two finally got to know each other. Gambo can't stand him—you probably figured that out. She won't have him in the house. Isn't that perfect? Just like somebody in Faulkner's books? Well, he's not one of her southern gentlemen, he doesn't bow over her hand and make pretty speeches. But Jeffie, I have to go out of town for a week, just a week, I wanted to tell you. You don't mind, do you?"

He minded terribly. "No," he said. "Where are you going?"

"There's a folk festival in the mountains, the first annual South Carolina folk festival and fiddling contest. All the proceeds, after expenses, are going to the environmental group that's sponsoring it. I don't know if you've seen some of the eroded areas, the rural poverty—little children, Jeffie, who never get enough to eat, or medicine or shoes. Max wants to write an article on the festival and I'll take pictures. We talked it over and he said there wouldn't be anything for you to do, so it's better if you stay here with Gambo. That's all right, isn't it?"

"Sure," Jeff said.

"And it's only for a week. And I have a picture I want to show you, I want to show you all my pictures."

"I'd like that," he said truthfully.

"Maybe this afternoon; we're leaving tonight. I'm really sorry, Jeffie," she said, watching his face.

"I'll be fine. Don't worry about me."

"I wouldn't go if I thought I needed to worry about you. I expect—living with your father—you're used to being left alone. That man left you alone even when he was with you."

"I'll be okay, I promise," Jeff said. He guessed he knew what she meant about the Professor; he knew he didn't want to argue with her. "Melody?" he asked, then waited until their plates were set down in front of them. "Can I ask you a question?"

"You sound serious."

"It's okay, I'm not. I don't have to know."

"Go ahead, you silly goose, ask."

"Why did you marry the Professor? I mean—" Jeff couldn't think of how to finish the sentence, so he let it dangle. Max had said she was pregnant and had to. The Professor hadn't said that.

His mother nibbled at a potato chip, drank some of her iced tea. "He was so handsome," she said. "I was younger then—well, of course. Distinguished is the word I guess, he was so distinguished-looking. I was taking a course with him, and we used to laugh because he got so embarrassed if you tried to talk to him. He was so—good-looking, and shy and stand-offish. I thought about how lonely his life must be and the more I thought about it, I began to feel sorry for him. So I set out to be friends with him, just to see if I could, to see if I could make him like me. It was kind of like a challenge. And—well, when he talked with me he laughed and wasn't so dignified. He'd been so lonely and I made him happy. The poor old thing."

That made sense. Jeff could see how that would make her feel and she might decide to marry him if she felt that way. "But—then you left—" he started to say.

"I was so unhappy, Jeffie. He didn't notice, he didn't care. That horrible little house and all the stuffy professors and their horrible frumpy wives, and he didn't *do* anything to make things better. We never had any money—I always had to pinch pennies, everything, no matter how small. There wasn't ever enough. You don't know how that can wear a person down." Her eyes grew unhappy as she remembered.

Jeff felt so sorry for her he didn't know what to say. He wished he hadn't brought up the question at all. He was angry at himself for making her unhappy. "It's okay, really; I understand."

"I don't think you can," she said, her voice low and sad. "Sometimes, I don't think any man can."

"I don't mind," Jeff said. "But tell me about this festival; does it last all week? Who's going to appear, do you know?"

That cheered her up. "Max will, that's the important thing, for a whole week." She smiled at Jeff as if they shared a secret. "And Gambo would be livid if she knew." Then she mentioned a list of other names, some of which he had heard before, and the rest of the lunch went too quickly by.

Melody returned to her darkroom after lunch, telling Jeff to wait in the kitchen, please. Then she took him by the arm and led him with her to the cellar stairs, to whisper in his ear: "Don't say anything about Willum to Miss Opal. He's in jail, for five years—he was selling marijuana. But if he'd been white it would only be two years and—don't ask about him, okay? It breaks her heart."

But Miss Opal did want to talk about Willum, explaining how Willum couldn't help going bad, with the friends he had and his parents living so far away, with her having to work for their living, with the schools the way they were, and the job situation. "That boy—he never did have a chance," she said, stirring sugar into her cup of tea. "But I tell him, his old Granny won't desert him, he always have a home with me. I ask the Lord to spare me for that time."

"How old are you?" Jeff asked.

"Why, seventy-eight."

Jeff stared at her. "But you're older than Gambo. I didn't know you were."

"Well, I always was," Miss Opal said.

Melody came back upstairs to show him a print so fresh she held it in tweezers and let it drip onto the table. "Look, Jeffie, what do you think?"

It was the happiest picture Jeff had ever seen. The boy in the picture had just seen something that he'd always wanted to see and never hoped to. Whatever it was, it made his eyes bright and his shoulders, all of his body that showed in the photograph, looked like he was about to run toward it.

"But that's me," Jeff said.

"A candid portrait. Now will you believe I'm good?"

"The boy never doubted it, Miss Melody."

"I'll make you a copy," Melody promised him, "and Gambo too—would you like that? You can keep this one."

Jeff didn't know he ever looked like that.

"But I'm going to have to work downstairs all afternoon, I'm afraid; you're going to have to find something to do. We took hundreds of pictures last night. You can find something to do, can't you?"

Finding something to do was what Jeff did—for a month, because Melody was away from the middle of June to the middle of July, as it turned out. The trip kept getting prolonged, for a few days, or a week. Jeff figured out in short order that Gambo's stroke had altered her interest in him, somehow. When he asked her questions, she answered impatiently and always concluded with something about "you young people." She wanted to talk, that summer, with the aunts, and their conversations began with the question, "Remember when?" Jeff didn't remember, but he would have liked to listen. The women, however, looked at him as if he were eavesdropping, moved closer together so that he couldn't hear, or simply ignored him. He didn't know what he'd done wrong, he didn't know how to do it right. Miss Opal, busy keeping the entire house, had no time for him and refused his offers to help her with her chores. "She'd be furious to see that. She'd fire me, and then what would I do? And then what would *she* do?"

After the first four phone calls, Jeff stopped hoping that Melody would be home soon. The disappointment of hearing her voice on the phone, after he had been expecting her to walk in the front door at any moment, of hearing her explain what had happened, asking if he could stand it if she was away for another few days, promising to really be back on Thursday, or next Saturday. . . . It was better not to hope.

Instead, he kept himself out of the house, wandered around the city, did some sightseeing, and took to riding buses out as far as they went. Gambo asked him every morning where he'd be going, how much money he needed, whether it was raining or not. She wanted him to be away. "I'm too old to entertain children," she said, opening her black purse. "I don't know what your mother is thinking of."

Jeff had more money than he could spend that month, because his father sent him ten dollars every week, the bill wrapped around with the yellow lined paper the Professor wrote lectures on. The Professor also had something to say, some sentence. "Hope your weather is better than ours," or "Here's your allowance." Sometimes he included a postcard Brother Thomas had sent from England to Jeff. So Jeff could take Melody out for as many lunches as she liked, when she got back.

One day Melody did return and was there in the living room with Gambo and the aunts when Jeff walked in the front door. He didn't remember where he'd been when he heard her voice and saw her face, her eyes shining at him, her hair damp and curly from a shower. "Where have you been?" she asked him.

Jeff just let the happiness grow inside him.

"Nobody knew where you were," Melody said. "You shouldn't just go wandering off like that." She was angry.

"I'm sorry," Jeff said. "I told Gambo this morning."

Melody stood up and took him out into the front hallway to say, "You know she can't remember anything. Honestly, Jeffie, I thought I could trust you."

Jeff felt ashamed of himself, although he couldn't be quite sure why, and he hadn't noticed Gambo forgetting, just not being interested. "I'm sorry," he said, and then said it again. "I'm sorry."

She wasn't satisfied. "And I told Max I'd go with him out to Santa Fe, and now I don't know if I can," she told Jeff. "All you can say is, 'I'm sorry.' Just like your father."

Jeff just stared at her. He couldn't have spoken. He was confused, between guilt at failing her, dismay that she was going away again, and the desire that she not be angry at him.

"Well?" she asked.

He swallowed. "When?"

"We have to leave tonight and drive straight through, to get there in time. I had to wash and iron everything, and Miss Opal is so slow—it takes her ages to do anything these days."

"But Melody . . ." Jeff heard his own voice complaining and saw anger rise in her eyes again. He didn't protest any more. "For how long?" he asked.

"A month, maybe five weeks. It's a really important chance for Max. And you're here to keep an eye on Gambo for me so it's all right. If you weren't here I don't know how I'd get away."

Jeff made himself accept it, right then. He knew that if he waited even for a second, he would start complaining, and then she really wouldn't like him. "Okay," he said.

"Oh Jeffie, I knew I could count on you," and she smiled into his eyes. But her smile was as painful to him as her anger. He didn't know what to do. But he thought, if he was careful, he could keep a grip on himself until after dinner, until he was alone in his room. He held his face expressionless. "Sometimes," Melody said, leaning forward to kiss him gently on the cheek, as if to take the sting out of her words, "you really do remind me of your father. That's silly, isn't it? Come and watch me pack? We can catch up with each other. Oh, I missed you, Jeffie," she said. She looked like she meant it. He felt like she was telling the truth, even though he knew she must be lying.

When Jeff was at last alone in his room that night, he lay across the bed and cried. He didn't even take off his clothes or turn on the lights. He felt so bad—sorry for himself, and angry at himself for losing her—and helpless. He didn't know what he should have done, what he could have done. He felt—rolling over onto his back and wrapping his arms across the pain in his chest and stomach, pain that wasn't even real—as if he had been broken into thousands of little pieces. Broken and then dropped into some dark place. Some dark place where he was always going to stay.

Because Melody was going away, again. Because she didn't want to stay where he was. And he wasn't sure he could stand that.

He had never suspected how easy he was to break.

He couldn't think of anything he wanted to do. Ever.

Jeff made it through several long days, trying not to think. He mostly stayed up in his room. He did not come down for meals, but ate sandwiches in the kitchen if he felt hungry. Nobody paid much attention to him. He paid no attention to anybody, just struggled with the sadness that always threatened to overwhelm him into crying again. He was ashamed of himself, but he couldn't help it. So he stayed upstairs. He watched out his window, but what the weather was he didn't notice. After several days, he realized that with the exception of Miss Opal, nobody in the house knew he was there. Not really knew. If you'd asked them, he supposed they would have looked vaguely around and said, "Jefferson? He's somewhere around, isn't he? Or has he gone away?"

Because he was easy to forget, easy to leave behind—Jeff understood that. He had interested them for the one summer, but that was more because of being a stranger and the last of the Boudraults than because of what he was like. He'd misunderstood that.

Everybody could leave him behind. But that was okay, he decided, waking before dawn one morning when he had fallen asleep fully dressed on top of the bedspread. If nobody owed him anything then he didn't owe anybody anything. So at least he could do just what he wanted. If there was anything he wanted to do.

That morning he rode the bus along the same route he had followed on his last day last summer. Then he walked down along the same road, through the live oak tunnels. The island lay as he had remembered it. Jeff stood squinting at it over the broad field of marsh, over the narrow river. He wouldn't mind going out there, he thought. He was hot—he could feel sweat running down from his armpits, over his ribs. His hair stuck on his forehead. Bugs buzzed around him. If he had a boat.

Jeff walked slowly back up the road to the bus stop. There, he went into the ramshackle store where the screen was ripped and the dim air inside uncooled even by a fan. He bought himself a Coke from the white-haired black man behind the counter. A strip of flypaper hung in coils down from the ceiling, covered with dead flies. A fly buzzed around Jeff's ear.

"If I wanted a boat," Jeff said.

"Suh?"

"Like a rowboat," Jeff said.

"Whuffo?"

"Never mind," Jeff said. He drained the last of the Coke from the bottle. His sorrow was rising up in him again, and he needed to get outside.

"M'neighbor's boy—he got him a barque he be glad to get shot of," the old man said.

Jeff hesitated. He didn't know why he'd asked. He brushed at the fly that hovered near his ear.

"Come wi' me, suh. It's just a pace out around back."

Jeff followed him, going by oil drums that overflowed with

garbage, down a short dusty road to a line of five wooden cabins, built up on cinderblocks. Cars were parked all over the place, some rusting away on wheelless axles, some shiny new. A creek ran behind.

A younger man, who wore only denim overalls, led him onto a sagging dock. At the end, a flat-bottomed, unpainted rowboat was tied up. Its oars had weathered splintery gray. The man's skin glistened with sweat, his dark eyes barely looked at Jeff. He yawned and scratched at his neck. Jeff looked down at the boat.

It had one seat, just a board nailed across at the center. There wasn't any water in it, so he figured it didn't leak.

"She be fifteen," the man said.

"I don't know how to row," Jeff said. He didn't know what he was doing back here, anyway.

The man shrugged and walked back along the dock. Jeff walked with him.

"It's not hard to row, is it?"

"Nosuh."

"Fifteen dollars?"

"Yessuh."

"If I give you another five, can I leave it tied up here? When I'm not using it?"

The man shrugged. He turned and faced Jeff, looking over Jeff's shoulder.

"I'll bring you the money tomorrow," Jeff said.

The dark eyes finally focused on him. "I be here," the man said.

It took Jeff three days to learn to handle the little boat well enough to dare an approach to the island. By that time he could row with confidence along the creek that ran behind the cabins.

He had run aground on the shallow creek bottom often enough to know how little trouble that caused, had asked the nameless black man about currents and tides, had looked at a map of the area and found the island on it. He bought himself a hat to protect his head. Out on the water, the sunlight was reflected and it scorched his face and his eyes especially. He had also heard a couple of songs he'd never heard before. "They's gospel," the man had answered his question. "She sings over to the church." Whoever she was. But the man was no more curious about Jeff than Jeff was about him.

One morning, Jeff pushed himself away from the dock, turned the boat around, and rowed down the back creek, heading toward the island. He had sandwiches in a paper bag and two quart jars of apple juice. He'd learned how thirsty you could get out on the water.

He rowed down between standing marsh grasses. It wasn't long before he was out of sight of human habitation, out of the sound of human voices. He could see only the low wall of grass and the bleached sky above it. An occasional bird burst out of cover when he came near. He could hear the silence made by the surf breaking on the other side of the barrier island, by the plashing sound of his oars in the water.

Although the map he had looked at was clear in Jeff's memory and he turned north when the back creek joined the deeper creek that separated the island from the mainland without hesitation, the strangeness of the scene affected him. The tide was up and made the water look deceptively deep. Over toward the island, across the grasses, he could see the line of trees and underbrush: it looked wild and dangerous. He was afraid.

He was always a little afraid in the boat. That was, in fact, why he liked it. That fear came from outside, from the unfamiliarity of the place, from his being so far from people that if he yelled for help nobody would hear him. He slipped into that fear like slipping into the water to go swimming. Because the fear that came from outside distracted him from the fear that was living inside him. The fear inside him threatened at any moment to take him over and sweep him away, and the only way he could manage it at all was by avoiding it. In the boat, alone on the water.

That first day he went only half a mile up the main creek. Then he tossed over the ten-pound anchor he had purchased and sat. The boat swayed gently on the water of the narrow creek. He sat and looked around him and listened and became easier in his spirit as the scene grew familiar. This had been the pattern of his days on the back creek, too: he would move the boat out until he felt more frightened than he had courage to match; then he would anchor and wait.

Jeff ate his sandwiches, drank juice, and watched the slimy underwater stalks of the grasses grow visible as the tide ran out. He sat on the floorboards, his back against the side, watching and listening. A rustle of wings announced the arrival of one of the great blue herons. The bird landed a few yards up from the boat and proceeded to walk along the water's edge, its long beak pointing down. The bird's legs, more like pipes than legs, bent backward at the knee, so it looked like the bird was going backward or was trying to go backward when it was actually moving forward or like it could only move forward by going backward. Every now and then it would halt and stand motionless, then plunge its beak into the shallow water, shake its head two or three times, and swallow its catch, whole.

The blues were always alone, Jeff had noticed. They came at low tide to fish along the edges of the marshes. They stalked the shallows, their flat, elongated, triangular heads facing down, to where their prey hid. This blue hunted up about a hundred yards, then backed up until he stood camouflaged against the grasses. The blues were big, awkward birds on land; in flight they spread long wings out, tucked their necks in against their chests, and trailed their legs out straight behind them, looping across the land or the water.

At the end of the afternoon, Jeff rowed back down the creek, then along up to the dock. The last bus to town left at sunset.

It was a week before he actually landed on the island, tying the boat up to the poles of an abandoned dock that sat beneath the overgrown lawn of a burned-out house. There, the steep mudbanks were inhabited by land crabs. Their holes, as large as fifty cent pieces, made the steep brown banks look like swiss cheese. The crabs came out into the sun—to eat, Jeff supposed. When he had first seen them, from a distance, he had thought they were large beetles, and not until he had come so close that they scurried back into their holes had he recognized them. The first time he landed, Jeff watched the crabs for a cautious half hour before he brought the boat close enough to tie up to a piling. As he had deduced, they scrabbled quickly into holes when he set his foot on the mudbank and scrambled up its slippery surface to the weedy lawn.

For several days, Jeff stayed around the shell of the house, venturing up across what must once have been a well-kept lawn, where bushlike trees were overgrown with vines and the Spanish moss on the live oaks grew down to the earth like old men's beards.

Gradually, hampered by the occasional day of rain, Jeff explored inland, along a double rutted path he found leading away from the house. The tangled woods closed in over him, low myrtle bushes, palmettos at various stages of their life cycle, honeysuckle, pines. These days he wore jeans over his swimming trunks and a long-sleeved shirt, because the mosquitos bit mercilessly in the dense woods. He left his hat at the boat—the sun couldn't penetrate much into the semitropical growth. He walked along cautiously, a dead branch in his hand, and his fear at the strangeness and solitude never entirely left him.

He discovered a pond, a long, narrow pond so large it might have been considered a lake. Sitting at its side to watch a chameleon, his hand waving away clusters of gnats, Jeff saw a log moving on the shallow bank opposite: an alligator, as brown as the mud beneath the grasses, slipped into the water.

Jeff leaped to his feet and ran, thundering along the now-familiar path. Heedless of the noise he was making, he ran until he had climbed back into the safety of his boat. An alligator!

He sat on the wooden board, his head held in shaking hands. An *al*-ligator. He was sweating. His chest heaved. He'd never been so frightened in his life.

After a while, the sun made him so hot he stripped off his shirt and shoes, then his trousers. He lowered himself gently over the side of the boat, paddled for a minute, carefully keeping his feet from touching whatever might be on the bottom of the creek, and then hauled himself back up over the side, cooled.

An alligator. Geez. He'd never thought— He'd thought of spiders and snakes and even snapping turtles, but never alligators.

One of the songs he'd heard the woman in the cabins singing had an alligator in it: "When a gator hollers, folks say it's gwina rain." Jeff ate lunch in the boat that day and then rowed to the dock. He got back to the city in time to look up alligators at the library, to see how much the appearance of the creatures might curtail his exploration of the island.

He should have gone straight to Gambo's, as it turned out, because Melody was there. He didn't know that at first, entering the cool hallway and picking up the Friday note from the Professor. He didn't hear her voice, just the television. He opened the note, read a postcard from Brother Thomas about brass rubbings, unfolded the sheet of yellow legal paper, and pocketed the ten dollar bill. This note was longer, three lines of bold, slanted script. "I expect you in a couple of weeks. Let me know the day and time. Sold a book—imagine that—I'll tell you about it."

Only a couple of weeks. Jeff guessed he could manage that, and he thought he would feel easier once he got back to Baltimore. At that thought, the spacious indifference of Gambo's house to his presence started to swell out from his belly and threatened to take him over. "Sold a book," he said loudly within his own brain, "I wonder what that means." The Professor sounded excited, for him. Jeff thought maybe he would write the Professor a postcard and ask. He thought maybe he would go out right then and get one to send. And a stamp, he reminded himself, feeling his tension abate as he planned out where he would go to get them.

But just then Melody came to the head of the stairs. "Jeffie?"

Jeff didn't have the power to just get out. When she stood there, so close, her voice unsure and asking him, her hair curled around her beautiful face, it took all of his strength not to run up the stairs and throw his arms around her. "Hello," he said.

"Come on up, Jeffie. I want to talk to you. Privately."

She went into Jeff's room, where only the brush and comb on the bureau and the picture of himself stuck into the edge of the mirror showed that anyone lived there. He had put the picture up to remind himself—of what, he did not know, but when he looked at it the cold, wet feeling inside him froze to ice and was easier to handle. Melody sat cross-legged on his bed. She spread her skirt over her knees and patted the space beside her. Hating himself for his inability to resist her and to resist an insistently happy feeling, Jeff sat down. But he wouldn't look at her.

"Oh Jeffie." She put her hand under his chin and turned his face toward hers. "It hasn't been the way you wanted it to be, has it."

"It doesn't make any difference," Jeff said. All he had to do was remember how badly she had hurt him and he would be all right.

"And I'm going away again tomorrow, and you'll be gone before I get back," she said, her voice sad.

Jeff couldn't stop himself from asking. "Do you have to?"

"Yes, of course; would I go if I didn't have to? Max is going to do an article on an Appalachian community, on rural poverty—but don't tell Gambo that"—she smiled into his eyes, mischievously—"she think's I'm the one doing it. What she doesn't know won't hurt her. But what have you been doing? Oh, I've missed you and thought about you all the time," she said.

Jeff knew he couldn't believe her, but he wanted to believe her so badly that he did. "I could take you out to dinner, just the two of us."

At that she laughed and hugged him, pleased. "You do love me, despite it all. But we can't. It would hurt Gambo's feelings. You don't want to do that, do you? She has only us, you know that."

Jeff nodded.

"So we have to stick around here tonight, even though it

would be good to have just the two of us, just this once. But what have you been doing all this time? Miss Opal tells me you're out of the house and she doesn't set your place for dinner unless she's seen you. You're not getting into trouble, are you?"

"No," Jeff said. He opened his mouth to tell her about the island and the boat and the black families in their houses beside the back creek.

"You should have come with us." She didn't give him time to speak. "We were up in the mountains—well, the foothills—and it's a wonderful countryside. The pueblos are a disgrace, outhouses, garbage. Whole families live in one room where the smoke isn't ventilated. When I think what we've done to the Indians." She went on and on about New Mexico and what to do about the Indians out there, how much help they needed; Jeff listened and did not let himself think. Because she didn't even mean her questions to him. At last, she wound down. "Are you awfully sad to be going back to Baltimore?" she asked. "I always was."

Jeff looked over at the picture on his mirror.

"No," he said.

"Jeffie, what a terrible thing to say—after all everybody's done for you. I hope you don't talk to Gambo like that, it would break her heart. It breaks *my* heart a little, truth be told."

Something burst inside Jeff. "Don't lie to me," he said to his mother. "I don't believe you. If you really cared you'd have stayed here, and you wouldn't be going away tomorrow and lying to Gambo about it, and—" He was making her angry, he could see that. But he couldn't stop. "And I don't like the way you lie. You make it sound like the Professor is so terrible, but you're terrible yourself. What you do to people," he said. "Lying to them so you'll get what you want."

Big tears rolled down Melody's cheeks. Jeff didn't mind that.

He got off the bed and went to stand by the window.

"I've made you unhappy," Melody said. "I'm so sorry, Jeffie."

"I'm not unhappy," Jeff lied. "I just don't care."

"Like your father."

"Don't say that. Don't say it that way just when you want to criticize me. He's not so bad."

"Well, what do you think of a man who lets you nearly die of pneumonia because he just doesn't notice."

"Bronchial pneumonia."

"Bronchial pneumonia, plain pneumonia, what's the difference? I don't know how you can stick up for him. It just goes to show—"

"Show what?" Jeff asked, angry himself. He'd never had a fight with anybody, and it felt oddly good.

"Show how men always take their own side. I should have known better than to try to get you down here, but I felt so sorry for you—stuck with him and sick and nobody noticed, I cried myself to sleep when I first heard. I thought I could at least help you a little—but men always stick to their side."

"That's stupid," Jeff said. His voice was loud in his ears.

She jumped off the bed and stood with her hands on her hips. "Are you calling me stupid? You don't know anything, do you? You don't know anything about the world; he hasn't taught you anything up there in his ivory tower, safe and secure, not about the dangers or what really goes on, not about the way some people have to live or what we're doing to the world—and you call *me* stupid. Well maybe I am, I was surely stupid to marry him, that was about the stupidest thing I ever did. Unless having a boy wins the prize. I wanted a girl. You didn't know that, did you; but you should have figured it out. If you're so smart. If you'd been a girl I'd have taken you with me when I walked out on him. I thought you were a girl when I got pregnant, I was sure of it."

"Oh yeah?" Jeff answered right back. He didn't know what to say to show her that he knew she wanted to break him into pieces. And he could see that; she wanted to hurt him, as badly as she could. Then he thought of something. "Well, Max told me why you got married, because you had to. So don't go blaming me for anything. You probably lied to the Professor too, he probably isn't even my father."

Jeff wondered where that idea had come from, where in the icy black spaces inside of him that idea had been hiding.

Melody's hand went to her throat. Her eyes were huge and gray. "That he is," she said, her voice cold. She wasn't saying it to make Jeff feel better, he knew that. So he knew what she was saying was true. "I'd never had married him otherwise, if I hadn't had to. You can bet your boots on that."

Jeff said the only thing he could. "Go away. Please, go away."

She went. Jeff stood at the window for a long time, so angry he felt he was shaking, all the little pieces of himself he had so carefully tried to put together broken again and rattling around inside him. Sorrow welled up in him again, and he was frightened. He had thought if he could just say what he thought, if he was just strong enough to do that, then he'd be all right. But he wasn't.

But he made himself go down to dinner, because Gambo might have her feelings hurt, and there was no reason for him to do that. He figured he could get through dinner with Melody, somehow. Nobody noticed much about him anyway; they'd probably miss noticing how upset he was.

But at the table Melody pretended nothing had happened. She sat next to him and kept trying to hold his hand as if nothing had changed between them. She was putting on an act for Gambo, about how much she loved Jeff and how much he loved her.

Jeff felt broken and bruised. When he looked at her, she smiled right into his eyes, so he tried not to look at her. He'd thought he wasn't really vulnerable anymore and maybe not even angry now that he'd let some of his feelings steam out. But there was some feeling like anger in him. He hated her, he thought, and he knew it was true when she left the table to answer the phone and came back to say she'd been invited to a party; nobody minded if she went, did they? She kissed Gambo's head when she asked permission and then kissed Jeff too, on the top of his head, with her perfume in the air all around him.

He thought: alligators stayed near water, if he kept well away from that inland pond he'd be able to continue exploring the island. And what did it matter if an alligator got him, anyway; at least it would hurt so much he wouldn't be able to think about Melody. Because he was beginning to hate himself for being so fragile, so easy for her to break.

CHAPTER 6

The day before he was due to leave Charleston, Jeff crossed over the top of a low, sandy dune, overgrown with scrub bushes. He saw the beach stretching away to the south; the ocean stretching out to the endless east; the line of waves breaking on the shore; sandpipers in nervous bands fishing the waves' edges; three pelicans flying in a line over the surface of the water. He breathed in the salty air, the wind against his face. He saw a world in which he was the only human inhabitant.

It was midmorning and hot. Jeff ran down the dune and across to the water. To the north, he saw a narrow spit of land and a turbulence of waves where the tip of the island made currents, marking the entrance of the creek into the ocean. To the south lay an unbroken distance of beach, thirty feet wide, sandy white. Jeff ran south. He had to run, he didn't know what else to do to celebrate what he had come to find here. And found. Sandpipers and gulls fled from his approach, circled and landed again behind him. When he had run himself out, he walked, mile after empty mile. The waves broke beside him, and he succumbed to the temptation to walk among them. When he realized how hungry he was, he turned around and walked the long miles back to where he had dropped his brown paper bag full of food on the duneside.

The afternoon flowed over him. He sat at the water's edge,

watching. Watching the birds, the waves, and once the gliding backs of porpoises cutting arcs through the ocean in front of him. He took off his clothes and waded out into the water to swim. He lay down to bake dry on the fine sand, first on his stomach, then on his back, soaking in the tireless whispering of the wind, the dry warmth of the sand, the heat of the sun, the spacious solitude all around him.

When the shadows grew longer and the temperature started to drop, he knew he ought to cross back, return to the boat. But he couldn't do that. He made no decision to stay the night, but he couldn't make himself leave the beach. Gradually, he understood that he would miss the last bus. That made no difference.

Jeff walked the beach again, this time picking up sand dollars, which lay flat and bleached white on the mudflats, and whorled conch shells. He made a pile of them by his empty paper bag and folded clothes. Then, sitting at the very edge of the waves, he discovered how the little pastel plaid cochinas tumbled down from the sides of pools his fingers dug. A shower of fragile mollusks poured down with the water that came to fill up the pools.

At his back the sun went down. The sky's colors, reflected by the ocean, went from orange to pink to velvet blue to midnight blue and then black. Stars—millions of stars—came out. The moon rose, just past the full, and shone down with its sad face. The path the moon made on the water glowed silver.

Jeff slept on the beach hungry, but that made no difference. He awoke to a sky the color of thick smoke. All the stars had faded but one: Venus, the morning star, low on the eastern horizon, large and white; it too shone bright enough here to make its own narrow silver path on the water. Jeff sat up and watched, watched light and sunrise. During the night the wind had shifted to the west and blew into his ears from behind, heated by the closer air of the inner island. He saw fishing boats hundreds of yards off shore, so distant they looked like toys. All morning long he walked, through puddles between sandflats left by the receding tide, until he came to the southern tip of the island. Then he turned to go back.

He felt—washed clean, healed. He felt if he could just live here he would be all right. He felt as if he had never been alive before. He felt at ease with himself and as if he had come home to a place where he could be himself, without hiding anything, without pretending even to himself. He felt, thinking his way back up the beach, as if his brain had just woken up from some long sleep, and it wanted to run along beside the waves, to see how far and fast it could go.

When he returned to where he had left his clothes, he put them on. He picked out one perfect sand dollar from his collection of shells, then walked back to toss the rest gently into the waves, returning them. He jammed the paper bag into the back pocket of his jeans and carried the sand dollar tenderly in his hand.

At the top of the dunes, under a blazing noon sun, Jeff turned to take a last look. He drank in the scene with his eyes, to be able to carry it away with him. The empty beach, the line of breaking waves groping up onto the sand, the restless ocean.

He crossed the island as quickly as he dared, giving the alligator pond a wide berth. When he came to the driveway leading to the burned-out house, he began to jog; his plane left at eight; he'd have to pack and get a cab. But when he sat in the rowboat again, the oars ready but not yet dipped into the water to take him away from the island, Jeff looked back. He didn't see the busy land crabs nor the overgrown interior; he saw the beach, knowing it was there just beyond sight, keeping the sight of it clear in his inner eye. He splashed the oars into the water. Behind him, a great blue squawked—Jeff turned his head quickly.

The heron rose up from the marsh grass, croaking its displeasure at the disturbance, at Jeff, at all of the world. Its legs dragged briefly in the water before it rose free to swoop over Jeff's head with a whirring of powerful wings. It landed again on the far side of the ruined dock, to stand on stiltlike legs with its long beak pointed toward the water. Just leave me alone, the heron seemed to be saying. Jeff rowed away, down the quiet creek. The bird did not watch him go.

PART TWO

CHAPTER 7

The professor stood waiting among the throng of people at Friendship Airport. He was taller than most of them, and the first thing Jeff saw was his glasses. Then the Professor raised one hand. Jeff made his way over to his father.

The Professor's brown seersucker suit was rumpled. He didn't wear a tie. He looked at Jeff as if he hadn't seen him for so long he needed to be reminded of what Jeff looked like. But Jeff had made himself a place, inside himself, a kind of tower room, round, without any windows. In that room, he had locked his memory of the beach on the island, all the memories from the day hours and from the night hours. He had discovered how to step inside that room and slide the curved door closed and bolt it across.

"You've only got a couple of days before school starts," the Professor said. "Is there anything you want to do? Go to Ocean City or anything?"

Jeff shook his head.

"Let's get your suitcase. Did you have a good time?"

"It was okay," Jeff said. They walked along with the throng, heading down the central aisle, then down the escalators to the baggage claim.

"I bet we're going to have to get you a whole set of new clothes," the Professor said. "You look like you're filled out some and gotten taller."

"Ummm," Jeff said.

"So," the Professor said, "what's new?"

"Nothing."

The Professor waited a long time before asking, "How's your mother?"

Rage surged up against the outside of Jeff's tower room, a tall, black wave. "She's okay," he said, holding the door safe. Inside the room lay miles of solitary beaches, a spacious, peaceful place. As long as he could go there Jeff would be safe. If the room were not there—he was afraid of what he might do, what he might say. If the room were not there, he would fall apart, disintegrate like music broken into individual melody lines, the lines turning into notes, the notes exploding into unconnected sounds, the sounds dissipating into space itself.

If the room were not there in his mind, Jeff thought, there would be just a sharp-stoned wall, and he would stand in front of it and whack his head against it. Until his head burst open like a pumpkin.

Protecting the room became the thing he did, the only thing, all of his days. He couldn't play his guitar, and neither could he look too carefully at the Professor or the house they lived in together, because all those things distracted him from his watch over the tower door. Luckily, the Professor didn't say much to him anyway; he was busy with his own life. At school, the classes of boys didn't bother Jeff either. The teachers left him alone as long as he kept quiet in class, although when they called on him and discovered that he couldn't answer questions, they looked at him in anger or suspicion or even pity. None of that made any difference to Jeff. He handed in his homework if he had done any, whether it was complete or not. He didn't even notice the other boys in his classes.

The only thing Jeff could do, could really do outside of his tower room, he discovered by accident. One Saturday afternoon in October he found that he'd wandered to the amusement park. He had money in his pocket so he took a couple of rides, the roller coaster and the Octopus. The sheer physical sensations of speed and swooping were exciting in the same way that the island beach had been exciting. He rode the roller coaster time after time, alone in the car, soaring out on thin rails over the edge of the city, rising slowly up, up, up a steep grade until the train finally made its way over the top of the hill. And fell down, dizzying and uncontrollable.

The Octopus was inside, within a huge warehouselike building, which held also a carousel, a few rides small children could take, bumper cars, food concessions, and a bingo hall. The Octopus turned in circles, the round covered motor section at the center, eight metal arms spreading out from that, and at the end of each arm four round cars, like the suction cups on a starfish. The cars circled on their own axles within the large circling machine. They swung so close to each other it seemed they must collide, but they never did. While the arms turned and the cars turned, music played, and colored lights flashed overhead, pouring down over Jeff like fragments of sunlight. He sat back alone in his car, facing three empty seats, wearing sunglasses to make it impossible for anyone to see him, his arms spread along the back of the seat. If he relaxed, as the car swung around building up speed, if he concentrated on the rain of colors over him and the wind rushing by his ears, he could feel—almost—as if he were back on the beach.

It was like trying to recapture a dream, and Jeff never could precisely feel as he had. But it was the nearest he could come. That first day he stayed at the park for hours. He went back every weekend and gradually, when he learned it didn't make any difference, during the weekdays too. As the weather got colder they closed down the outside rides; but Jeff only wanted to ride the Octopus anyway. The indoor rides stayed open all winter, so Jeff would be all right. The only times he could relax his vigilance at the door of his inner room was when his body swung with the movement of the Octopus, and calliope music drowned out human voices, and the shattered prism of color poured over him.

Jeff knew that somewhere outside of his tower room he was flunking courses; but the Professor didn't know because Jeff had forged the Professor's signature on his report card. He checked the mail before the Professor saw it, to throw out unopened any envelopes that came from the University School. Jeff didn't ever know for sure what day of the week it was, so it wasn't exactly as if he was cutting classes. Some days the park was more crowded, some days not. Fall turned into cold weather, and on Christmas Day, it was closed. Then it opened, and Jeff had someplace to go again.

It was on an afternoon in deep winter that Jeff sat in the round seat of the Octopus, alone, whirling under a waterfall of color. Inside himself, he was within the tower room. He could almost really taste the salt in the air, he could almost feel that what was pouring down over his skin was the sun. It was only almost, but almost promised so much and was so much better than nothing that he concentrated on losing himself into it.

When the ride stopped he rose carefully from his seat. If he moved slowly, he would not shatter his inner concentration, even when he went to give the man another ticket. So that when he heard someone call his name, it was as shocking as if somebody had slugged him in the face. He whipped around, frightened.

The Professor stood just beyond the gate. Brother Thomas,

back from England, was with him. Jeff looked around for someplace to run. They couldn't catch him. They were going to hurt him, he knew that, and he knew how easy he was to hurt. There was no way out, so he just stood still, inside the tower. He made them come to get him while he stayed safe.

Each man took one of his arms and led him out of the enclosure. Brother Thomas stood in front of him, staring into his eyes. Jeff lowered his eyelids. Brother Thomas pulled them up with gentle fingers. He looked worried, puzzled. "Are you on anything?" he asked.

Jeff shook his head.

The Professor's hand was on his shoulder. "I was so afraid," the Professor said.

"I'm sorry," Jeff said.

They all went out to the Professor's car. Jeff sat in the back, but they both turned around to stare at him. "You're supposed to be in a math exam now," the Professor said. "You missed English and geography yesterday. Exams, Jeff. I don't understand. They called me, the principal did." He knew everything.

"I'm sorry."

The Professor looked at Brother Thomas. "Take him home, Horace," Brother Thomas advised. "Take him home and feed him and make him talk to you. Your father," he said to Jeff, "wanted to leave you be, since you wanted to be left alone. But you're going to have to tell him. Whatever it is."

Jeff didn't say anything at all. He had an hour, anyway, for the drive back into the city, he had an hour for the sun-bleached stretch of beach, where waves broke and spread.

When they sat across from one another at the little Formica kitchen table and Jeff had finished his peanut-butter-and-jelly sandwiches and the Professor had brewed a mug of coffee, the Professor said, "I'm sorry, Jeff; you're going to have to tell me about it. You've been different, and I don't know what it is. I didn't think it was drugs—I didn't think you'd be that stupid—but people say it's so hard to tell. . . . Look at me Jeff," he said, making Jeff meet his eyes. "I don't care about the schoolwork. I'm not angry, I'm frightened. Tell me what's bothering you, and we'll figure out the best way to handle it."

"I'm okay," Jeff told him. "There isn't anything."

"No, you're not okay. I'm not much of a father, but I can see that. You're not even really here, are you? You act as if you're a hundred miles away. Where are you?"

"I'm sorry," Jeff said.

The Professor sat back in his chair. He looked at the coffee in his mug. He moved his glasses back up his nose. His voice, when he spoke, was expressionless. "I thought myself, the way you've been acting, that it was probably Melody. I thought it had to have something to do with her. Judging from my own experience, I've been assuming that she told you, somehow, the way only Melody can, that she didn't love you. And you thought she did."

Jeff saw his own hands clench up into fists. His stomach too, was clenched. He started to talk, fast. "I'll tell you where I was. The last day, I went over to a beach. The last full day. An island, one of the sea islands, uninhabited. I had a boat, I bought it. I'd never explored that far before, and I spent the night there. And—it was so beautiful. Nobody but me was there. I spent all day and all night and half the next day too. I have a sand dollar I found; it's upstairs, I can show you." He looked down at his fists. "I can remember it; I can go there, inside."

"It wasn't the worst time when Melody left me," the Professor said. "The worst time was the years before. Because I didn't know I could hate anybody that much, I didn't know I could be that angry, I didn't know what to do except concentrate on my work. I didn't know anybody could hurt anybody else that much; it was like she'd stuck a sword into me, one of those Japanese samurai swords, do you know the kind I mean? Heavy and razor sharp—and curved—and she'd stuck it in me and then she was . . . pushing it around." His hand rested on his stomach, remembering. "I couldn't get free from the feelings. I didn't know how frightened I could be, all the time. But whenever we had to go out together, she'd smile at me and talk to me and listen and look at me the way she did—and I wanted to hit her," he said, his voice low and ashamed.

Jeff let his head down to rest his face on his fists.

"When I found out how many lies she was telling me, I finally realized that she had always lied to me. About my lectures. About boyfriends; and even after she knew I knew, she'd still lie about it. I hated her. Or the bills she ran up, without asking, without telling; then she'd say she'd taken care of them but she just—ignored them. I know I looked all right to other people—maybe more of a dry old stick than usual, maybe even more boring than usual—but inside I was knotted up, all the time, because I hated her so much, and I hated myself, and I was scared."

Jeff looked up at his father.

"I didn't think she'd do that to you, Jeff," the Professor said. "But she did, didn't she?"

Jeff nodded. He knew he was crying, but he didn't know what to do about it. Neither did the Professor. He just sat and waited, until Jeff got up to blow his nose.

"It was the lies," the Professor said. "They were what really scared me. Even now, if I think about her—and the kinds of things she says. . . . I don't know what she told you, but I never was sorry I'd married her or loved her because of you. You always made a difference, made a real difference, from the very beginning. I always knew that, inside me, but I didn't bother to learn how to show you. I'm sorry, Jeff, I should have taken the trouble."

Jeff didn't know what to say, didn't even know what to think. He could see, as if it were familiar, his father during those early times. And see too what his father had seen: his son, unchanged by Melody's leaving, everything going on the same, although never the same because Melody had left, taking her own light with her. He could see what the Professor's days had looked like to him: long, empty, to be endured until he could get used to things, day after day of waiting to get accustomed. And he could see the Professor now, too; what the Professor was seeing now—his father was frightened and worried about Jeff. Jeff knew that; suddenly, he knew it as clearly as if the Professor had said it aloud. He could receive the feelings, like some musical instrument, whether he wanted to or not. He could see what the Professor saw as the Professor saw it.

"Jeff, please, say something," the Professor asked him.

"She told me she wanted a girl, she told me if I'd been a girl she would have taken me with her."

At that, the Professor laughed. It was shaky, but it was a laugh. "She's still a liar," he said. "Besides, I wouldn't have let her."

"Really?"

"Really. I may be a dry old stick, but I'm not a fool," the Professor told him. He got up from the table, spooned coffee from the can into the top of the coffeepot, and poured the boiling water through. Jeff washed his plate and poured a glass of milk.

"What was that about a boat? How could you get a boat?" the Professor asked in a normal voice.

"I had the money you were sending. It wasn't much of a boat, it only cost fifteen dollars. Plus five to tie it up at the dock. It was only a dinghy, not even painted." Jeff remembered how it felt, once he'd learned how to handle it. He remembered going a little farther each day. "It took me time to get used to it, to be not as frightened. I explored the island the same way. There was a lot to see. And the day I left, I saw this great blue heron—have you seen one?" The Professor hadn't. "They're so beautiful and ugly—awkward—it flew over my head, right over. Because I'd disturbed it, but it landed not very far up at all, and it stayed there when I rowed away. It didn't mind me."

"Where is the boat now?"

Jeff looked at his father: "I sank it."

"You what?"

"I didn't want anyone else to—have it. I won't be going back there."

The Professor, calmer now, thought. "You haven't played your guitar since you've been back. Have you?" It wasn't easy for the Professor to think about how to say to Jeff what he wanted to say. Not like it was easy for Jeff to see. But the Professor was doing it, trying as hard as he could, making himself. Because Jeff mattered to him, and Jeff saw *that* now, too, and saw that he could count on that. He could feel himself relaxing.

A memory that had been blocked away somewhere with other things Jeff didn't want to remember at all struck him like an unexpected wave. "You told me you sold a book."

Now the Professor looked surprised.

"You did, in one of your notes, the last one. What happened to it?"

The Professor didn't know what to say. Jeff could see that. He didn't understand, now that he had remembered, why the Professor had had nothing further to say about the book since Jeff's return.

"Tell me," Jeff asked. "Unless you don't want to." Unless whatever the deal was had fallen through?

"No, I do want to; it's just—I thought you weren't interested, I thought—"

"I'm sorry. I just forgot. You mean . . . you wrote a book—to be published?"

The Professor nodded.

Why did he look embarrassed? Jeff wondered.

"What kind of book is it?"

"It's a sort of history book, biography; it's due to come out next fall. I'm finishing up revisions now."

"Is the university press going to publish it?"

"Actually"—the Professor looked even more uncomfortable—"it's not one of the academic presses, it's a regular publisher."

"Is that . . . does that make a difference?"

"Evidently. It will be . . . more available to the general public."

"It must be good," Jeff said. "What's it about?"

"It's a series of short biographies. Just some people who have—caught my attention."

"Can I read it?"

"I thought about that. I'd like you to wait until you're fifteen. I think—then you'll be old enough. Will you promise me that?"

"Sure. I promise. What's it called?"

"*Earth's Honored Guests.* Not a very scholarly title. I don't know, I can't tell—the scholarship in the book is solid. I think they're afraid it'll be too scholarly. I don't know who would want to read it, but that's their business. I mean, they bought it—which means we have some extra money, and more when I get the revisions done and the second half of the advance. It gives us some leeway. Brother Thomas says."

"Leeway for what? Aren't you proud?"

"I am proud, yes. Well, sometimes I am. It's pretty foreign country for me, Jeff. Leeway about you. About school. About what we're going to do about school. You can't possibly pass the year, they told me that. So we have to decide what to do."

Jeff began to feel frightened again. "It doesn't make any difference," he said.

"And you sank the boat?" the Professor asked. "How do you sink a boat?"

"It was old. I pounded the oar on the floorboards; it wasn't strong at all, really. Then I swam to the dock."

"I'll try to make it all right, Jeff," the Professor said. "Whatever we decide to do."

While January turned to February, and a week of warm weather was followed by sharp, sporadic storms of snow and sleet, the Professor didn't do anything about Jeff. Jeff stayed home and played on his guitar. Brother Thomas came around frequently, but if he had anything to say about Jeff, he kept it for the Professor. He brought Jeff a thick volume of songs, collected in England by a man named Childs. Jeff put the volume aside for later and went back to relearning the songs he had once been able to play well.

In mid-February, the Professor took Jeff for an appointment with the principal of the University School. Jeff sat silent while the two men talked—he had worn the gray flannels and blazer—and stared unseeing at the toes of his polished shoes. The Professor wanted to withdraw Jeff from the school, and the principal agreed that that might be all for the best. He talked about academic pressures on a student of less than average ability, and he didn't look at Jeff. He suggested testing, to get a precise fix on just what the limits were, he suggested therapy because "socialization was well below norm." The Professor didn't disagree. When they finally walked out of the office, down the hall, and out onto the icy brick front steps, Jeff said, "I'm sorry."

"We'll see," the Professor said. He didn't seem to be listening to Jeff. "We'll give it some time and then we'll see. Don't *you* worry, Jeff." Jeff left his father alone to think it out. His father needed time to think things out.

They also went to visit Dr. Baker, who did a complete physical; then listened as the Professor recounted what Jeff had done. Jeff listened too, as if they were talking about somebody else.

"It sounds as if some counseling is in order," Dr. Baker said. He smiled at Jeff as he spoke. Jeff didn't say anything.

"I'd like to give it some time," the Professor said. "I'm not ruling the possibility out, but—I don't believe anyone can understand as well as I can what effect his mother could have had on him."

The doctor laced his fingers together and said to the Professor, "It's not only his mother. He hasn't been primarily in her care, has he?"

The Professor didn't answer that right away. "I understand," he said at last. "I see what you must think—and you're correct, I understand that. I guess I'd like a little time, myself. Circumstances permit a little more freedom this year." He looked at Jeff. "I would like to keep him out of school and have him repeat eighth grade next year. Somewhere else."

"Jeff?" Dr. Baker asked. Jeff looked up at him. He had been

thinking about the beach again and how the pelicans swooped low over the water, scooping up their prey with buckety beaks. "What do you think?"

"It doesn't make any difference to me."

Dr. Baker studied him for a long time. Jeff kept his face expressionless and looked right back.

"I don't know, Dr. Greene. I can testify to his being run down, and it certainly doesn't sound as if he should go back to school—especially not if the year is already shot. I have to say that I think counseling is strongly indicated. But not urgent. Not at this point. But I'd have to have your word to get in touch with me if . . . I don't know, if there was any smallest sign of trouble. Or even lack of improvement."

"You have my word. Thank you," the Professor said. "I hope I've learned; I think I'm learning. We have a family friend who's much quicker than I am—Brother Thomas," he said to Jeff's raised face. "You have my word," he said to Dr. Baker.

The Professor didn't speak to Jeff again until they had arrived back home and Jeff was about to go up to his room to play the guitar. "I can't change, not really," the Professor said.

"That's okay," Jeff told him. He already knew that, and he liked that in his father.

"But even if we can't change me, I've been thinking, we might change this." The Professor waved his hand around, indicating the hallway. Jeff didn't understand. "Would you mind moving?" the Professor asked him.

"No."

So they became acquainted with a real estate agent, who carried a large zip case with her wherever she went, wrote everything down with a quick, nervous hand, and talked constantly, called the Professor, "Dr. Greene." She drove them around to show them houses, in the city, in the suburbs. She advised them not to fix their house up. "I thought about that, Dr. Greene, and while it would cost you thousands just to have it painted inside and out, you wouldn't ever realize what you'd spent in the sales price. I think we should sell it as a bargain." She drove them around in her big white car and walked them through other people's houses. She even showed them a mansion out in the western suburbs, built out of white stucco with a tall fence enclosing a garden and green hills rolling behind it.

"We can't afford it," he said to his father.

"Hardly. A pity, except if you think about trying to keep the lawns mowed," the Professor said.

"Yeah," Jeff agreed. What he really liked about the property was the garden and the hillsides around.

It was at that point, in April, that they started looking farther afield. They drove out to the north, but that was being developed too rapidly; to the south, but Annapolis was too much like a city; and over the long Bay Bridge to the Eastern Shore. As soon as he saw the flat landscape, the sky stretched out flat like a blanket overhead, the water appearing at unexpected places, Jeff breathed easier. The Professor had no Friday classes, so they spent weekends driving around, going farther south each time, to find something they could afford that still suited them. They spent nights in motels, where Jeff played his guitar and the Professor made notes on pages of books or wrote lecture notes. They spent days with real estate agents or just driving around towns. They saw houses they liked on land they didn't; land they liked with a house neither of them wanted to live in. It seemed that if they liked a town they could find nothing for sale in it, and if there were a lot of houses available they didn't like the town.

Until, deep in the western corner, an agent drove them down a dirt road to a little cabin that sat on high land—high for that part of the country. A one-room, red-shingled cabin that faced across a broad creek to marshes, that sat right on a point where the creek emptied into the Chesapeake Bay. The cabin was just one room, with a bathroom tacked onto the back; the whole front wall was plate glass doors that looked out over to where the creek flowed by, hurrying into the bay, and where the level tops of marsh grasses were all you could see, except for a line of low trees at the distance. Mice and roaches scurried away as they entered the room. Spiders had made complex webs at the places where bare roof beams came together at the peak. A bunk bed, a stove and refrigerator, a chipped sink, a table, three chairs, two rollaway beds, a woodburning stove made out of thin tin and rusting through in many places, stacks of newspapers—the room was crowded. The walls were bare plywood, the floor plywood laid down in sheets. The air was damp and musty.

Jeff stood by the window, looking out, not listening. He went outside, leaving the two men inside, looking around and talking. He made his way down to the creek, down a five-foot muddy bank to a band of sand too narrow to lie down on. He had to force his way through honeysuckle vines and the branches of low wild cherry trees, so his approach was clumsy, noisy. As he slid to his feet, a great blue heron croaked loudly just off to his left and at the same time rose out and flew away—complaining—to land on the far side of the creek. From there, the bird stared at Jeff. Jeff stared back, not moving, except for the smile on his mouth. The bird decided Jeff was harmless and paced slowly upstream, its attention on the shallow water where prey might be found. The long stilty legs, the long curved neck, the awkward perfect body moved inland, away from Jeff.

He watched it. He watched it not find anything to eat, watched it come to a rest and blend into the stillness of a dead tree that had fallen out into the creek.

The two men were still inside when Jeff rejoined them. The Professor looked at his face and said, "You like it."

Jeff nodded. "I saw a blue heron."

"They're common around here," the agent said. "You-all birdwatchers?"

But the Professor remembered and understood what Jeff meant. "You take that as a sign from the gods?" Jeff nodded. "Well, I like it myself. Let's take a walk around and see. If you'll excuse us?" he said to the agent. The agent dusted off a wooden chair and sat down, ready to be patient.

Behind the cabin grew loblollies, wild cherries, holly, swamp oaks. The small area of lawn that circled the cabin was sparse and untended. Jeff and the Professor walked to the bank and looked down the creek to the bay. "There'll be mosquitoes," the Professor said. "There are only these three high acres in the property, it'll never be worth anything for development."

"Good," Jeff said.

"It's awfully isolated; you'll be alone a lot."

"That's all right." Jeff waited for his father to finish thinking out the major objections. That was the way the Professor did things.

"But I agree with you, it's like an island, isn't it?"

Jeff hadn't thought of that, he'd thought only of the quiet water noises, the sense of space and peace. "I guess it is. I really like it, Professor."

"Not at all what I imagine Charleston looks like."

"Not a bit," Jeff agreed. "Except—it's like that island, just like you said."

"You didn't see alligators?" The Professor sounded alarmed.

"No, Professor, I didn't. Alligators need a warmer climate. Just the heron."

"Then we'd better make a bid on it, don't you think? It doesn't do to disregard a sign from the gods. Back to the office. We'll have to add on some rooms—redo the bathroom entirely—finish off that room for year-round living—maybe gravel the driveway so it won't wash away in bad weather. I guess the septic system's all right; he says it's only two years old. And a dock, we'll need a dock."

"What for?"

"For your boat. Let's go get the business over."

"I thought so," the agent said with satisfaction, "I thought you were the right people for this, soon as I saw you."

"You appear to have been correct," the Professor said. "What's the nearest town, and how far are we from it?"

"Crisfield," the agent said. "You're about eight miles out, as the crow flies. Maybe ten or a little more by road."

"But what about you, Professor?" Jeff had a picture of the map of Maryland in his mind. He remembered where Crisfield was and where Baltimore was in relation to that. "How will you get to work?"

"I can arrange my schedule so that it's only a couple of nights a week I'd need to be away. I can stay at the Faculty Club or with Brother Thomas. As long as you can take the solitude, it shouldn't be hard to arrange."

"I can take it," Jeff said. "You know that." He thought his father might be teasing him.

The Professor bought the property, as he called it, and sold their little house in Baltimore. Before they moved, they had a lot of work done on the cabin. They added hallways and two bedrooms going off opposite sides of the kitchen. They ripped out the old bathroom and had an entirely new one put in. They had the cabin insulated, its walls finished. New double-paned glass doors replaced the old ones in the kitchen. They both wanted to leave the ceiling unfinished, so they did. They had the long driveway graded and covered with oyster shells. They put a short dock out into the creek and steps down the steep bank leading to it. They drove down frequently to check on the progress and watched the swarming workmen; carpenters, glaziers, roofers, painters, and listened to the sounds of saws and the pile driver.

Brother Thomas seemed to find unflagging humor in everything about the new house. "How big is this piece of wilderness?" he asked, and "How's Jeff going to get to school—dogsled?" and "You putting in any crops, Farmer Greene?"

The Professor answered him mildly. "When it's done, you'll come down to visit. On the property."

Jeff didn't call it that. To himself, he called it a safe place, and when they were finally settled in at the end of July, living in the three-room house where windows gave out over the water and woods and sky, he knew he had been right. When they had bought a little skiff, an eleven-foot wooden boat, painted white, with a seven and a half horsepower outboard motor and he took his father exploring up the creek, winding among the branches of fallen trees, staring up at the backs of little cabins or waterfront homes, or meandering across the marshes on one of the canals that ran into the creek—the water so shallow they had to raise the motor and pole the boat—he knew he had been righter than he'd thought. The Professor didn't seem to mind the inconveniences: the distance from the grocery store and libraries, the mosquitoes that rose up like mist on windless evenings, the necessity of keeping Coleman lanterns available for power failures when thunderstorms moved up the bay. Sometimes the Professor would even suggest himself that Jeff take him out in the boat. "I need to get away from myself for a while. Want to go up the bay shore a ways?" They didn't talk much on such trips, but looked about them. The Professor wore a floppy white spinnaker hat to protect his face from the sun and looked out over the water where a fish would often reward his vigil by leaping up out of the water. Jeff wore only shorts, or trunks, and studied the shoreline. He was learning the names of birds and trees, learning also how to scan the water's edge for where a great blue might be standing in camouflage, looking like a branch of one of the fallen trees or blending into the grass. The blues roosted, he had learned, on the high branches of trees. If he wandered outside at night and let the door slam behind him, he could hear them taking off—squawking—from their roosts. They never traveled together, they never shared fishing territory; he liked to think that they squawked their displeasure with one another and him and the state of the world. Great Cranky Birds the Indians had named them.

He told the Professor this as they sat in the boat at the mouth of the creek, rocking gently as the tide carried them out onto the bay. "I don't know why they're so jumpy," Jeff said. "There isn't anything that preys on them, is there? What spooks them?"

"Women with big hats," the Professor said.

Jeff looked at the back of his father's head. His neck was getting tan, Jeff noticed. Jeff always ran the boat because the Professor couldn't seem to learn how to handle it. He tried to figure out what his father meant. A fish jumped off to starboard. An egret, snowy white, fished along the muddy shallows, its path crossing with two of its fellows. Egrets shared their fishing territory with one another. "C'mon, Professor," Jeff said. "I was serious."

"Oh, so was I." The Professor turned around to look earnestly at Jeff. "When women wore those picture hats, with hat pins—one of the prized adornments was heron feathers."

Jeff thought about that and thought about his father's response to his question. He started to laugh, a small bubbling of humor in his stomach. "But that's funny, what you said."

"I have my moments," the Professor answered, and turned back to the water. But he was pleased, Jeff knew that.

In the evenings, the Professor studied or wrote or read a mystery. Jeff played his guitar. They had decided against a television, had bought a stereo, instead, and a radio, so they could hear the news and weather. Sometimes the Professor joined Jeff in the kitchen, which they had turned into what magazines called a family kitchen, with sofa and chairs near the Franklin stove the Professor had insisted on having. Sometimes he worked in his room. "Are you writing another book?" Jeff asked his father, one night, watching him wander to the window to look out over the water, which ran red under the last light of the setting sun.

"Hmmm?" The Professor turned, but didn't focus his eyes on Jeff. "I think maybe," he said.

Jeff began playing on his guitar again, softly. The Professor didn't mind, he'd given Jeff only a fraction of his attention, Jeff knew, because he was thinking something out. Jeff worked out a background for one of the songs he'd heard in Charleston. It needed, he thought, a kind of jingle to it, almost like a tambourine, as if the guitar were one of those cigar box banjos. He thought the Martin could make that kind of sound, if he could figure out how to get it out of his fingers. "Oh Lord, you know, I have no friend like you," he sang. He almost had it, but not quite. "And I cain't feel at home in this world, any more."

The Professor drifted back to his room. "This world is not my home, I'm only passing through," Jeff sang. He was getting closer to the sound he wanted.

They registered Jeff in school and got him a ten-speed bicycle, for days when he didn't want to take the bus. The guidance counselor didn't even ask him why he was repeating the eighth grade. The Professor didn't ask whether Jeff was strong enough to bike the miles to the school, but he did suggest that Jeff might want to build up his muscles. So Jeff packed sandwiches and took long rides on the empty roads, roads that went along for miles between intersections. He learned every turn of the flat road into Crisfield, became familiar with the farms set back behind fields, their barns bright tin or bright red, with the little houses set up close to the road, with the clusters of trailer homes, the rectangular fields framed by loblollies. He learned the names on the mailboxes along the road to school, most of them standing opposite trim driveways, as erect as soldiers. Only one mailbox was neglected, tilted over, its door always hanging open, its paint chipped, its name faded away to *llerma.* He became familiar with the stores in the shopping center, a mile before the school—the large antiseptic supermarket that carried medicines as well as school supplies and even some clothing—and with the less modern stores down at the town center, the hardware, the restaurant, the small grocery whose windows were streaked with grime.

On good days, Jeff took the boat out. He learned to dangle chicken necks at the end of pieces of string to catch crabs. He could, he knew, set pots out in a line, then run the boat along the line, pulling up the pots to see what he'd caught. That would have been more efficient. But he preferred the quiet of the boat anchored in the middle of the creek, he preferred the lazier pace. He'd bait five or six strings and dangle them over the side of the boat. He left them undisturbed until he saw, by the movement of a string on the gunwales, that a crab was feeding on the bait. Then he would take the string in his fingers and pull it gently in, feeling the crab at the other end, knowing it had one claw firmly fixed on the chicken neck while the other ripped off pieces of flesh to eat greedily. Gently, smoothly, so the crab wouldn't sense anything unnatural, Jeff pulled the string in, until he could see the crab, now a few inches beneath the water's surface. He held the bait steady by stepping on the string and picked up his net. He scooped the crab up in the net, dumped it into the bushel basket, and tossed out the string again, feeding out line until the bait came to rest on the creek bottom. They often had steamed crabs for dinner, eating them with cornbread made from a mix, or biscuits, and glasses of beer or wine or iced tea.

Jeff tried to teach the Professor how to catch crabs, but his father's hands were clumsy. Somehow, his crabs always swam off from the bait before the Professor could net them. Jeff, watching, admired the crab's sideways retreat. The crab slipped away, angling into darker, deeper water. "I don't know how you do it," the Professor said to Jeff.

"I don't know how you can't," Jeff answered.

"High natural ineptitude," the Professor said. "I'd rather read anyway." He sat and did just that most of the time, moving his legs out of Jeff's way when Jeff moved around the boat to check the lines.

Brother Thomas, who came to stay for a week in late August, took a more voluble interest in crabbing and in Crisfield, especially the workboats that moored up at the town dock, especially in the history, especially in everything. "Look at all the churches," he said, walking along the residential streets that ran back behind the town. "Look at those old Victorian houses, the gingerbreading. I'd think someone would fix them up. Who do you suppose built them?" Brother Thomas, in the bright Hawaiian shirts he wore on vacation, wandered happily through the stores, talking with anyone nearby. He met the local priest, he talked with the old men who sat in the shade of shacks by the dock, among miniature mountains of oyster shells. "This is a wonderful life. I don't know how you found this place," Brother Thomas said. "It must be your background as a geographer, Horace."

"Your what?" Jeff asked. They were all sitting outside on low chairs. The men drank a chilled white wine and Jeff watched the egrets feeding on the opposite side of the creek. A wind blew the mosquitoes away, so they sat in comfort.

"I started out specializing in geography," the Professor explained to him.

"Why?" Jeff asked.

"I was interested. It seemed like a good way to get grants to travel."

"Did you know your father won a Rhodes Scholarship?"

Jeff didn't know that.

"But that was in 1945, so he couldn't take it. Honestly, Horace, it's almost pathological, your secretiveness."

"It never came up," the Professor said.

"Besides," Jeff said, "it's not the kind of question you think of to ask—'By the way, what academic prizes did you win?' It's not like 'What do you want for dinner?' or 'Can I take any library books back for you?' Is it?"

They were all stretched out in their chairs, and the quiet stretched out around them.

"*My* only question now is, how often can I come back?" Brother Thomas asked.

"As often as you like. The sofa bed is there for you," the Professor said.

Jeff heard in their voices their contentment. They were two of a kind, he saw; two quiet men, each able to respect what was central to the other's life, both intellectuals. Brother Thomas had a deep, stabilizing faith; although he didn't talk about it, it was always there in him. The Professor had his study of history, whether reading it, writing about it, or thinking it over; it was always there in him, always important. Jeff saw why they were friends.

"You going to get a dog to keep Jeff company?" Brother Thomas asked.

"And a red wagon too?" the Professor asked.

"Why would I need a red wagon?" Jeff asked.

"It's what every boy should have, a dog and a little red wagon," the Professor told him.

"No thanks. Not that I'm ungrateful. But a dog would chase away the birds and the raccoons."

"But," Brother Thomas said, "it could pull you to school in your little red wagon."

Jeff chuckled.

CHAPTER 8

Jeff knew what the Professor wanted from him in school, although the Professor never said anything about it. He wanted the same thing Jeff wanted, just for it to be okay. He didn't expect top grades. He didn't expect Jeff to get popular or play varsity sports or join activities. The Professor's classes didn't start until two weeks after Jeff's so the Professor was there every day when Jeff came home. "Everything okay?" he'd ask.

"Okay," Jeff would answer.

That was the truth. The school was pretty big, so a newcomer could be invisible among all the old friends. Everybody was new to the school, because in Crisfield grades eight through twelve were in one building, an old two-story brick with tall oaks beside the path to the main entrance. Jeff took six classes, five academic courses and mechanical drawing. He hadn't wanted to take mechanical drawing, he'd wanted to take home economics—after all, the way they lived, that would have been really useful to him, cooking and sewing. But the guidance counselor told him he couldn't recommend home ec, not to a boy and new to the area, there was an unwritten policy. The main sport was football, which Jeff didn't play and didn't want to, so he took the regular PE class where he ran laps, played soccer, and did exercises with the other unathletic boys. He sat quiet in classes, moved quiet through the halls, ate quiet at the lunch table, and nobody paid any attention to him. Not that he wanted attention. He paid attention himself during classes, did his homework without any trouble at all and made sure it was neat, answered questions when the teachers asked him, answered exactly what he knew they were asking to find out if he knew. The work wasn't hard. Jeff thought maybe that was because he'd done it the year before at the University School; but he couldn't remember much of anything about that.

The first night he spent alone in the house, Jeff expected to be uneasy. The Professor would stay up in Baltimore for two nights. Jeff rode his bike home and leaned it up against the wall by the back door. He entered the empty house, made himself a bologna sandwich, then wandered down to the dock, getting himself used to being alone. He'd promised the Professor not to go out in the boat when he was alone, which seemed fair enough. He sat on the end of the dock and looked around. Behind him, on the low rise of land that passed as a hill in this flat country, the house sat, its windows bright. Before him, the creek ran slowly, the long field of marshes swayed like waves under a breeze not strong enough to do more than rustle the leaves on the trees. A great blue paced its territory down to the west, toward the bay, where little waves rippled. In the opposite direction, the creek twisted up off to the east, going inland. The boat floated beside him, the dock was sturdy beneath him.

Unable to sit still, Jeff went back to the house and brought his guitar down. He hesitated, trying to decide what song to sing. Far up in the sky an osprey circled. Jeff ran the pick down across the strings—and the heron rose, complaining. Jeff watched it, the great wings spread out smoky blue, the long neck tucked in until the bird seemed full of dignity, full of ridiculous dignity, looking pompously ahead, the long legs held stiffly out behind him.

Jeff sat and played, song after song, until the mosquitos rose with the lowering sun to drive him inside. There he made a supper of steak and salad and baked potato. After he had washed up, he began on his homework, spreading the books and papers out over the kitchen table. The silence and solitude wrapped themselves around him.

As he was diagramming the last of a dozen sentences for English, the silence was shattered by a harsh, clanging sound: the telephone. Their telephone never rang, and Jeff knocked over his chair in his hurry to answer it. It was the Professor. "How is everything, okay?" he asked.

"Okay," Jeff said. "Really, Professor—except for the phone scaring me half to death. It's going to be okay."

"I thought so, and Brother Thomas thought so too, but we thought we'd just call and check in."

"Thanks," Jeff said. Then he asked, "Is everything okay up there?"

"Everything's fine. I'll see you the day after tomorrow."

"See you then. Thanks for calling."

As the first weeks of school went by, Jeff worked out how things went in Crisfield. He learned to wear jeans to school. Most people wore jeans. It didn't matter what you wore for a shirt. Some people, girls especially, dressed up more, some always looked ratty, but if you wore jeans you didn't stand out. His homework papers, then quizzes and tests, kept coming back perfect. It wasn't because the school was easier than his old school, because it wasn't; and it wasn't that the other kids weren't smart enough, because they seemed smart enough. Maybe not like some of the brains, the really brainy kids up in Baltimore who planned to finish high school in two years and go straight into college—but smart enough, and most of them did their work. They were just regular kids, each one different, everybody a lot alike.

They hung around in packs, the girls in one pack, the boys in another. They didn't know anything about Jeff and didn't seem very interested, but by listening he learned about them, what they thought of themselves, what their fathers did, when they had parties, how they got along with their families. They thought Crisfield was a dull and dumpy little town, the boonies they called it. They liked to go up to the mall in Salisbury, where life was more exciting. They longed to have cars so they could get away. They liked the mechanical drawing teacher all right, they thought the science teacher was the best ever, they were awed by the elderly Latin teacher, a minister's wife who never raised her voice at a class but was so steely and strict nobody dared talk back or come unprepared. They thought the English teacher was a phony, the PE teacher a hero because he rode a Harley to school and was rumored to race it on the weekends. Jeff agreed with them, on the whole. If he hadn't, it wouldn't have made any difference.

A couple of the guys played in a band, a rock band they had formed; Jeff learned that. A couple of other guys, one from English, the other from science, struck him as more interesting than the rest. He couldn't have said why, precisely. Phil Milson, in English, was pretty funny, without being a clown about it. They were talking about stories by then, and Phil usually had some unusual angle on a story, which the teacher didn't appreciate. But Phil was funny in a subtle way, which Chappelle, the teacher, didn't always get, Jeff suspected, along with most of the rest of the class. Then Andy Barrows in science always had questions and questions and questions, why and how. Listening to his questions and the answers he got, Jeff learned a lot more than the book taught. He wondered how Andy figured out what questions to ask. He didn't talk to either of those two, they had their own friends, but they made his school day more interesting.

The girls giggled and whispered, passed notes, combed their hair, talked about being too fat or too skinny. In class they were more serious, and they were always willing to try talking about what the teacher wanted—but Jeff wasn't much interested in girls. He had the feeling that they were pretending, looking around to see who noticed them. And there was something else, something secret, that they were always trying to get.

Jeff's first report card surprised him by being all A's. He brought it home for the Professor to sign. The Professor didn't seem surprised or particularly overwhelmed. "I guess that's good enough," he said.

"It's okay," Jeff said. He thought he knew what his father might be thinking, so he told him. "Even if it had been all F's I would have shown it to you."

"I hope so. Do you like the school?"

"Yeah, sure."

"Is it easier?"

"Not really. At least, I don't think so. I don't know why my grades are so good."

The Professor stared at him for a long time, making up his mind about something. They sat outside, on low chairs. Jeff ate an apple. "You've got a high IQ," the Professor said. "Not genius or anything, but high. Of course, the relevance of IQ tests is under question, and their accuracy. But you've always tested at the top percentages in any standardized test."

Jeff stopped chewing. "But—"

"But what?"

"But—I don't know. The principal up at the University School said . . . and Melody told me. . . ."

"The principal hadn't read through your file, he just wanted you out because you were messing up his class averages. But what did Melody say?"

"She said I'd gotten her brains and you must be disappointed."

"I don't know why she said that—it's not true," the Professor said. "She's smart enough. I never thought she would have—I should have told you sooner. I'm sorry, Jeff."

"I'll forgive you," he told his father, who smiled back at him. "I don't mind. So I'm a classic underachiever?"

"Not this year."

"How come I never did well in school before?"

"What do you think?" the Professor asked. Jeff didn't know the answer. "It might be worth thinking about," his father said.

Jeff tried, off and on. He couldn't remember much from school, or before that, kindergarten, and before that the day care center. He remembered some of the teachers, some of the other kids, but not himself, Jeff Greene. It was almost as if he'd been a ghost in all those rooms, all those days, a ghost in his own life.

At the end of October, the Professor showed Jeff a copy of his book. He brought it out one night after dinner and put it on the table in front of Jeff. Jeff looked at it: a book, *Earth's Honored Guests,* with a picture on the cover of the outline of a man's head and shoulders, with a medal hanging down from where his shirt pocket would have been if more than the outline had been drawn. By Horace Greene. Jeff just stared at it.

"That's what I said too," the Professor said.

Jeff sat there wishing he hadn't given his word to wait until he was fifteen to read the book. He turned it over and saw a photograph of the Professor. His hair shone white, his tie was slightly askew. "Horace Greene is a Professor of History at Baltimore University," he read. Jeff turned the book over in his hands, feeling the weight of it.

"I'm really impressed," he said.

The Professor's face was expressionless.

"C'mon, Professor," Jeff insisted. He knew that that expressionless face was put on to hide something, and he was pretty sure he could guess what. "Aren't you proud of yourself? Just a little bit? You can tell me."

"Don't pick on me, please," the Professor said, giving way and smiling. "Yes, I am—proud. I think it's an honest book. I'm just not very comfortable with having a book published. Maybe it will fade into immediate obscurity; I think I hope it will."

Jeff handed the book back to his father. He didn't want to do that, he wanted to read it, right away; but he had given his word. He knew he'd better give it back, because if he didn't, he wasn't sure he'd be able to keep his promise.

They were assigned an essay in English, to write about conflict in a real character. Jeff decided to write about John C. Calhoun of South Carolina. He'd often visited the park in Charleston that was dominated by a statue of Calhoun.

When Chappelle finally returned the paper Jeff wrote, Jeff's grade was a perplexing A/F. Chappelle talked a little about all the essays, then read a couple aloud that he thought were good, then hauled one girl over the coals for not writing it herself. Then he called on Jeff. "Greene," he said, his face serious under carroty hair, one hand on his narrow necktie. "Do you have any questions about your grade?"

Jeff shook his head.

"You should. I rather suspected you hadn't taken the trouble to write down the assignment. Do you write down assignments?"

"Yes."

"Have you got this one written down?"

"Yes."

"Do you think you could trouble yourself to look it up?"

Jeff was suddenly nervous, even frightened. He didn't think he'd burst into tears and have to leave the room, but he remembered—he'd forgotten it for so long, he'd been stupid to forget it—that he was easy to break down. He read out the assignment nervously. "Write about conflict in someone real." He remembered, it had been written on the board; he didn't think he'd have forgotten to copy down an assignment written on the board. But what if he had? "At least one thousand words," he finished reading.

He could remember, as clearly as if it was still on the board, the assignment written out in Chappelle's irregular print. He could trust his memory, couldn't he?

"It was supposed to be somebody you knew, as well," Chappelle said. "I'm presuming you didn't ever meet John Calhoun."

His sarcasm was so clumsy it couldn't frighten Jeff. And Chappelle wasn't exactly angry, Jeff could tell, just super-patient and patronizing.

"You'd be right in that, sir," he agreed. He heard a rustling of attention in the class around him.

"So the grade is fair, even generous," Chappelle said.

Jeff breathed easy again. If that was all he'd done wrong that was okay. "I didn't question it," he said.

"You'll have to work hard to get your average back up, if you want to stay on high honor roll," the teacher told him. "Do you want to do an extra credit assignment? Write another essay?"

Jeff thought about that, because he didn't want to. "No, I don't," he said. "Thank you anyway, sir."

Chappelle was staring at him, but the bell rang so that was an end of that. It was Friday, and Jeff hoped the whole thing would have blown over by the next Monday. A question waded along at the edge of his attention, like the blue heron fishing the creekside. But somebody nudged him in the ribs. He turned his head sharply.

It was Phil Milson. "Man, you are as cool as a cucumber," Phil said. "Old Chappelle couldn't get you nervous at all, could he?"

"Oh, yeah, he could," Jeff said, glad it hadn't shown.

"He could? I like that even better. See you around, okay?" Phil ran ahead to join his friends. But he came over to the table where Jeff sat in the cafeteria and said, "I don't know if you know this, I've got a brother and a sister who've been through it with Chappelle, but you're new this year, aren't you?"

Jeff nodded.

"He'll sulk, a week, maybe two—then he'll forget about it. He's a case of arrested emotional development. Just keep a low profile for a couple of weeks."

"Thanks," Jeff said. "I'll remember." He thought he ought to say something friendly, but he wasn't sure what that would be. "What do you mean arrested emotional development?"

"I mean, we're kids, so we're supposed to act like jerks; it's okay for us. But it's supposed to be a phase you pass through." The bell rang and Jeff didn't have to think of anything else to say.

He went out crabbing that evening, while the Professor did some shopping so they'd have something for Brother Thomas to cook when he came down the next day. Jeff didn't expect to catch anything, and he didn't. In the cooler weather most of the crabs moved on south or buried themselves in the deep mud at the bottom of the bay. The herons and egrets too were growing scarce; only gulls remained in any numbers.

Jeff sat back in the boat, which he hadn't even untied from the dock, and let it rock under him. He didn't even look at the strings hanging over the gunwales.

He didn't think Chappelle had said it had to be somebody you knew, but probably the man had and Jeff hadn't registered it. He hadn't registered it, even though he usually listened well and remembered accurately; so he hadn't let it get into his head. Sometimes he did that, he knew; and then he would remember suddenly and wonder why he had forgotten. That was the way he was.

Why hadn't he ever done well in school before, if he was smart, and the Professor said he tested smart. The Professor didn't actually say he was smart though, did he?

If he was a ghost in the life he remembered, Jeff thought, he was also a ghost in his present life, just the same way. Except, in all the fourteen years, just a couple of times. With Melody that first summer he had felt alive. On the beach on the island. And when he played the guitar.

Most of the time, he thought, he practiced not being anybody. If you weren't anybody then nobody could—what? Hurt you or leave you behind? Make you unhappy? But then they couldn't make you happy either, could they? If you played it safe, then you kept safe. Jeff figured he was pretty good at keeping safe—he didn't even look in mirrors because he didn't want to see Melody's eyes. But one result of that was that Jeff didn't know anything about himself. And he thought, sitting in the little boat, alone on the creek, alone with the creek and the sky and the marshes, that he might want to know more.

But as soon as he thought that, he got scared that there wasn't any more to know. As soon as he got scared, he thought that being scared was one of his problems. As soon as he thought about one of his problems, he got impatient with himself, irritated—and that felt better. The Professor, after all, had loved Melody and lost her and been hurt by her too, Jeff suddenly realized. Probably at least as badly as Jeff had been; and now he'd written a book, and before that he'd made friends with Brother Thomas, so the Professor survived. Hadn't Melody said, meaning to criticize, that Jeff was like his father? Jeff hauled in the baited strings and climbed out of the boat. He hadn't stopped thinking. But he was going to take it slow and quiet, this thinking about himself.

Chappelle did act funny about Jeff for a couple of weeks, calling on him every day at the end of class to read off the exact assignment, paying exaggerated attention to whatever Jeff said in class. Then he seemed to forget about it. Thanksgiving came, and a short vacation from school, which Jeff and the Professor used to haul the boat out of the water and stock up on some food in case they got snowed in. "It's always good to be safe," the Professor said, placing cans of beans and soup in a row at the back of the shelf, lining up cans of ravioli, boxes of grits and oatmeal, as well as dry mixes for cornbread, biscuits, and milk.

"As a general rule?" Jeff asked. This was, of course, something he had been thinking about.

"As a general rule, well—I'm not the one to ask about that," the Professor said. "If you mean, as I take it, a general rule for life. I'm awfully good at playing it safe and not good at all at taking risks."

"But you have," Jeff pointed out.

"Never by my own choice," the Professor told him. He turned around to look at Jeff, who passed him more cans and boxes. "Always somebody else pushed me. Even my book; Brother Thomas is the one who pushed me into submitting it—the man is implacable, once he gets his teeth into an idea. I'm very grateful to him."

"I like him too," Jeff said.

And he did. All the more when, after Christmas vacation, on one of the days when the Professor stayed up in Baltimore, he picked up a brown manilla envelope from the mailbox. Brother Thomas had sent him some xeroxed copies of newspaper articles, he saw; also a note. The note read: "If I know the man you won't have seen these. I thought you'd enjoy them. BroT."

There was a review (from *Time* magazine, Jeff noticed, impressed; more impressed when he read it and saw words like *intelligent, readable, thought-provoking*) and an interview from the Baltimore paper. It was the interview Jeff read three or four times. Because he didn't know any of this stuff about his father.

"Born in 1924," he read, collecting the facts, "graduated from University of Chicago in 1943." So the Professor had accelerated through school. "PhD, University of Chicago." The Professor had told the reporter that he had studied political geography, because he wanted to travel, but had gone to work for Army Intelligence instead. He'd worked in Washington, analyzing information from aerial photographs of central Europe, mostly, because he knew about the countries. After the war, he'd read philosophy at Oxford for a year, then taken the job at Baltimore. He guessed it had taken him fifteen years to write his book. He'd finished it two years earlier and a friend had bullied him into submitting it to a publisher. The Professor told the reporter that he thought that was an awfully long time to spend on one book, but he'd enjoyed the work so much he had been almost sorry when he finished with it. Yes, he said, he might write another, he had file cabinets filled with notes. At the end of the article, there was a paragraph of personal information: married in 1962, separated, lives with his teenaged son. "A handsome, ageless man," the reporter described the Professor, "whose eyes twinkle with dry humor . . . a thoroughly charming man, who weighs his words and is worth listening to." The article closed with a quote from the Professor: "Some of my best work is in that book, which is, I take it, what a book should contain."

Jeff put down the papers. He didn't know what to think. He didn't really know his father, not this way, not as this kind of man. He guessed he was pretty proud of the Professor, and thought he was going to have even more trouble now keeping his promise to the Professor. He went to his room and got the Martin, sat strumming on it, looking out over the winter brown marshes and winter clear creek water and winter gray skies. Good for the Professor, he thought.

Jeff felt a little embarrassed, greeting his father after school the next day. He didn't know why the Professor hadn't told him about the review or the interview. Or about his life. He didn't know why he himself hadn't asked the Professor more about his life. Riding his bike back from school, arguing with himself whether or not he'd been a fool to take the bike on such a cold day, Jeff didn't know what he was going to say to his father. What he finally said was, "Your eyes don't twinkle."

The blue eyes, of course, did look bright and amused at that. "I agree," the Professor said. "Am I to gather then that Brother Thomas has been in touch with you?"

"I'm really impressed," Jeff said.

"Thank you. It's probably as well he warned you, because I'm afraid the book is successful."

"That's okay, Professor, I won't hold it against you. How successful?"

"British sales and a contract for a paperback edition. Is there anything you need money for?"

"No," Jeff said. Then he thought. "Don't you want an electric typewriter?"

"Yes, but I've got one on order. What about you? Schools? I don't know, what do boys want these days?"

"Just a dog and a little red wagon," Jeff said. "But you aren't serious, are you? You are, aren't you. I want a Martin, and I have it. I want to live in a place where it's beautiful, and we do. And a boat. I think getting rid of the money's going to be your problem, Professor, not mine."

"I meant, we could move back to Baltimore, to one of those houses we couldn't afford before." His father's face was expressionless.

Jeff made his face expressionless too. "Is that what you'd like?" After all, it was the Professor who supported them, who had the work. Jeff carefully didn't look out the window.

"I asked you first."

"No, you didn't. You suggested, you didn't ask. I asked you first."

"But I want to hear what you want."

"Then you should have asked first," Jeff insisted. This was crazy, like two little kids quarreling.

"But . . . all right. The truth of the matter is—no, I don't want to leave. But I always was a hermit. I don't know about you . . . if you're making friends, if there's enough for you to do, if the school is good enough."

Jeff did get up from the table then. He walked to the glass door and looked out, across the marsh then down to the sweep of bay, larger now that the deciduous trees had shed their leaves. "I love it here," he said, trying to say it as clear and true as he could.

"You really do," the Professor said. After a pause, "I don't mind it myself," he added.

As spring approached, Jeff began preparing the boat. He scraped and repainted the bottom and had the motor overhauled. In late March he began to see ospreys. By mid-April, the trees started to produce new leaves. The egrets returned and, during May, the herons. Jeff saw his first heron of the season one sunny afternoon after school. The blue stood on the trunk of a tree that had fallen over into the creek, stood motionless and unaware. For a long time, Jeff watched it from the dock. The sun-warmed air smelled of moist earth, and somehow green, of growing things. Without moving, Jeff watched. The heron stood on stiff thin legs, its long neck tucked in, its flattened head still. Finally, Jeff couldn't contain himself: "Hello!" he called down the creek. "Welcome back."

The bird didn't even look toward him. It took off, raising itself awkwardly from the tree, and flew up the creek, squawking its resentment as it disappeared into treetops. Jeff laughed aloud.

At school, he often joined Phil for lunch. Phil's father was a farmer, so they didn't get together outside of school—Phil had chores and had to help plow up the land, then plant it. He didn't seem too curious about Jeff, but he seemed to like him all right. They talked about classes, mostly, although sometimes Phil made cracks about girls, and he asked Jeff what his father did, and if he had brothers and sisters, and how his mother liked living in the boonies. Jeff just said his mother lived in Charleston. "I wish my mother lived in Charleston," Phil answered.

Jeff liked Phil; he liked his sense of humor and the practical turn of his mind. Phil's life was so normal, so practical—and Phil couldn't see that. Phil figured, Jeff thought, that everyone was pretty much like him; he didn't have the imagination or experience to see what differences there could be. He was a four-square, solid person, and Jeff liked that. They weren't friends, exactly, but he wouldn't mind being friends.

Everything was going smoothly and Jeff slipped through the days, until Mr. Chappelle asked one day in class if Jeff's father was the one who wrote the book. After that, people seemed to look at Jeff with more interest and give him a wider berth. Except Phil, who tackled the subject head on. "He wrote a book? What are you doing down here?"

"We like it here."

"Does that mean he's an egghead? Or you?"

"I don't know."

"You *are* high honor roll, every time."

"I'm sorry." Luckily, Phil thought that was funny, so Jeff, hearing how stupid it sounded, had a chance to say, "I'm repeating eighth grade—I don't know how I'll do next year."

"You don't *mind* being high honor roll, do you?" Phil looked surprised.

"You know, I don't know."

"Greene, you're unbelievable. I can't tell if you're a total fink or a really unusual guy."

"Probably something in between," Jeff said.

Jeff did have the chance to ask Phil if he'd like to go out in the boat, crabbing or something, once school let out. Phil knew where they lived, "on the old Mitchell place; they used it for hunting." He said he'd call if his father took the chains off for a day. The Milsons sold some of their vegetables and all of their eggs in Salisbury during the summer, as well as having a roadside produce stand, so he was pretty busy. "I wouldn't mind a day off, I'll tell you," Phil said. This was as they left school on the last day, when everybody burst out the doors, and some of them yelled aloud their joy. Jeff took his bike from the rack and rode home alone. He was satisfied, he thought, with the way he'd spent the year. He hadn't made any enemies and he might have made a friend. That made it a terrific year for him.

Brother Thomas spent two weeks with them that summer. He and Jeff learned how to bait and set out a trotline, then how to run it, the motor at its slowest speed, one of them steering while the other netted the crabs that clung to the pieces of bait as they rose to the surface. It took them most of the two weeks to get good enough at it, and it wasn't until the last week that they made the kind of haul Jeff read about, three bushels in two hours. They couldn't, of course, eat all those crabs. They culled out the very largest to cook and turned the rest loose, dumping the crabs overboard, like a living landslide. They were out in the bay that day, wearing just shorts. When the sun got too hot they slipped over the side to cool off, avoiding the translucent jellyfish who had arrived in mid-July to make swimming unpleasant. The jellies clustered near the surface of the dark water and clung with stringy formless tentacles to anything that caught them, the net, the line, a shoulder. Jeff had been stung often enough to learn that, while it hurt some, it only lasted for about half an hour.

That day was, he thought, just about perfect. Brother Thomas liked to sing, so they sang as they waited between runs down the trotline, and Brother Thomas taught Jeff the elements of harmony singing. They watched workboats run by single men or crews. They saw sailboats and motor yachts trailing fishing lines and a little red motor boat run by a solitary woman whose hair was a tangled mass of gray curls. She went up along the coast then turned into a dock that seemed unattached to any house. They went back home so baked by sunlight that Jeff felt as crusted with salt as a pretzel and was surprised not to see large salt flakes on his arms and legs.

One day, when they were downtown so Brother Thomas could soak up local color, Jeff was killing time wandering up and down the sidewalk by the town harbor, waiting to meet Brother Thomas for a Coke before driving home. Brother Thomas had gone into the fish market to get them some lobsters, "for a housegift, to go with that champagne I brought." A woman came out of the little grocery store, carrying two huge bags. Jeff looked at her and thought he should offer to help her carry them. She looked old, but she didn't move as if she was old. He hesitated, inching toward her. She had leathery, tanned skin and wore a long skirt with a baggy blouse over it. Her hair was iron gray, and her eyes looked at him as if she was angry at him. Over her shoulder he saw Brother Thomas approaching, so he stepped aside without offering to take the bags. She walked on by him, but as she passed she said something that sounded like "manners of a chicken."

Jeff felt her anger toward him, and he felt unaccountably shaky. Why should he be afraid, he asked himself. He didn't even know her. She couldn't possibly do anything to him. But he felt—inside himself, and he didn't lie to himself about it—as if she could, even though he knew she couldn't.

"Who's that?" Brother Thomas asked. "What did you say to her? I'm trying hard to imagine—I mean *you,* I've known you for years—what could you have said? Tell, Jeff, I'm going crazy with curiosity." His humor masked genuine concern for Jeff, Jeff saw that.

"Not a word." Jeff still felt quivery from the odd encounter. "Honest, I didn't do anything. I was even thinking about offering to carry her bags."

They watched the woman go out on the dock, then climb down into a motor boat and rush off.

"That's the same red boat, isn't it," Brother Thomas said. "Wait here." He went into the grocery store and came out in a few minutes, carrying a bag of potato chips. "Well"—he justified the purchase—"I couldn't just go in and pump her for information. Her name's Abigail Tillerman, she's a widow, had three children, all of whom left home years ago. The youngest died in Vietnam—she might be a little crazy with solitude, at least that's what people say. That store is withering of neglect."

"How'd you find out all that?"

But Brother Thomas was watching the now-empty water of the harbor. "When you think of all the lost souls in this world. What life does to people. Do you know what I mean?"

Jeff did, because he was one of them. "I guess," he said.

"And that store—the woman in there was another one. But this Tillerman woman—at least her spirit wasn't broken, wouldn't you say?"

"I wouldn't like to meet her again," Jeff said, "and not in a dark alley." He'd need to be tougher than he ever could be, and it wasn't just this one old lady, it was most people in the world. Jeff felt as if he'd been keeping a secret from himself and had come around a dark inner corner to rediscover it. He felt shaky, but as if he'd learned something. Probably it was good for him. He thought it was. It wasn't good for him to get confident; just like he'd been confident about Melody. It was when you got confident you got taken by surprise and really banged around.

It was strange, he thought to himself a couple of weeks later, that he'd thought of Melody. It had been such a long time, since they lived in Baltimore that strange fall, that he'd even mentioned her name to himself. He had put her away and shut the drawer on her. The coincidence struck him because the Professor sat him down in the long summer twilight to talk about her. "Your mother has written me—about you."

"I don't want to go there. Professor? I don't have to, do I? Can she make me? I *can't*."

The Professor's eyes studied him. Jeff looked away, to the scrubby grass of the lawn. He didn't want to hear what the Professor would say. For a long time, the Professor didn't say anything. When he did speak, it took Jeff a minute to figure out that he hadn't changed the subject. "Right after she left, I was miserable and ashamed. I just wanted her to come back. It was like that for a long time. But then, when I got used to it, I began to be afraid she *would* come back; just thinking of it scared me. Really scared me—it took courage just to answer the phone if it rang. In case it was her. I think I understand how you feel, Jeff."

Jeff appreciated that, but it didn't answer his question. "Can she make me go see her?"

The Professor sighed. "Let me tell you what she wants; it's much easier and much harder than what you think. She wants a divorce; she doesn't say why. She wants custody of you."

"No!" Jeff couldn't sit anymore. But he couldn't go too far

away because then he couldn't hear his father. "No, I won't," he said. He walked away, to where the lawn sloped down. "You can't make me."

"I don't want to make you, you know that." His father's voice spoke from behind him, patient, trustworthy. "Come back, sit down. I've talked to a lawyer, and they never guarantee, but at your age a court will listen to what you want. A judge will. The lawyer says he's pretty sure of that. But she wants to divorce me, she wants it uncontested, for incompatibility."

Jeff was back, seated again. "That's okay."

"Well," the Professor said, "the lawyer doesn't think so. He says that if it goes through uncontested she could make a strong appeal for custody, at least half the year."

"What can we do?" Jeff asked. He heard how small his voice was. He looked up at the sky, above the smooth line of marsh grass and the ragged line of trees. The sky was streaked with pastel clouds, yellow and orange and pink.

"I can divorce her for desertion, or adultery if she contests that."

"You mean with Max?"

"Only you'd have to be willing to testify against her, if she contested it. In court. And that seems like an awful lot to ask of you. She is your mother, after all."

Jeff looked at his feet. They were bare and brown. The soles had thick callouses. "But it's true; why would she contest it?"

"I don't know." The Professor sounded tired, really tired, and discouraged.

Jeff's attention focused on his father. "Professor, how long has this been going on?"

"She wrote me in March, the first time."

"That's five months ago, you should have told me."

"I didn't want to worry you. I was hoping not to have to. Maybe you'd better read her letter."

The Professor had kept Melody's letters in a manila file folder. Jeff opened it. The first one—he had to read it twice, because on first reading he was thinking about Melody's handwriting, the shapes of the letters and the way her sentences sounded, eager and happy, just the way her voice sounded.

The first letter talked about how she had been surprised to read about his book and asked wouldn't it be a good thing if they formalized the separation by getting divorced. She couldn't possibly give up Jeff, she said, so she would ask for custody. "Unless you've changed radically, Horace, he'll be better off with me. He needs affection and attention, and I know you don't want to deprive him. Do you?"

The second letter sounded like her feelings had been hurt. She said she didn't think the Professor would go to a lawyer; but if he wanted to be that way he was lucky to be able to afford it; she said she missed Jeff and had become suspicious at not hearing from him. Was the Professor allowing her son to communicate with her?

The third had a photograph clipped to it, the picture she had taken in the Charleston airport. "Did you ever see him look like that?" she asked. "Was he ever so happy when he was with you? Have you thought at all about Jeff in this or only about your own convenience?"

Jeff looked at the photograph. The boy was so young, and his smile so broad it made even Jeff smile to look at him, and he knew better. "I'm sorry," he said, not looking at his father. Everything Melody wrote, every word she used, showed how well she could guess what the Professor was like, how he would react—as if she could see him. That was her real talent, Jeff thought, for feeling what people were like; and he had, he could see, that same talent. But she was using it to get what she wanted from the Professor.

"Oh, well," the Professor said, accepting the facts as he had been told them by Melody.

"But—but she's lying, I know she's lying. She *lies.* She doesn't mean it. She didn't take any other pictures of me. You know you can't trust her, Professor. Don't let her get to you."

"What I want to know is, if you're absolutely sure," the Professor asked.

"I am. Honest. I'm sure."

His father didn't speak.

"Don't you believe me? You have to believe me. If you don't believe me, then who will?"

"It's all right, I do. So—we'll fight her. She says she knows I'll be a gentleman, which really means she's counting on that. As a weakness."

"Can we win?"

"The lawyer thinks so, with your testimony. About Max. About—I told him I thought she'd never answered your letters that first year when you came back. I was correct in that, wasn't I?"

Jeff nodded. "Does she know where we live? I mean, these letters all came to the university."

"I didn't tell her."

"Good." Jeff picked up the photograph.

"What are you doing? Don't rip it up. I'd like to keep it, if you don't want it."

"Is the lawyer sure?" Jeff gave the photograph to his father.

"Pretty sure. I wouldn't even have told you about it except—I never knew what Melody would do. When there's something she wants, she's unpredictable. It'll take a long time, of course. The law always does. Don't brood over it."

"I'll try," Jeff said. Even the Professor was scared of Melody. And what if she could make Jeff live with her?

"You wouldn't like to serenade me for a while, would you? I feel like—a glass of wine and some music—to soothe the savage beast."

So Jeff brought out his guitar, and they ignored the mosquitos while the sun set. After a while, Jeff felt better, and he thought his father did too.

But Jeff couldn't shake the vague, unsettled feeling. He didn't think about Melody, he didn't want to; but he was aware of her, without thinking about her, like clouds rising up at the horizon or footsteps behind you on a dark and solitary street. He didn't mention her to the Professor. Carefully, he didn't think about her. Carefully, he kept on with his usual life.

A couple of days before school opened, when Jeff was sitting on the dock, playing the guitar and singing while he watched the little waves at high tide bouncing against the sides of the creek, Phil Milson came to join him. Phil's hair was bleached white blond, and his skin tanned to coppery brown. "Would you believe this is the first day off my father's given me? How've you been? I'm about ready for a vacation, aren't you?"

Jeff stood up awkwardly. He didn't know what to say.

"Keep playing, you sound good. Are you good?"

Jeff shrugged, he didn't know. "How'd you find us?"

"This is a small town, I keep telling you. I told you I knew the place you'd bought. You've done a lot with it, and it's not half bad now. What do you play, not rock, I can hear that. Country? Bluegrass?"

"I don't know," Jeff said. They settled themselves on the dock. A midmorning sun shone down hot.

"Play me something. I already heard you so there's nothing left to be modest about."

Jeff was glad to be able to look at the guitar, rather than at the boy he didn't know how to entertain. He strummed a few chords, thinking, then decided to play the song about the Springhill Mine Disaster. "Through all their lives they dug a grave, two miles of earth for a marking stone, two miles of earth for a marking stone."

"That's folk," Phil said, happy to have labeled it.

"Now I know what I play," Jeff joked.

Phil grinned at him. "You been playing long? You look good too, you look like you know what you're doing, but—I hate that kind of song. It's depressing. I mean we all know we spend our lives digging our graves, but I'm not interested in writing songs about it." They talked about that for a while, then about their courses, then Jeff asked about Phil's summer, which had been consumed by backbreaking labor, Phil said. They decided to take the boat out. "Did you see my father?" Jeff asked.

"No, I just followed the sound of music."

They went back to the house, had some juice and a couple of sandwiches, and introduced Phil to the Professor. In the boat, Phil asked, "Your mother's still in Charleston?"

"They're getting divorced."

"How come you're with him not her? I thought women always got the kids." There was nothing subtle about Phil.

"She left home when I was in second grade," Jeff told him. He didn't look at Phil when he said that. He didn't really want to talk about it, but he didn't want to sound unfriendly.

"She walked out on you? Women are something else, aren't

they? They don't play by the same rules. You ever think about that?"

"No."

"Yeah, I agree; it's too depressing to think about."

In ninth grade, he discovered, people began to pair off, to talk about dates and steadies. Jeff wasn't interested in girls, but decided that since he'd had good luck with Phil he'd try to be friendly with Andy Barrows as well. Pretty soon the three of them were hanging around together a lot. They suited one another. Phil refused to be serious, and Andy was always serious, so no matter what they did things were pretty lively.

Sometimes they went out fishing or crabbing, and once they tried tonging for oysters. Sometimes they just hung around at Andy's house in town, up in his room where his mother and sisters couldn't get at them, Jeff playing his guitar and listening to the other two quarreling about the tax advantages given to farmers or the relative importance of theoretical and practical physics. "What do you think, Jeff?" one or the other would ask him, and he'd tell them.

Phil went to parties and on dates and decided he was in love with someone for a couple of weeks before he decided he was in love with someone else.

Andy had a crush on one of his older sister's classmates, which they teased him about. "Well, she might get to like me, when I'm older; age difference doesn't matter so much when you've grown up," he told them.

Jeff suspected that Andy didn't really care, except he didn't want to be freaky. What Andy was really interested in was science. He read science books and science magazines, he often skipped other assignments to work on science and was surprised when the teachers of his other courses yelled at him about that.

He was smart enough to see how odd that made him, and he was frightened of being too odd, Jeff saw, because he was afraid of being laughed at. Jeff could sympathize with that.

A girl named Carol Sutter put notes on Jeff's desk in math class and tried to get him to talk to her in the library and cafeteria and stared at him in the halls. But he didn't talk about that. He felt sorry for her and embarrassed for her. She was pretty, he guessed; she had long blonde hair that she wore loose down her back and big, violet-blue eyes. A lot of the boys liked her, and Jeff wished she would like one of them back. Phil found one of the notes before Jeff did. "You're the cutest boy in the whole school." It wasn't signed, they never were, but Phil recognized the handwriting.

"Greene, you're wasting opportunities," he said. "Do you know how many guys would kill for this?"

"Oh, well," Jeff said.

"You ought to take her out, or something. Why not?"

"I don't like her."

"So what? She likes you."

Jeff shrugged.

"That's weird, really weird, Greene. But I forgive you. I'm glad you decided you wanted to be friends with me, whatever weird things you say," Phil told him. "You'll outgrow this phase."

Jeff was stopped in his tracks by that. Was that what had happened? Had he, in fact, chosen his friends? And not the other way around?

For Christmas that year his father gave him a book, his book. They also had a tree they'd decorated, and Jeff sat beside it in his pajamas, with the book on his lap. "It's okay for me to read it now, isn't it?"

"I didn't know you wanted to," the Professor said.

"Professor—you made me promise not to until I was fifteen. And then you didn't give me one for my birthday. What do you mean I didn't want to read it?"

"I'm sorry," his father said.

"No, that's okay," Jeff tried to reassure him, tried to keep his eyes off the book, which by then he wanted to read so badly he wanted to end the conversation and get started.

"I never know how to communicate," the Professor said.

The Professor looked half asleep. Jeff had no idea from his face what he was thinking. "Hey," he said, "that's not true. That sounds like the kind of thing Melody would say, the way she does. Has she been—?"

The Professor looked up. "Now I think of it, yes. You'd think I'd learn."

Jeff opened the cover of the book and turned the blank first page. He read the title, turned the page, read the copyright information—he had no idea of what he'd find in this book, how it would read, what its subject was. He saw the dedication: *For my son.*

He put his fingers on the page. He stared and stared at the words, especially at the one word, *son.* "Professor," he said, "I'm honored."

The Professor didn't answer. "She knows we don't live in Baltimore, she knows we moved."

"It's okay, it's going to be okay. Trust me; I'm your son, it says so right here." He pointed his finger at the word. "She can't make me live with her. She doesn't even want me to, I bet. There's something, and if she thinks I won't tell the truth she's making a big mistake about me."

"But—she's your mother."

"So what?"

He wouldn't choose Melody, not now. He knew that, but he tried to think about why: he'd liked her being beautiful and the sound of her voice, but he didn't trust her and he didn't like the way she talked about need. He suspected that it made her feel good to feel sorry for people. She was dangerous, the way she pulled at your emotions. No, he wouldn't choose her now.

Jeff continued to be satisfied with his two chosen friends at school. They even, at the end of the year and a couple of times over the summer, went to a few parties, where Jeff would play his guitar and sing or jam with some other people who played. Jeff and Andy got along all right at parties, but it was Phil who really fit in, dragging the other two along with him. Jeff even learned how to dance and put his arm around a girl and how to kiss one, although he never took a date and always arranged it so he didn't have to take anyone home. He figured he was still learning how to have friends, and he wasn't interested in having a girlfriend. So he kept his distance clear. There was no sense in hurting anyone's feelings. There were enough hurt feelings in the world without him adding to that.

By the time tenth grade began, the Professor was well into another book. "Like the first," he told Jeff. He wouldn't let Jeff read it in manuscript. "What if you don't like it?"

Jeff didn't pester his father. He was taking driver's ed and would get his license by the middle of October. He didn't mind school, he liked the way he'd gotten along so far, and he kept his eye out for anybody else he might choose for a friend. One girl, an eighth grader, kept catching his eye in the hall—a mature-looking black girl with a ringing laugh and lively, intelligent eyes.

Wilhemina Smiths; he found out her name. Everybody knew her already, even though she was just an eighth grader. "A real fireball," they said. Jeff thought she looked strong, inside and out, and he thought to himself that he wouldn't call her a real fireball, but a real person.

Except for the permanent uneasiness of what Melody might do, he felt pretty good. She had sent him a note. Why would she do that? How stupid did she think he was? And she'd enclosed it in a letter to the Professor. He knew why she'd sent it that way, instead of sending it separately. The letter accused his father of being unnaturally cruel to her and trying to get back at her by using Jeff and being selfish and having no sympathy for what she'd been through. The note to Jeff was short. It said she missed him, he knew that, and if he was allowed to see the note, which she doubted, she'd know that if he answered it.

Jeff didn't believe a word of it and didn't answer. It didn't make any difference what Melody got up to now, because she didn't matter to him anymore. He had locked her out of his mind and out of his life. She could no longer get through to him, to make him feel the way she used to. He just wanted to forget about her and the way she played on his feelings—the same way she used to play on the guitar, he thought, remembering for a minute. He knew now just how badly she had played the guitar.

CHAPTER 9

Sophomores on high honor roll didn't have to go to the study hall for their free periods, so Jeff had the last period of the day entirely free. He liked to spend it outside, sitting on a low wall by the bicycle racks, playing his guitar and working out songs. When the bell rang to end school, he would watch the kids emerge from the double doors, hurrying out and talking. Then he would either join up with Phil or Andy for the afternoon or just say, "See you," before getting on his bike and going home. Some days the Professor came and picked him up. On those days, Jeff drove the car and the Professor rode beside him, because Jeff had his learner's permit. The afternoons were slow, easy hours, and Jeff savored them, whatever happened in them.

Early in October, he was working out a song he'd heard on a record, trying to figure out how to keep the rhythm in his backup without losing the sense of flowing melody. It was a matter of balancing, of keeping things in proportion. He kept trying to get it right. "When first unto this country, a stranger I came, and I courted a fair maid and Nancy was her name."

About one second after the final bell rang, a kid came out through the doors. A kid with somewhere to go, Jeff thought, continuing to play. The kid wasn't anyone he knew, a narrow head with ragged, dark hair, cut-offs, T-shirt, and long, skinny legs. What held his eye, as he sat playing his guitar in mild

October sunlight, was the lift of the kid's chin. That chin raised—not high, not angry. Brave maybe. Purposeful. He looked at the kid's face. Even features and a straight nose, eyes dark and the mouth large. His hands played as his mind wandered.

The kid turned in Jeff's direction, as if the music were some kind of string winding around the long legs. Jeff kept his eyes down, watching at the periphery of his vision the awkward and reluctant approach, as if the long legs were trying to move away from him but moved instead toward him. He'd never seen more tired-looking sneakers in his life, he thought, and looked up into a pair of dark hazel eyes, brown shot with greens and golds—a girl? What did she want? An eighth grader, probably; she had no figure—especially in those clothes.

"I never heard that song," she said. She didn't want to say that, she didn't want to be drawn over to him, but she couldn't do anything to stop herself. She couldn't stop herself from coming over or from asking, even though she wanted to.

Jeff sang the song, all the way through. Her presence affected his voice, which had settled down over the summer: she listened so intently he was confused; she stood so still he barely dared look at her. Or maybe it was her eyes he didn't want to look at, because he had seen the way the music coiled around her and drew her to him, in her eyes, seen something helpless in her against music and melody. She stared at his hands playing and soaked in his song in a way that made him think—for the first time in a long time—of the island, of solitude and space and the waves tumbling up onto the broad white beaches. He finished the song and looked up at her. She had her hands jammed awkwardly into her pockets; the melody of the song still played behind her eyes, he was sure of it. He played a couple of chords so the thread of music wouldn't be broken between them. "Have a sit, kid," he said, himself awkward, and that broke the spell, and she was free because he'd said it wrong.

She shook her head and turned abruptly away. He watched her back, her straight shoulders, the long-legged way she walked.

About a week later, she marched back up to him, wearing a boy's shirt this time, chin high, and demanded: "What are the words for that song."

Jeff didn't know how to take it, and why she came up cross to ask a favor. He felt like smiling at her, but kept his face expressionless, because he didn't know how she'd react. He recited the verses, without playing any music. He had all of her attention and he was willing to bet she'd remember the words. Her face and expression looked intelligent, alert. She didn't thank him, just went to get on her bike and ride off.

He saw her a couple of times in the hallways, always alone. He watched for her after school. He would cast out his song like a fisherman his line, and she'd get drawn in because she couldn't help it. Finally he introduced himself. "My name's Jeff Greene." She nodded her head, her eyes wary. "What's yours?" he asked. He kept on playing, not even a melody, just any music so she wouldn't take off.

"Dicey Tillerman," she told him.

He knew the name and remembered the old lady with the red boat. "You related to that old lady with the farm?" he asked. That was the wrong thing to say, he could see it in her eyes, in her chin. He held her with music. "What are you, a grandchild?" She nodded again. She wasn't going to say anything: stubborn. Jeff kept himself from grinning: stubborn and prickly.

"Listen, can you sing the melody for 'The Coat of Many Colors'?" he asked on impulse. "I want to try a harmony."

She didn't want to, she didn't sit down, but she started to sing. He kept the guitar soft, listening to her voice and trying to harmonize with half of his attention. She didn't have a great voice, but it sang true notes. She sang the song plainly, her voice round and strong; he could hear in her singing how much she liked the song. He had her now, and he thought he'd say something she wanted to hear. "You sing pretty well."

"Not particularly. Just better than you." Jeff didn't know how to take that. He didn't know what to say next. "My sister is the one who can really sing," she continued. "You should hear her sing this song." She liked her sister. And she wasn't fishing for compliments—that was for sure—and she sure wasn't trying to flatter him. He couldn't imagine her telling a lie.

He put a friendly expression on his face, "I'd like to." He waited for her to ask him out to her house.

"I gotta go now," she said.

Jeff was surprised. He felt things shift on him, like a shift in the tide. She was about to run away on him. "Why?" he asked. "I've got another song you might like."

All she answered was, "I gotta go."

Well, he probably couldn't stop her, he guessed. He bet nobody could stop her when she wanted something or had something she had to do. Probably that was what appealed to him, her determination; opposites attracted, they said. That, and the way he could hold her helpless with music. That and the way she didn't act like most girls, saying one thing and hinting at another with her eyes. She just went her own way, in her own way—she didn't ask or even want anything from him. She was as distant as the ocean, even when you're up close to it. Independent, but he could pull her in with music.

He saw her in the downtown grocery store, working there. So

they must need money, her parents, because eighth grade was young for a job. She didn't expect to see him, and her chin went up when she did, so he spent his time talking with the owner while Dicey stubbornly swabbed down the floors.

One day, just before Thanksgiving, there was a story Phil told him, about how this squirty eighth grader had flattened Chappelle, something about whether or not she'd cheated on the character sketch essay. The kid, Phil said, delighted to be telling such a good story, had stood up to the teacher, and then Wilhemina Smiths had joined up with her and between them they'd reduced Chappelle to nothing. To a puddle of nothing on the floor. "You've got to feel sorry for the guy," Phil said. Jeff heard the same story, with several variations, over the day and wasn't surprised to see Dicey walking out of school that afternoon with the black girl. It was too cold to play the guitar outside, so he had to keep it in a case, but he tried greeting her anyway. "Hey, Dicey. I hear you put Chappelle into his place." He waited to see how she'd react to the greeting, to the compliment.

"That wasn't me, that was Mina," Dicey told him. "Do you know Mina?"

Jeff looked into a pair of laughing eyes. She was as tall as he was. "Everybody knows Mina."

"Yeah," the girl answered. "Everybody knows you too, friend."

"That's what they think," Jeff told her, thinking how nobody knew at all what he was really like, inside. She chuckled, amused, friendly. He relaxed.

"So, was this essay as good as everybody says?" he asked Dicey. He watched her eyes, wondering how she'd react to a question not about music.

She didn't know what to say, and her eyes looked back into his, brown, green, gold, distant and close, both. "No, of course not," she said, and he grinned at her. He knew she'd tell the truth. "But it was pretty good," she said, to be exact. The two girls walked away from him, and he felt his face, smiling goofily, watching them.

That afternoon he risked going back to the little store on purpose, because he had the car for their Thanksgiving shopping, which the Professor didn't want to do. A little kid was with Dicey, a little blond kid with the same hazel eyes, only rounder and not as dark, and the same prickly attitude, her brother. Jeff made his purchases and offered her a ride home. It turned out she was taking her brother with her on her bike, so she was glad of the offer. Sammy, she called him. Jeff didn't mind waiting. He tried some music on Sammy, who wasn't glad to meet him, but who obeyed Dicey.

"Does she always ride you home?" he asked the boy, after he'd played the longest song he knew and the kid had settled down.

"Nope."

"How come today?"

The kid shrugged. He didn't want to answer the question. Jeff saw marks on his face and decided he'd been in a fight. He looked tough enough to be able to do well in a fight. Jeff tried another question. "You live with your grandmother?" He thought he'd say next how he lived farther out along the same road.

"So what?" Sammy asked, a wave of anger coming at Jeff. But it was kid's anger and he knew how to answer it.

"So nothing," Jeff said. "I'm innocent, officer; I didn't do nothing," he teased.

Sammy giggled. He wiped his hand across his cheek, still smiling. He sat cross-legged on the floor, a sturdy little kid in sneakers.

"You and your sister have the worst-looking sneakers I've ever seen," Jeff said.

"Oh, yeah?" The kid was ready to fight again. Jeff changed the subject, puzzled:

"What're you in, third grade?"

"Naw, second. I've got a sister in third."

"The one who sings?" At that his face changed again; he liked his sister a lot.

"Yeah."

"Boy, do you remind me of Dicey," Jeff said.

Sammy looked at him for a long time, then nodded his head. "Good-o."

Dicey told Jeff it was all right, so he went to their house the next Saturday. He rode his bike over through unseasonally warm weather. He walked it up the driveway, trying to avoid puddles where Thanksgiving snow flurries had melted. He walked it up because he was nervous about getting there.

The driveway went between two neglected fields and then under a stand of pines. At the front of the house, which looked like nobody ever went in that way, a big tree stretched out bare branches, held firm by thick twisted wires. The path went around the side, past a screen porch. Jeff didn't see anybody around. He had his guitar slung across his back and he stood for a minute, looking around him, feeling awkward, thinking maybe he'd go home, noticing that they had a big garden out behind the house and a path through it that led down to the marshes. He considered just turning around and riding home, but he was curious about this singing sister. The door of the barn, its bottom rotted away in large pieces, had been braced open. He looked inside.

Dicey had her back to him. She wore cutoffs and a T-shirt. She didn't know he was there. She was scraping paint off the hull of a little boat, a sailboat he guessed from the deep curved keel, and he could see a mast laid on the ground over by some stalls. She moved like she was dancing, leaning into each stroke, her legs long, her shoulder blades outlined under the T-shirt. Her short raggedy hair shone dark in the warm sunlight. Except for the noise of the scraper it was absolutely quiet. "Dicey?" he said.

She wheeled around and she was angry at him. He could feel it.

"Whatcha doing?" he asked. He felt like saying I'm sorry.

"I'm the one to ask that," she said, anger in her eyes and in her face. She held the scraper like a weapon, up against him.

Jeff looked over her shoulder to the stalls, then over her other shoulder to the worktable. Back and forth. Her feelings washed over him, like waves, and he didn't know how he'd let this happen. He had been in this scene before, with Melody, with the anger and dislike attacking him and breaking him down. He could feel himself cracking, inside. He didn't know why he kept forgetting what he was really like. He didn't know it mattered so much to him. If he'd known that, he never would have come out here, he never would have wound her around with music. He'd been fooling himself. Again.

Dicey stared at him and he could see in her face that she didn't think much of him. He agreed with her, he wasn't much. But she didn't have to get angry. He didn't understand women, girls, he never would; he didn't even much want to. Except he hadn't thought Dicey was like that. Kidding himself that he understood her. Thinking he had cast out his line of music, baited with glittering song, cast it out into the water and slowly reeled her in, so gently that she didn't even know what was happening.

"Look," he said, keeping his voice expressionless, hiding everything about himself. "I thought I'd come out and see you, and I want to meet this sister of yours. If you're busy, I'll go. If you don't like the idea"—he thought for the right, unemotional words—"of me being here—you just have to say so."

"No," she answered quickly, her face relaxing, her hostility flowing away and out, like a wave, washing past and gone. "It's not that. Come on in, I've only got a little more to do here. I was just surprised to see someone."

Jeff was surprised himself at how relieved he was to hear her say that. But if this was what she was like when she was only surprised, she would be a terror if she was angry. He leaned his bike against a post and came closer, cautiously. He took the guitar off his back. "If that's the way you react to surprises, I'll be careful not to surprise you again," he promised her. It was, now that he thought about it, pretty funny, the whole scene.

For a long time she kept looking at his eyes, and then she smiled at him, just briefly, because her smile disappeared as fast as it came, even though it stayed, somehow, bright behind her eyes. He was glad he'd stayed out her anger. Glad because of the smile and glad because he'd had the courage. Her smile told him she liked him for fighting back.

When she asked him to play a song while she finished, he had to strum chords for a while and pretend to be tuning up until he settled down. He didn't want her to see how unsettled he'd been by the whole thing. How unsettled he still was. He had thought he was the fisherman, but he saw now—

She had pronged him, with a single stroke, pronged him through the heart and he was caught. Just like with Melody, caught. But this wasn't Melody, Dicey wasn't. And besides, he didn't feel pronged, he felt—overwhelmed, out of breath, breathless.

Dicey watched him, but he did not look up to meet her eyes: he had things to settle inside himself first, he thought, recognizing that he felt easy, at ease, and also alert, eager, as if he had just fought his way through some thick overgrown jungle to the ocean beaches beyond.

CHAPTER 10

Jeff's life that tenth grade year became suddenly crowded, with people he liked, with things he wanted to do. Sometimes he caught himself protesting to himself: life is too rich. Like one of the French meals Brother Thomas cooked for them, where when you concentrated on the taste of chicken you knew you were missing out on the sharp, winy sauce and the sweetness of onions or mushrooms sauteed so briskly that their musty flavor got locked inside each slice. Life is so rich, Jeff said to himself gratefully.

Much of this had to do with the Tillermans; especially Dicey, but—since you couldn't separate her from her family, and Jeff didn't even want to—the whole crew of them, individually and together. He spent a lot of time at the farmhouse after that first day. One way and another, he did a lot of work with them. That first day it was Maybeth who knocked him out. She was almost ten and so lovely Jeff had to be careful not to stare at her. Staring at her, he knew, would make her more shy. He could feel how frightened she was, of anyone strange.

Her eyes were large and round, clear hazel, and looked right at him once she got her courage up. They were the kind of eyes that you could look all the way into and know there was nothing ungentle in her. At first she was shy and silent but, like Dicey, she could be looped in with music. He watched the way the songs and the singing won her over slowly. He watched how quietly she moved and how quietly she sat, her hands still. He watched how her skin shone as if from within, like fine porcelain. All of her reactions were slow. When he asked her how she liked a song, or if she wanted to choose one, he had to wait for her answer while she looked at him out of clear eyes. You couldn't hurry Maybeth, and he didn't want to because he felt how that might hurt her. Once he caught on to her particular rhythm, the slowness didn't bother him.

Walking their bicycles down the driveway at the end of the afternoon, he asked Mina Smiths the question he didn't dare ask Dicey. "Where are their parents?"

Mina was tall enough to look him straight in the eye, a measuring glance, wondering if she could trust him. "Do you gossip?"

"No."

"That kid can sing, can't she?"

"Yeah," Jeff agreed wholeheartedly.

Mina kept looking at him until she finally said, "I'll tell you what I know. Their father's been gone since before Sammy was born and never married their mother anyhow. Then, last summer, their mother went nuts. She's in a mental hospital somewhere."

"So their grandmother took them in," Jeff finished. "Poor kids." He could see them, just the four of them standing alone in a hostile world.

"You stupid, friend?" Mina asked. She was laughing at him. "You know how they got here? They walked. Dicey brought them, just the kids, just the four of them. There was some cousin in Connecticut, and that's where they started if you want to look at a map. Dicey didn't like it at the cousin's, so they ran away and came down here. Mrs. Tillerman wasn't going to let them stay—"

"Why not? She seems to like them."

"I think Dicey convinced her. I guess when Dicey wants something she gets it."

"They're alike, Dicey and her grandmother, don't you think?" Jeff asked.

Mina hadn't thought of that. "Maybe they are. That would be funny, because Dicey said their grandmother didn't even know they were alive. They hadn't even heard about her until Connecticut."

"You mean they came down here without knowing anything?"

"That's it."

It would be like jumping off a cliff and hoping the water was deep enough, Jeff thought. Only Dicey had to jump with the three littler children holding on to her. And traveling all that way, too. It would be like whistling in the dark and following the sound of your own melody. He couldn't have done that, he knew; he hadn't had to, but he could see the kind of courage it took, and the kind of hopelessness. He just shook his head. "I guess they're not exactly pitiful," he told Mina.

"Not exactly," she agreed.

"And they really feel like a family, all of them," he said.

"More than mine, and mine hasn't ever been disrupted," she said. He looked across at her and began to see why she liked Dicey.

"I'm an only child," he said.

"And you're not stupid, are you, friend," she said, her eyes still laughing, but friendly.

"Not a bit of it, friend." He was sure of that.

What he liked about the Tillermans, he decided—after knowing them for winter and spring, after taking care of the little kids when Mrs. Tillerman took Dicey out sailing, after working with the stubbornly energetic Sammy on the spring planting, after arguing ideas with James, after learning how to play the Martin behind Maybeth's voice and how to sing harmony with all of them . . . What he liked was the person he became around them. He liked the complicated interactions, trying to keep aware of what each person was feeling. He liked being able to move comfortably among them.

With Mrs. Tillerman, you had to stand up to her and not let her bully you and also let her just be herself, let her wander around in bare feet, let her say what she thought even though half the time Jeff couldn't tell how she made the connections between one idea and the next. With Sammy you had to wrestle and play catch and be ready to tease him into laughter or let him clown at you until you laughed. With Maybeth you had to go slowly, gently, let her open up like a flower. With James you had to be smart like the Professor and Brother Thomas, carry on the argument, but not tell James what to think. You had to understand that some of his wrong thinking was right for a smart kid in fifth grade and trust him to grow out of it at the proper time. Jeff could do all these things, he discovered, and do them pretty well.

With Dicey—he didn't know, he could never be sure. Sometimes she wanted to be left alone, and sometimes she wanted to chase down crabs with everybody running around in circles. Always she liked music, of any kind, and she was smarter than she'd figured out yet, he thought. He'd watched her turn quiet and inward after her mother died. That had happened just before Christmas—the mother had never gotten well—and

Dicey was as private as the Professor in her sorrow, as solitary. He had known she needed to be left alone, just as he had known that Sammy needed to be wrestled with, hard, during that long time of grieving, that James's absorbed interest in entomology came from the same source, and that Maybeth was all right, stronger, somehow, for this than any of the others. Stronger even than Mrs. Tillerman, whose temper flared, whose eyes watched Jeff warily.

If he stayed too long she would come into the room. "Go home, boy, we can't feed an extra mouth."

"Yes, ma'am." He would leave quickly, knowing that her greeting when he returned would be as direct.

"It's a good thing you came by, James keeps talking about bugs at me."

Jeff kept up with his friends, with Phil and Andy, partly because they were his friends and partly because he couldn't crowd the Tillermans. Phil asked him, that spring, what was going on with Dicey. "What is it, you have a thing for that Tillerman kid?"

"She's not a kid. She's a girl."

"Yeah, but Greene—okay, okay, none of my business, right? Don't bother telling me to stuff it, I know what that kind of stiff-faced look means. We'll drop it. I mean, for all I know, she's as sweet as honey and a real hot number, for all I know."

Seeing Dicey as Phil saw her, Jeff just laughed. Phil joined in, and Jeff didn't say what he might have because Phil wouldn't have understood. Honey, Dicey wasn't. She was tart, bitter—alive; and she made him feel alive too, awake. They all did. And he thought she liked him too, anyway more than she liked most people—and that was pretty good.

Jeff kept up his own friendships, pestering Andy with the

questions James asked about insects, until he finally introduced the two of them and left them to their discussions. He kept up with his schoolwork. He kept up with his guitar and his hours appreciating the water, marshes, sky, birds, trees—sometimes just the whole world. He kept up with the Professor, too, especially; listening and talking, living together.

That summer, because Andy was going up to Baltimore for some advanced classes at Johns Hopkins and Phil worked at the business of farming, Jeff set up in a crabbing business with the Tillermans. They had to learn how to lay and run a trotline, but between Mrs. Tillerman's experience and James's research, it didn't take them long. Dicey had a couple of regular babysitting jobs as well as her grocery store job, so it was Sammy or James who waited at the dock for Jeff, a shadowy figure in predawn light. Sammy had more endurance for the work. He had the energy to pick up a badly set line and reset it, never complaining about the sheer hard work. James had the kind of mind that never rested quiet. Either way, Jeff enjoyed the long hours.

It was James, sitting in the back of the little boat while Jeff did the job of hauling in the trotline, who asked him about his parents. "Is your father really the one who wrote that book?"

Jeff stood up straight, relaxing tired back muscles. He looked back to where the younger boy leaned against the silent motor. "Yeah, why?"

"I read it, it was good," James said. He rested his feet on top of one of the bushels of crabs they'd deliver downtown.

"He told me, asked me anyway, not to read it until I was fifteen," Jeff said. He had to wipe sweat from his forehead and the smell of ripe salted eel assaulted his nostrils. "Ugh," he said.

"What about your mother?" James asked. But then he

changed the subject. "So I shouldn't have read it? I could reread it later; it was a good book, I don't mind. It was dedicated to you."

"I know," Jeff said, making himself bend to the task again.

"Why not your mother?"

"She walked out on us, when I was in second grade."

"I didn't know that. So did my father, but I wasn't that old. I guess it's not so uncommon. So did my mother, but that was different. I used to think it was me, or us."

Jeff didn't turn around, but he thought hard. "I guess everybody thinks that. Kids. Maybe adults too."

"I don't know why people have kids if they're just going to walk out. Did you ever ask your mother? Did you ever see her after?"

"A couple of times," Jeff said. "I asked her, but she lied."

James didn't answer right away, then he spoke quickly, the way he did when a new idea had just occurred to him. "Maybe it's women; maybe women are liars, maybe that's one of the differences. Dicey knows how to lie, you should have heard her. When we came down here, and it was just us? She would spin stories—sometimes I thought I'd bust out laughing. Every time different, every time perfect. Cripes—now I think of it—she was really something."

"Dicey doesn't lie," Jeff said. His stomach felt cold, even with the heat and sweat out on the water.

"Sure she does."

Jeff heaved the cinderblock that anchored down the line's end, heaved it up and into the boat.

"No, she doesn't."

"Why shouldn't she? Cripes, Jeff, you don't know what we were up against, even I didn't and I'm glad I didn't. Sometimes when I think about it . . ." He stared at Jeff. "Never mind," he said, closing Jeff out. "I shouldn't have told you. I know what you're thinking, but you're wrong." Jeff just shook his head. He couldn't answer, he didn't trust himself to speak.

The whole day had gone black and cold around him. James couldn't know what he was thinking, and Jeff didn't want to be thinking what he was thinking, about Melody. He knew James was closing him out, but he didn't care.

He felt as if he'd just learned that Dicey was dying of some incurable disease. He felt the fragile inside part of himself cracking. He could hide it, he felt pretty sure about that; he knew he was strong enough to hide it. From everybody but himself.

So that when Dicey finally did what he'd been wanting her to do for a long time and asked him if he'd like to go for a sail, he almost said no. It wasn't that he liked her any less or expected her to be perfect. He knew she wasn't perfect—she was often bossy, and she always knew what she wanted, so she was impatient with anyone less decisive. She was harsh, sometimes; too quick to judge, especially people who didn't work the same way she did. He knew that. But he didn't want her to be imperfect in that one particular way. And if she was (and James would know) Jeff didn't feel necessarily safe with her alone. He looked over her shoulder, thinking up excuses.

"Hey. You don't have to," she said, puzzled, irritated. Well, he'd certainly hinted, so he could see why she was puzzled. Her eyes studied his face, trying to figure out what he was thinking; but he kept his face expressionless. "I mean, if you're scared because I'm not very good yet, that's okay."

How did she know he was scared? Jeff wondered. The same way he knew she was more puzzled than angry, however she sounded. "It's just that I promised the Professor," he said, seizing the half-truth.

"You don't need to make excuses," she told him.

Jeff didn't know what to say. He had let himself get tied up in his feelings with Dicey and through her with them all; and this was what happened, it was probably bound to happen.

"I've got life preservers. Gram made me plunk three weeks' earnings into them," she told him impatiently, "and I don't care if you don't want to."

That was true, Jeff knew, she didn't care if he didn't want to, even though it meant a lot to her. He was confused and kept looking at her. She waited impatiently for a couple of minutes, chewing on her lower lip, then turned her back on him and started walking down the path to the dock. He watched her walk, her long legs and bare feet, the cutoffs and T-shirt, and he followed her. He hadn't made up his mind, either to go or not to go. He felt that he'd disappointed her and he should apologize; he didn't want her to be angry at him. He got into the boat.

She hoisted the sails and cast off from the dock without saying anything. They moved out onto the bay, and still she didn't say anything. When Jeff finally turned to look at her, he realized that she didn't even know he was there. She paid attention only to the boat, to the tiller and to the wind in the sails. She looked the way she sometimes did when they were all singing. She caught Jeff's eyes and grinned at him.

"You really like this." He was surprised at the intensity of her happiness.

"Yeah."

"But you said you only sailed once before you came here," he reminded her, checking up on the truth.

She brought the boat about, heading to the southwest on a reach, and instructed him to sit on the gunwales so that it would ride level. Waves slapped up against the side. Dicey sat back, her legs stretched out, her hand brown on the tiller.

"Across the bay, on a yacht. Boy, that was a time. Because we had to get across, to see what Crisfield was like, if we could live here. And Gram. We got to Annapolis, and we were sleeping out on this lawn—that was pretty easy because they were renovating the house so there was nobody there to know about us. We had to convince these two guys to sail us across. They wouldn't have done it to help out, they weren't that kind. So I told them we were going to visit relatives, an aunt who worked full time, in Easton, whose children were in day camp so it didn't matter what time we got there, and I told them we were staying with an old lady who knew our parents, but was too old to keep close tabs on us." She stopped speaking, thought. "The hardest thing, all the time, was trying to remember all the different ends you had to cover and let it slip out in conversation, not as if you were making it up. And trying to look casual, too, because if these guys had figured out that we really needed help they wouldn't have offered it. James kept asking them if the boat could sail all the way across the bay—and I kept thinking to myself what a dumb question. Until I figured out what he was up to. Then it had to be some kind of a dare, because—it was a funny kind of friendship, no friendship at all. I couldn't have pulled it off without James that time."

"That time?"

"Other times—I just kind of knew what to tell people so they'd leave us alone."

"How come you wanted them to leave you alone?"

She ignored the question.

Jeff remembered that they had come down alone from Connecticut, and he saw a picture of the four of them, and those sneakers. He didn't feel sorry for them at all, anymore, just impressed. "But you could have gotten help from someone, the police, or welfare. Couldn't you?"

"Once we tried. Once. They wanted to put Maybeth into retarded classes, or something, and Sammy kept getting into trouble. My cousin dressed Maybeth up, and they all fluttered around her, because she was pretty, and talked about her marrying a rich man. My cousin didn't want to keep Sammy, she wanted him to go live somewhere else. There was this priest, he meant well but . . ." Her voice trailed off. She didn't want to talk about it.

Listening to her, imagining it, knowing them all, Jeff knew he couldn't understand; but he understood the important thing. James had tried to tell him, saying, "what we were up against." Jeff hadn't understood before he heard Dicey's voice, telling it. He saw now what they had had to fight through to get to Crisfield. He felt his insides ease up, relax—and he felt tears behind his eyes. And he understood himself a little more, too. He changed the subject. "I know a priest, he's okay. Actually, he's a monk, a brother, but a priest too. He's—a really good man. Where'd you live, before?"

"In Provincetown, out on Cape Cod. Right on the ocean. Not right on, but back behind the dunes, but it really was right on it."

"I was at the ocean once. Not Ocean City, that doesn't count, but—" Because he felt suddenly like talking, Jeff told her about the island, about the beach there. Then, when she asked him, he told her about how he'd bought a boat and gradually worked up the courage to explore because of being frightened.

"What were you doing there anyway?" she asked him, not interested in his fears.

"Visiting my mother. But she took off with her boyfriend. There was just my great-grandmother and a couple of elderly cousins we called aunts; they weren't interested in what I did. So I did what I liked." He could hear in his voice some of the feelings of that time, and he made a business out of adjusting the jib. Because he didn't want Dicey thinking he wanted her to feel sorry for him, because he knew he'd been lucky after all. In the long run. And the long run counted more than the short run.

"Where's the boat?" Dicey asked.

He told her about the last night in Charleston, on the island, and how he'd sunk the boat. That made her smile. Then he told her something he had only just remembered, wondering why the memory had sunk so far back into his mind that he hadn't ever recalled it. "The man who sold me the boat and rented me docking space, he was waiting when I swam back to the dock. I'd thought that nobody knew or cared where I was, what happened to me, as long as I was out of the way. Well, I was right. But he came out onto the dock with a towel. He'd known where I was, it turned out. When I hadn't come back by sunset, the way I usually did, he'd gone out looking and seen the boat tied up. Listen, Dicey, I can't say it the way he did, but he said he figured *if she gator gotchuh you's already a goner.* He called me *suh.* He said—I wish I could imitate it the way it was—*Suh, you come down here looking like she hounds of hell be chewing at your heart and no gator bites so bad. So I be watching this morning.* I guess, if I hadn't turned up, he'd have found my bones. Or something. I guess."

Dicey didn't say anything. He thought she might ask about his mother and was glad she didn't. Then she said, "I wouldn't have sunk the boat. I wouldn't ever."

"I wasn't in your kind of trouble," Jeff pointed out.

"I guess you were in your own kind," she said. "It's time to bring her about. Will you please get your weight back into the boat so I can do it?" she asked impatiently.

Brother Thomas came down for a week at the end of July, and the week stretched out to two, then three. He seemed tired, Jeff thought, subdued, and he didn't get rested up. He talked late with the Professor, night after night. Jeff fell asleep to the sound of their voices. Jeff went to bed early because he got up so early, before dawn. One dark morning, Brother Thomas sat drinking a mug of tea and watching the silky gray sky when Jeff came into the kitchen. He didn't greet Jeff, didn't even seem to know he was there.

Jeff went to the bathroom, took a quick shower, brushed his teeth, and was awake by the time he came back. Brother Thomas sat in the same position, his hands in his lap, not leaning back against the chair. The level of tea in his mug hadn't changed. "Good morning," Jeff said. "It's early."

Brother Thomas greeted him then, his face pale above the black suit and white collar he had never, on that visit, gone without. "Couldn't you sleep?" Jeff asked. "Can I get you a bowl of cereal?"

"No, thank you; I'm not hungry."

Jeff sat down to eat. "You look like you didn't sleep."

"I guess I didn't. Do you always go off at this hour?"

"I have to pick up whoever is coming with me, then get the line set. Sunrise is about six," Jeff explained. Then he had an idea. "Do you want to come?"

But Brother Thomas wasn't interested.

"You might like it," Jeff said. He couldn't understand Brother

Thomas's lack of energy; it wasn't like him, not like him at all. Something was wrong, he knew that, and he realized that this same barren feeling he was getting from Brother Thomas now was the only kind of feeling he'd gotten from the man this visit. Something was very wrong.

Jeff chewed and thought. Whatever it was, even talking with the Professor wasn't doing any good. But what was it? Okay, Jeff said to himself, surprising himself, if you're supposed to have a talent for knowing how people feel, what's Brother Thomas feeling?

He glanced at the man sitting hunched, staring out at the sky but not seeing it. Bleak, Jeff felt, bleak and hopeless, some inner landscape as barren as the moon's surface, cold and lifeless.

What can I do? Jeff asked, inside himself. He figured, if the Professor's intelligence couldn't help, then that wasn't the way. He wondered if he should do anything, even if he could think of what. But he thought he would try. Something was wrong, he didn't know what, but he wondered what he could give to Brother Thomas—who had given so much to him one way and another. "You ought to come," he urged him. "You ought to try it, you used to be good at netting crabs off the line. Besides, you'd like my friends. I don't know who it'll be today."

"Are these the Tillermans?"

"Yes. It would tire you out, too; we'll let you do all the work. You remember how much work it is, don't you? So you'll sleep well tonight." Jeff worked to persuade him. "But it gets hot."

"I don't mind," Brother Thomas said. Although he didn't say he wanted to go along, he went. They needed a flashlight to get to the boat and check the supplies, but once they were away from the dock, Jeff told Brother Thomas to turn it off. The motor worked noisily as Jeff took the boat out to the deep center of the creek, then along into the bay. In predawn darkness, black waves made the boat buck slightly. Brother Thomas's shape was black at the bow of the boat. The last stars faded from the sky, but Brother Thomas didn't notice them.

It was James who waited at the end of the Tillermans' dock, in sleepy untalkativeness, two apples in his hand. But after the dawn had begun, a pool of light on the eastern horizon spreading out to illuminate the whole sky, and after he had eaten the apples and tossed the cores into the water, he began questioning Brother Thomas, as Jeff had known he would.

"Apple cores are biodegradable, so it's not like throwing garbage. Do you worry about garbage, are you an ecologist?"

"Isn't it because they're garbage that they're biodegradable?" Brother Thomas asked.

"Yeah, maybe. No, wait, that's not true, garbage means everything even tin cans and plastic. Who are you, anyway?"

"He teaches at the university with the Professor," Jeff told James when Brother Thomas didn't answer. James was off, what did he teach, what did that mean, what kinds of books did he teach out of, what did they say, how did you get interested in teaching stuff like that, how did you learn about it, were his students smart? Brother Thomas answered all the questions, and at last his eyes met Jeff's—humorously—over James's head. Jeff just smiled back.

In between, they ran the line, culled through the haul, waited a few minutes then ran it again. Jeff drove the motor, because James got impatient at the slow, careful speed you needed to maintain. Brother Thomas and James took turns netting the crabs. Brother Thomas tried to pick up an escaped crab with his fingers and got bitten for his trouble. That seemed to please him.

"You'll have to wash that out with antiseptic," James told him. "Crab bites tend to get infected. We think they have some kind of mild natural poison on their shells for protection. Either that or it's because they're scavengers—they'll eat anything, you know."

"Apparently," Brother Thomas answered, sucking on his bleeding finger. James grinned. "What grade are you in, James?"

"Going into sixth. Why don't you take off your jacket, or is it one of the rules of your order that you can't? Aren't you hot?"

By then they had three bushels, more than enough to sell, as well as feed both families dinner. Jeff tried to ignore the stiffness in his back muscles, tightened by hours of sitting on the hard seat, leaning forward to watch where the trotline rose up out of the water, and now straining against the weight of anchor, boat, and line as he hauled the trotline in. He hoisted up the final cinderblock and set it gently down on the bottom of the boat. He stretched his arms out, trying to relieve his back. "You wouldn't like to run us in, would you?" he asked Brother Thomas.

In the round face, the brown eyes were awake again. "And I shall make you fishers of men," he joked to Jeff. "It would have been, in those days, more like crabbing than the fishing industry is now. That's something I don't think I understood before."

"You mean, with the nets they used?" James asked. Then he yelled—"I'm so hungry!"

"You're always hungry," Jeff reminded him. "The line needs rebaiting—"

"Let Sammy do that. Maybeth's busy helping Gram can beans, Sammy won't mind, and besides, he got to sleep late."

"Usually," Jeff explained to Brother Thomas, "we unload at their dock, then I go home to get the car to take the catch down to the restaurant. You can stay there and help cull—"

Brother Thomas held up his finger in mute protest.

"We've got tongs," James told him. "Gram used them when she was a little girl. Her uncle made them. They're wooden. He was a bootlegger."

Brother Thomas's face shone red with heat, and beads of sweat speckled the top of his head. He decided to stay at the Tillermans' to clean his hand, maybe to cull, at least to set eyes on these historic tongs.

Jeff drove the car back to the farmhouse. He parked by the barn. Dicey, he knew, worked downtown all day Saturday. Mrs. Tillerman was in the big vegetable garden, her hair wild and her loose shirt flapping in the breeze as she crouched over bushy green-bean plants. At the other end, Brother Thomas in his black suit worked with a hoe around the staked tomato plants, bending to pull out clumps of weeds and toss them into a heap, chopping at the dirt, to loosen it. His face was even redder, and sweat ran down his cheeks.

"Do you want to come downtown with us?" Jeff asked him.

He stood up straight and leaned his weight on the hoe. He was breathing heavily. "I'll finish here. She doesn't talk much, does she?"

"No. But when she does you better look out," Jeff said.

"Hostile?"

"Just sharp. She's pretty terrific. Why don't you take off your jacket and vest and all?"

The brown eyes moved from Jeff's face down to the far opposite end of the garden, where Mrs. Tillerman hunched over the beans. They moved to the green marsh grasses beyond. "If I do I might never get it on again," Brother Thomas said. "So I think I'd better not."

"Ummm," Jeff said, wondering how he should respond.

"There's a Botticelli angel inside, snapping beans," Brother Thomas said.

"Maybeth."

"Yes. She didn't say a word, looked frightened of me. She applied antiseptic, bandaged my finger, stared at me. Then back to the beans. She doesn't look a bit like James. Why was she frightened? Who *are* these people?"

Jeff didn't know what to say. He went on down to the dock, said hello to Sammy, who was rebaiting the long trotline at a steady pace, then lifted one of the bushels while James carried the other. They delivered the crabs and split the money—putting aside enough for a five-gallon tank of gas and ten pounds of salted eel. Jeff had tried not to split the money, because he certainly didn't need it; but the Tillermans didn't work that way, although as far as he could tell they did need it.

Brother Thomas yawned all through dinner that night, and when they sat afterward over the bright-colored glasses of wine he was, he said, so tired he couldn't talk in complete sentences. "You could sleep in Jeff's room, you could go to bed now if you want," the Professor said. "You don't have to entertain us."

Brother Thomas shook his head, sunburned above the white collar. "You know? I'm enjoying the fatigue. But Horace, what's Melody up to? We've been talking about nothing but me, and I'm too tired to agonize tonight. You agonize."

The Professor smiled at Jeff, who was playing softly on the guitar. Outside, the sun slid down the western sky, and the creek ran beside the marshes, blue shot with ripples of gold. "We had the hearing, uncontested. I should get the decree next week, then there's a thirty-day period during which she can appeal. If she doesn't, the thing is finished. So it's been easy, in the end."

"The machinery of the law," Brother Thomas said. His eyelids drooped and he lifted them, sipped at his glass, held it up to turn it around in the light, then asked, "How do you feel about it, Jeff?"

"It doesn't make any difference to me," Jeff said. "I mean, I wouldn't have gone to live with her. I'm almost seventeen, they couldn't have made me."

"You never can tell what people can make you do," Brother Thomas told him. "You can't even tell what you'll want to do. My brother's daughter just got married, and his son is starting college in the fall. It's all the future with them. And they're right. It was in California, Horace, I was out among the beautiful people. They think I'm an anachronism. Something of a lost soul. A funny old man."

"And what do you think?"

"Me, I don't know. I don't know what I think. Except, I'm tired, bone tired." He yawned.

"I've never met these friends of Jeff's," the Professor said. "I know Phil and Andy, but not the Tillermans."

"Why not?"

"No reason," Jeff said.

"There are even a couple more I didn't see, one of them a girl, about Jeff's age, I take it." One eyelid raised and one curious brown eye looked at Jeff.

"She's much younger," Jeff said. He put down the guitar. "Her name's Dicey," he said, looking at his father's face. "She's a lot like her grandmother."

"That is one strong old lady," Brother Thomas said. "She could work me into a stupor without even straining her own resources." He yawned again and admitted that he had to get to bed, if it was okay with Jeff if he used Jeff's room.

After he'd left, Jeff picked up the guitar again and played what he called to himself Dicey's song. He didn't sing it, just played the melody against a strum, the words inside his head: "With my hands all in my pockets and my hat slung back so bold, and my coat of many colors like Jacob of old."

"How'd you come to take him with you today?" the Professor asked.

"He was awake and I asked him. Why?" He wondered if his father felt left out. "You don't want to, do you? Do you mind not meeting them? If it ever works out, you will. It's just that I go there, not them coming here."

"No, no and no." The Professor smiled at him. "It's clear that it was good for him, that's why I asked. He's at a bad time—"

"I thought, this morning. He hadn't slept, he said. He seems better, tonight."

"Sometimes, I think, it's hard to accept exactly who you are. And there can't be much harder to get through than a genuine spiritual crisis."

"A spiritual crisis? But . . . I don't understand." Yes that would make sense, Jeff thought, that would explain the barren feeling Brother Thomas seemed to have—if you lived your life in faith, with faith, and then something made you question how you'd lived your whole life.

"I don't know and neither does he," the Professor said. "But he seems to have had a good day, and that's the first in a long time for him. I'm grateful to you."

"I didn't do anything. It was mostly the Tillermans. But they didn't really do anything, either."

"We never do. But sometimes, things get done. Don't they? And I wouldn't mind meeting these Tillermans, if it ever works out."

Jeff nodded his head.

"Are you courting this girl?" the Professor asked.

Jeff felt his face grow hot. "You don't court Dicey," he told his father. "That's not what she's like."

"What's she like?"

Jeff didn't know what to say. "She's—I guess—she's straight. You know? She likes to sail. She works hard. Smart, I think, very."

"I can't picture her," the Professor said thoughtfully. "No, that's okay, I'm not prying. I'm only trying to behave like a responsible father and be familiar with my son's social life."

"I appreciate the effort," Jeff teased him. "If there's anything to report, I'll tell you, maybe. Is there such a thing as a one-woman man do you think?"

The Professor's face went expressionless. Then he met Jeff's eyes and answered Jeff's real question: "I wouldn't be surprised if you were; it seems to be in your character. And what's in your character is what you've got to deal with."

The next time Dicey asked Jeff to go sailing with her, he waited until they were heading out before he asked if she'd come by his house.

"Why?" Dicey asked.

"Well, you've never met the Professor and when Brother Thomas was here he met your family—"

"Gram said—do you know what she said? *I don't dislike the man,* as if—as if that was a big compliment." Dicey grinned.

"He said she was one strong old lady," Jeff told her.

"He sure was a help."

"The Professor said he hadn't met you, you Tillermans. And if he wanted to, I thought—he doesn't ask for things, and he didn't ask but he said he'd like to, and for him that's asking. Would you mind?"

"We should get somebody else. James is home; he'd love to meet someone who wrote a book. Ready to come about?"

"No. Just one at a time, he's—" Jeff didn't know how to say what he was thinking, because it was so complicated. Something to do with treating the Professor gently, or maybe letting him meet them the way Jeff had, sort of one at a time, or naturally and not as if it was arranged. He didn't want to explain, he just wanted Dicey to go along with what he wanted.

She shrugged and gave her attention back to the sail. He pointed out the entrance to the creek. "We'll have to tack up it," she said, and that pleased her, because it was harder. "When we get past the point, haul up on the centerboard. Your creek is broad."

"It's not my creek."

Jeff pulled up the centerboard and set it down on the floorboards. They negotiated the entrance. "Is that your house?" She looked up at the windowed front of the low building. Jeff nodded.

They had to tack six times. Dicey decided to sail up above the dock so they could approach it with the wind behind them. As they turned around to head down—and Jeff crawled onto the deck to pull down the jib—he saw a blue heron standing on a little muddy point of land across the creek. He pointed and Dicey followed his eyes.

The blue raised its flat head to look at them. Its feet were in the water, its feathers slightly ruffled as if by a recent annoyance. Jeff watched the bird, waiting for it to take off, anticipating the squawk with which it would trumpet its disapprovals.

But the blue seemed not to find them threatening. It stared

across the creek at them, then turned its back on them in a stately gesture of dismissal. Jeff knew the bird knew they were there. But, from all you could tell, the bird had never noticed them. It raised its head to look out across the marsh, unconcerned, solitary, ignoring them with great determination.

Dicey's low voice told him to pull down the mainsail, and he did. When he had it gathered around the boom, he looked back to the bird. The great blue still stood there, its back still to them. It wasn't going to let the suspicion that they were there chase it off of its fishing territory.

Jeff wrapped the sheet around the loosely furled mainsail and went up to the bow to fend off. Dicey concentrated on maneuvering the boat, propelled now only by its own weight. Her hand rested on the tiller as she waited patiently for the sluggish hull to respond to her directions. The landing was perfect.

Jeff held onto a piling with one hand while he looped a clove hitch around it. Then he looked back at Dicey. "You know who that bird reminds me of? You."

Her expression changed, and he didn't know what he'd said wrong. Then he saw that the change was caused by Dicey trying to hold back laughter. "I was thinking how much it was like you," she told him.

He didn't know what to say. "Come on up to the house." He didn't offer her a hand. Dicey liked to do things for herself.

"Are you sure you shouldn't have James here?" she asked him. "James would really like it."

Jeff was sure. He turned for a last look at the heron, now glancing over its shoulder to be certain they were leaving. "Who's that?" Dicey asked.

A woman stood at the top of the steps leading down to the dock. Her skirt blew around her slim legs, her dark hair blew back from her face. She raised on arm to wave, although she was close enough to have called out. She looked like a photograph of a dancer, Jeff thought, a dancer caught in one gesture of the dance. She looked eager and happy. She ran lightly down the steps.

"Melody," he told Dicey.

"Who's she?"

They stood side by side, watching.

"My mother," he told her, wishing she would stop asking questions.

Dicey stood away as Melody wrapped her arms around him saying, "Jeffie, Jeffie, it's so good to see you, I've missed you so terribly." Melody was shorter than he was now, and she had grown her hair out straight, but shorter than she used to wear it. Her perfume was the same. In the sunlight, the sounds of the little creek behind him, Jeff didn't know what to do.

"And who is this?" Melody asked, looking at Dicey. Jeff didn't answer, so she went over to Dicey and held out her hand. Dicey shook it briefly, looked at Jeff, looked back to Melody. "I'm Jeffie's wicked old mother," Melody said, laughing. "He didn't know I was coming—did you, darling?" Her face turned like a flower briefly back to Jeff, who shook his head. "I hope I haven't interrupted your plans for the day. Your father—I might have guessed—had no idea of what you were up to, where you were, when you'd be back—"

"Yes, he did," Jeff said, his face expressionless.

"Well, maybe he did, and I just wanted you to be right here, right then, so I could see you right away. You don't have any plans that can't be postponed, do you?"

"No," Dicey said when Jeff didn't answer. "I'll go along then."

"Maybe tomorrow?" Jeff asked her.

Her eyes, trying to read his expression, were bright with their secondary colors, green, gold. She shook her head. "We've got some friends—they have a circus and we're all going over to Ocean City. I was going to tell you, there won't be anybody to crab with you for a couple of days."

"Okay," Jeff said.

"Oh dear, it *is* just the wrong time, isn't it?" Melody said. "I'm so sorry—what did you say your name was?"

"Dicey." She wanted to go, and fast, Jeff could see.

"A good, old Southern name," Melody said. She tried to get Dicey to like her, to smile at her. "And I am sorry to ruin your day, truly I am. But you know how demanding mothers can be." Melody smiled as if she and Dicey shared an amusing secret.

Dicey's chin went up and her eyes snapped. "No," she said, "no, I don't." She turned abruptly and got back into the boat. Without looking at either of them, she raised the jib and unfurled the main.

Jeff looked at Melody, who had said about the wrongest thing to Dicey anybody could say.

"Well, I am sorry, Jeffie; whatever your little friend thinks."

Dicey had the main up and cleated. The sails flapped in the wind, snapping with a sound like whips. As she waited by the tiller for the boat to swing around and catch the wind, Dicey stood to sudden attention. Jeff looked where she was looking. He saw the great blue, alarmed now by the sound of the sails, draw itself clumsily up out of the water. It spread out its great wings and looped out toward the bay. Dicey turned to grin at Jeff and raise her hand in farewell. He had his face under too careful control to grin back, but he waved.

"Let's go where we can talk, really talk," Melody said to him.

She tucked her hand under his arm and he looked down at her face. She wore makeup on her eyes now, and her hair shone like the night sky. "I'm sorry I drove your little friend away, Jeffie."

"It doesn't make any difference," Jeff told her. He said it just to say something, but he realized when he heard himself that it really didn't, not to his friendship with the Tillermans. He wondered who these circus friends were, but James would tell him if Dicey wouldn't, because James liked to talk. If they were all going, then their grandmother must know them too.

"It doesn't make a difference to you, of course," his mother corrected him as they climbed the wooden steps then stood staring at the windows along the front of the house. "But you ought to think of her, what it might mean to her. She looked like such a bedraggled, lonely little thing. I felt really sorry for her. The poor girl probably has a crush on you."

Jeff bit at his lip to keep from smiling.

"But I can't feel too sorry for her, not while you're here. I was so im*pa*tient."

"Have you been here long?" Jeff asked. Where was his father?

"It felt long to me. Your father said you're getting A's in school. I'm so proud of you. I always knew you were smart; I was always on your side. I'd love to sit out here. See? I've been sitting and waiting. He even gave me a glass of iced tea. Really, sometimes he seems perfectly civilized, just like a real human being. Then he went inside to work. What work does he have during the summer?"

Jeff sat down in the chair, and she sat on the grass close beside him, her body turned eagerly to him, her eyes fixed on his face, all of her attention on him. "I think he's writing another book," Jeff said.

"Well," she said. "He is clever after all, isn't he. I haven't had a chance to read it yet, but I saw it in a bookstore. 'That's my husband,' I told a perfect stranger next to me. A perfect stranger, I was so proud. Of course, I can't say that anymore, can I?"

Jeff just shook his head.

"Poor Jeffie, I was so worried about you in all this. It's the children who really suffer during a divorce. It must have been so hard for you. But I just knew, somehow, we haven't been communicating properly, you and I. That's really why I'm here. If he wants a divorce, that's all right with me, and goodness knows I wouldn't say I've been much of a wife to him. But really, this selfishness with you—I just couldn't believe it. So I thought it over and decided to come right up here and get the question settled openly. Your room is all ready for you. Gambo—she's failing so badly she even made a will and she never would do that before—she needs to see you again. The schools are at least as good as the school here, I'm sure of that. So I just came right up here to collect you."

"But—"

Melody waited, her eyes smiling into his, light gray rimmed with dark, lovely. She didn't look any older, she never did, she probably never would, somehow. She was always beautiful.

"But I thought that was all settled," Jeff mumbled. What was he supposed to say and *where* was his father? He looked over his shoulder to the house. A shadowy figure stood by the kitchen window.

An expression of great sadness washed over Melody's features, and she turned to hide her face from Jeff. Her voice changed, to a hesitating, little-girl voice. "He said that. Your father. He said you were sixteen and knew what you wanted. But I guess I have to hear that for myself. I couldn't just believe what someone else told me about my own son. Could I?"

"No," Jeff agreed. He felt how sad this made her and how brave she was being, how hard it was for her to be reasonable when she was so sad.

She stood up slowly, dusted the back of her skirt, subdued now. She walked back to the house. They slid back the big door to enter the kitchen. The Professor stood with his back against the stove, like a man facing a firing squad. Jeff took Melody's glass to refill it with iced tea, and she smiled sadly at him, sitting down. He glanced out the window of the kitchen door and saw Max's car, parked down the driveway, almost hidden by bushes and trees. He wondered why she hadn't pulled it up behind their car.

Melody leaned her elbows on the table and said, "Well, you win Horace."

"Oh, Melody, it's not that way at all, you know that."

The Professor sounded terrible. Jeff looked at his father, whose face was absolutely expressionless, but whose eyes behind the glasses stared at Melody.

"I don't know *what* way it is. I only know—when lawyers get into it the human beings go out. I even hired a male lawyer—me! I thought it was practical; you don't go up against men with women; I thought I'd have at least an even chance. You're going to make me beg, aren't you?"

"Oh, Melody," the Professor said.

"I can talk to him, can't I? I don't need permission to do that, do I? Sit down, Jeffie, and just listen. Just hear my side of it. You know your limits, Horace; you know the kind of man you are."

The Professor lifted his mug and swallowed helplessly, nodding his head.

Jeff looked from his mother to his father. His father's expressionless face masked something, he couldn't see what.

"Although this book—you must be very pleased. And the dedication—moved me. Jeffie tells me you're working on another."

The Professor nodded again.

"I wouldn't mind a dedication." Melody smiled across the room into the Professor's eyes, warm and amused at herself, confident again. "A girl would like a little immortality. Isn't that right, Jeffie?" She reached across the table and put her hand over Jeff's. He studied the turquoise rings.

"After your last visit"—she switched topics abruptly—"I did some serious thinking. About myself—I wasn't any too pleased with myself, I have to admit it. Or with Max—and I finally figured out that he was jealous, jealous of you, Jeffie. I broke it off with him." She was lying again, Jeff knew. "He was a bad influence, on me," she went on, "and on everyone he came in contact with. I don't know how he managed to fool me for so long. Some real soul-searching went on that winter, I can tell you. I had neglected—so many things. Even Gambo—it's Gambo I'm thinking of too, Jeffie; she needs to have you around, especially now, because . . . you let her know that the family goes on. She's dying and she knows it, and she'd like to have her family around her. Did you think of Gambo? Did you?"

Jeff shook his head, no. But the decision had been made, it was settled. She couldn't do anything now.

"It's a secure life for him, Horace; it's safe for him. And civilized, too, and not just because it's lovely there, gracious and—" She laughed, stood up, and walked to the window. She turned around to face both of them, where they were frozen into place. "I must admit, with all the money you must have made, I don't know why you moved down here. It's not much of a house, nothing like Gambo's, is it, Jeffie? And the bay—you could have done so much better than that, the bay is a dying body of water, between pleasure boaters and those factories up north dumping who knows what into it, it can't flush itself clean, you know that, Horace, in ten years. . . ." Her voice trailed off on the threat. "John Smith wrote about the bay and how fertile it was. You could stick a sword into it and fish would jump onto the blade. It's not like that anymore, is it?"

The Professor cleared his throat. "John Smith was a terrible liar," he said, but there was no humor at all in his voice.

"He's my son," she said. Her voice was low and sad. "He's my only child. I don't know how you can be so uncaring and selfish. You didn't used to be so uncaring and selfish. You didn't used to be unreasonable, Horace; I always admired you for that, and that's probably the reason I've never been serious about another man. Can you honestly say it's right to grudge me my only child? The only child I'll ever have?"

The Professor didn't answer. He held onto the handle of a mug as if it were a lifeline. He looked at Jeff.

"I'm not asking for everything, not for all the time, just for the summers, just for a month, or a week, just for a little bit I can count on."

Jeff didn't think he could stand it. It hurt him to feel so sorry for her.

Melody kept looking at the Professor, talking to him, with the sun behind her making her hair shine gold around her head. "What can you offer him, Horace; be honest, you always were honest. Don't you think he needs what I can give him? What you can't give him and never could?"

Jeff had to break the tension, somehow. He couldn't think, not even about what he wanted. He only knew that the longer she talked, the worse he felt, and the Professor too, if his face was any indication. The Professor was looking from one to the other of them, back and forth, his head moving in a helpless and bewildered gesture. His father was frightened, miserable and frightened; Jeff saw through the mask to that. Because the Professor still loved her, even though he didn't want to, even though he didn't like her or respect her. How could he still love her? The Professor was helpless, and he knew it. And she knew it too, Jeff saw; she was taking advantage of the Professor's weakness. Somebody had to protect the Professor, or she would really get to him again.

"How'd you find us?" Jeff demanded. He sounded angry; but then he was angry. Somebody had to stand up for the Professor; somebody had to defend him against what she was doing to him—and doing on purpose too. Jeff knew that intuitively.

Melody looked as if she had forgotten Jeff was there. "I called the publisher—it's a wonderful book, Horace, I loved it. I explained who I was, and your editor gave me the address. I thought I might telephone first, but—well, I knew I had to be brave and face you two head-on. I was right, wasn't I, Horace?"

"But how'd you get here?" Jeff interrupted again. He could figure out what she was up to, and he tried to keep her attention on himself.

"I rented a car and drove. It's quicker than flying, with the bridge-tunnel highway. My goodness, Jeffie, why are you grilling me? Then I asked directions. You're quite a famous man down here, Horace."

She hadn't changed a bit, Jeff thought to himself. And he hated her as much as ever. He thought he had put her behind him, put himself beyond her. He hadn't changed either, after all. He made himself say it, she made him; well, it was her own fault.

"It's my choice." He heard how cold his voice was. "It was up to me, the Professor said; he always let me choose. I don't want to live with you. Not all the time, not for the summer, not for a week. Not ever. It's my decision, not his. It's what *I* want."

All of her attention turned onto him; and he already felt like he'd been battering at himself. He didn't need her to add to that. He looked briefly at his father, to remind himself what was at stake.

Her beautiful eyes looked into his, hurt, surprised. "How can you say that? To me. I'm your mother; doesn't that mean anything to you? I carried you inside me, under my heart. I'm the one who endured giving birth to you. I nursed you, took care of you. He doesn't love you the way I do. He can't, he doesn't have it in him."

"I mean it, Melody. I don't love you. I really mean it." Jeff kept his voice level.

Her eyes were wide and beautiful, drawing him in. "You're killing me," she said. "Here," and she drew one fist up under her heart and pressed the other hand against it.

"I'm sorry," Jeff said.

"You owe me more than that. I'm your mother," she said, angry now.

"I'm sorry," Jeff said again.

She stared at him. He stared back at her. His shoulders hurt from holding them stiff. After a long time, tears poured out of her eyes. "You've made me very unhappy—you, Jeffie." He nodded, expressionless. "I hope you're pleased, Horace," she said.

"It's nothing to do with him," Jeff reminded her, and she just walked out of the door. He heard a motor start.

Jeff didn't look at his father, who hadn't moved. "I'm sorry," he said, yet again, but meaning something entirely different.

"Me too," the Professor said. His eyes were now on the door, and he didn't really hear Jeff at all, Jeff guessed.

"I was bringing Dicey over too."

The Professor did look at him then, like a man waking up, and asked, "Were you? Well," and a little humor was back in his eyes, Jeff thought, or hoped. "The best laid plans gang aft a-gley. Don't they? Another time, maybe."

"I couldn't have picked a worse one. Anyway, she won't be back again."

His father understood who he was talking about. "You can't predict what Melody will do," he told Jeff. "I wonder what made her do this," he said thoughtfully. "Are you okay, Jeff?"

"I'm fine," Jeff lied. "I'm just glad it's over. How about you, are you okay?"

"I think so," the Professor said, without confidence.

CHAPTER 11

Jeff wasn't fine, and he knew it. But the Professor didn't know it, which was the important thing.

Five days after Melody's visit, school started. During those days the subject of Melody didn't come up. In fact, both the Professor and Jeff avoided it. Jeff didn't see that there was anything left to say. What he was thinking—about himself and how he'd acted, about the Professor and what Jeff had guessed—he didn't see any reason to burden the Professor with that. Jeff knew he'd done what he really wanted to do, and he knew why, and he even thought it was the right thing. But he wasn't too pleased with himself, all the same.

On the first day of school, Phil came up to him smirking, his face so tan his grin looked like a TV advertisement for toothpaste. "I met your mom. I'm still recovering. I mean, Jeff—"

"How'd you do that?" Jeff asked. It was the end of lunch break and they sat outside, while people with new school clothes and deep summer tans made themselves reacquainted. Jeff figured Phil had made some mistake.

"I was covering for my sister at the stand, last Wednesday afternoon—and to think I almost didn't do it. This dusty old car pulled up, the kind you expect fusty middle-aged people to ride around in, you know? And look at every tomato before they decide which to buy then try to argue down the price. And then buy exactly three ears of corn because she only eats one, and more than two is bad for his digestion. This car pulled up. I didn't pay any attention, except to notice that it had South Carolina plates, because we don't often see those. Then the legs emerged—and the rest of her. By then I was riveted to attention. And that voice. And those eyes—they're like yours only . . . not the same. I mean, she looks right into your eyes with hers. Wow."

Jeff didn't want to talk about Melody.

"When she asked for *you,* I almost asked if she was your mother. She asked if I knew your address, as a matter of fact. I said you were in my class. She said I looked older than you. She couldn't remember the directions, which makes sense, I guess; we're so rural and she said she lives in the city—so I drew her a map. Is she still there? I'd sure like to see her again. She knows about pesticides and herbicides—she liked our tomatoes."

Jeff just shook his head.

"I mean, what a great mother for anybody to have," Phil went on. "Did she say she'd met me?"

Jeff shrugged. He guessed, in her way, Melody was something special.

"With women like that in the world, it makes you glad to be a man, doesn't it?"

That too, Jeff couldn't answer, because he judged himself to have acted like not much of a man in relation to Melody. He had acted the way he felt: scared, and cruel because he was scared. As far as he was concerned, nobody should ever be as cruel to anyone as he had been to Melody. There was no excuse. Phil drifted away from his unresponsive company, and Jeff continued his own thoughts. He'd do the same thing again and the same way if he couldn't do better, but he'd never kid himself about liking what he'd done.

It wasn't that he regretted it, it was just that he couldn't forget. The knowledge was always with him, wherever he happened to be. Nobody else knew. Nobody else could know. Jeff felt as if there was an invisible wall around him that separated him from everybody else. Because he had done to Melody just what she had done to him: she had thought he loved her and he had told her he didn't. It was the truth, but that didn't make it any better or make him any better.

Except occasionally, when he saw Dicey in the hall, he didn't see the Tillermans, now that school was in session and their crabbing business closed for the season. He was still friendly with her and with Mina and with Phil and Andy. He still played the guitar and got straight A's. He even went to football games and to parties. But he didn't tell anybody, not even the Professor, what he was thinking. It wouldn't do any good, and it would be like asking for comfort. He didn't deserve comfort, or even sympathy.

He was responsible for what he had done, and that responsibility buzzed around his head like birds—like sea gulls in a flock, squabbling in midflight about some morsel of food, trying to grab it from whichever bird had it, attacking each other so greedily that the food fell into the water. He and only he had done that—that knowledge flapped inside his head. He couldn't undo it. He didn't even want to.

So he kept himself aloof, inside himself. When he remembered—waking up in the middle of the night—what he had said, how she had looked, what he had answered, shame washed over him like waves, and he buried his head under the pillow. He woke frequently at night that fall and would wander out from his bedroom to the kitchen. Hang on, he told himself, just hang on and it'll get easier.

He drank a glass of milk, looked out into the blankness of the night, and reminded himself that it was just what he deserved; it was fair enough. He had known what he was doing and he had done it. He thought, he hoped, that the vivid memory would eventually fade. He was young and in good shape: he didn't need eight hours of sleep every night. He would endure, like the Professor had, until his feelings faded a little.

He was sorry the Professor hadn't gotten to meet Dicey, and the Professor even mentioned that once, but not again. He also missed seeing the Tillermans, but that was just something he'd have to put up with. A part of some punishment, a part of the gulls quarreling and reminding him he wasn't to be trusted—like Melody. Not exactly like her, but enough. Phil and Andy were all wrapped up in talking about colleges that fall, and Jeff listened to their conversations, adding in his opinion when he was asked. Jeff didn't think about colleges for himself.

One November day, when an icy rain sleeted down from the sky, making it chilly even inside the heated car, Jeff passed Sammy Tillerman riding on his bike, a sack of newspapers over his shoulder. The kid's yellow hair was pounded down over his ears by the rain. Jeff pulled the car over and waited for Sammy to ride up. He made Sammy put his bike into the back, and the two of them drove the rest of Sammy's paper route. Sammy was starting to grow. His legs, in soaked jeans, were getting longer and his feet looked big. He was going to be a big, muscular man, Jeff thought. He looked pretty strong, even shivering beside Jeff in the car.

Instead of taking Sammy straight home, Jeff took him to his own house and told him to take a hot shower while he put Sammy's clothes in the dryer. He couldn't stand looking at Sammy so cold, even for the ten minutes extra it would have taken to drive him to his grandmother's house. Jeff made cocoa while Sammy called up to explain where he was. It was Maybeth he talked to, saying Jeff would bring him home in a little while. Jeff knew it was Maybeth without asking, because the pace of Sammy's conversation was slower than usual.

"She says hello to you," Sammy reported. He wore one of Jeff's long-sleeved T-shirts while his clothes dried. "She's funny. She asked me if you were all right, because we haven't seen you, I guess. She didn't ask about me."

"Well," Jeff said. "That's interesting."

Sammy stared at him, as if he'd said something pretty stupid. "But she's right, isn't she? I mean, she knows I'm all right, so she doesn't have to ask. They used to say she was stupid—retarded. Dicey never believed it, but I did. And she is, in some ways, anyway she acts it sometimes—sometimes it drives me crazy she's so slow."

"Not me," Jeff said.

"I used to think," Sammy continued, sitting at the table, drinking cocoa slowly, "that she was going to end up like Momma. I used to think that was bad. Because of how Momma was. But Momma wasn't just one thing or another, she was more than one, all at the same time. And now I'm older, when I think about it I can understand her better. She's dead. She died."

Jeff could see that Sammy was making himself say that. "I never knew her," he said, because he thought he ought to say something, and the Tillermans didn't like sympathy.

"She was a lot like Maybeth, I think," Sammy said. "I was too little to really know."

"If she was like Maybeth, I would have liked her," Jeff said.

"Yeah."

"Liked who?" the Professor asked. He had come out from his study. "I heard voices. Is there enough cocoa for me? This is miserable weather." He sat down with them, and Jeff introduced Sammy, then explained why Sammy's clothes were in the dryer. Sammy told the Professor about his paper route, and how much money it brought in. He boasted a little. Then he said, his hazel eyes mischievous, "James'll be jealous I met you. Won't he?" he asked Jeff.

"Why should he?" the Professor wondered.

"Because of your book."

"How old is James?"

"Eleven."

"That's too young to read my book."

"He's smart," Sammy explained.

"But it doesn't have anything to do with being smart," the Professor said, a little surprised.

Sammy sat back and grinned. "Good-o. Wait'll I tell James you said that. It'll serve him right."

"Serve him right for what? Being smart?"

Sammy squirmed in his seat. He didn't want to answer that question.

"But I didn't even let Jeff read it until he was fifteen, and he's smart too."

"Is that true?" Sammy asked Jeff. Jeff nodded. "Why?" Sammy asked the Professor.

"Because there's more to it than just brains, or just being able to read the words. You have to be able to read the ideas, too."

Sammy studied the Professor. "Could James meet you? He'd like that."

"I might like it too," the Professor said. His eyes, full of humor, met Jeff's.

As Jeff drove Sammy home, the boy asked him, "Is that what fathers are like?"

"I guess so. What do you mean?"

"I never had one," Sammy said. "Mine left before I was even born. I never wanted one, but yours has thought about things. He's really steady, isn't he? Mine wasn't—he couldn't have been, and Gram met him and she said so too. I guess, maybe, they're all just different. Do you think?'

"I think," Jeff said. He didn't go inside to say hello to anyone, just dropped Sammy off in the yard and waited while he unloaded his bike.

"Thanks a lot," Sammy said.

"Any time," Jeff told him. He ought to bring James over, he thought, because the Professor would like talking with him. He wondered what the Tillermans' father had been like. He guessed a man could walk out as easily as a woman. He guessed he was sorry he'd met up with Sammy, because he knew now how different remembering was from being there, being with them.

Melody didn't try to get in touch with Jeff or, he thought, the Professor. He couldn't be positive about his father, who was perfectly capable of keeping a secret. But he thought, watching him, that the Professor kept on in his usual way. He thought also that the Professor would tell him this time, rather than trying to keep it secret. Sometimes Jeff worried over Melody and almost wished she would get in touch just so he would know if he'd really hurt her. Most of the time, he was just relieved not to have to deal with her, or think about her—he had enough trouble living with his own sense of guilt. He had bad days, when he despised himself and guilt gnawed at his heart; he had not-so-bad days, when he felt responsibility buzzing around his head like flies. He was managing, he reassured himself, getting through the bad days all right, trying to measure if they were growing easier.

All that winter, Phil and Andy were preoccupied with the future: where they were going to apply to college, what they were going to study, what jobs they wanted to have when they were through with school. Even the Professor started to talk colleges. Jeff, feeling that he couldn't make any decisions, tried to put the whole subject off. "Have you thought about it at all?" the Professor asked him.

"No."

"Why not?"

"I don't know what I want to do or study, I don't have any plans or ambitions. It seems like a waste of time."

"What, college?"

"Thinking about it. Thinking ahead, maybe."

"Why?"

Jeff shrugged. He didn't want to answer. His father couldn't guess, and Jeff didn't want to tell him about how much energy, and work, it took to make it through every day. His father would worry and feel responsible, if he ever did guess.

"Jeff, you know I don't like to pester you or nag at you, but—"

Jeff waited.

"But I'm afraid I'm losing touch with you."

"No, you aren't," Jeff said. "I'm not. I wouldn't let you."

"Maybe not, but I'm getting the feeling—the way I got it that fall before we moved. I'm trying to learn from experience—what kind of an historian would I be if I didn't? I get the feeling something is worrying you, and I thought maybe it was college."

"I'm not worried about college," Jeff told his father. His father wouldn't ever guess what it was, because his mind didn't work that way. "Honest. If you really want to talk about it, I will." There was just the one thing he wasn't going to talk to his father about. In a way, it was for the Professor's sake he had done it. The Professor had needed him to do it. If the Professor could forget about Melody then that was the best thing for him.

"I've been sort of thinking about it. For example, I sort of think I'd like to go into ecology." The Professor's face went expressionless. "No, not saving the world or getting back to the good old prehistoric days, not that. But responsible management of it, somehow. I'm thinking about marine biology—with some chemistry and some economics, because it's never going to be a simple problem—and computers too, because that's the only efficient way to collate material, so you have to know programming, I guess. Don't you think?" The Professor nodded, watched, waited. "Nobody understands the bay, nobody really knows how it works. It's an incredibly complex system, but . . . I want to preserve it, I'd like to do that for a job. Maybe even enrich it." The Professor nodded. "Or be a waterman, that would be okay too; it's hard work, but I can do it."

"You are thinking about it then."

"Of course. What did you think?"

But the Professor didn't answer. Anyway, Jeff knew what his father had been thinking, and he hoped he had reassured him.

"And you haven't seen your friends the Tillermans, have you?"

Jeff shrugged. He hadn't, and he really missed them—missed the singing and the way they were always working at some project, and the way when they laughed together they egged one another on. The first time that had happened, he'd gotten so choked up he'd had to pretend he had to go home. "I know," he said, and heard the sadness in his voice.

"I don't understand," the Professor asked.

Jeff could see that, and he was glad, because it wasn't the

Professor's responsibility, it was his own. If the Professor couldn't understand, that meant Jeff had done something right, at least in that one respect. "I'm going to be okay, I think, Professor."

"I've never heard you say that before."

"Anyhow, I think it's the truth," Jeff said. Keeping an eye on the truth was one of the hardest parts; accepting what he'd done to Melody. No matter what anyone would say she'd done to him, he had still done what he had done to her.

That year, Brother Thomas didn't come down for Thanksgiving or for the days after Christmas or for any weekends. He sent Jeff a postcard at Christmastime: "*Adeste fideles.* Did you know that the preferred meaning of *fideles* is trustworthy? Seasons greetings to the Tillermans. Thinking of you. BroT." During the Christmas holiday, Jeff saw a couple of movies with Phil and Andy, went to a couple of parties, but didn't go to the Tillermans'. The reason he didn't go was simple: he didn't go because he really wanted to.

Dicey never said anything about it, but she didn't seem angry at him or anything. When they ran into each other at school she'd talk to him in the ordinary way. She didn't say anything much except she'd answer his questions carefully. They were usually "How are you?" or "What's new?"

There was no snow that winter, only a long spell of cold weather that froze the muddy fields into ruts, as if they had been fossilized, that sharpened the edge of the winds so that Jeff rode the bus to and from school every day.

The weather broke in February, near the end of the month, into a long thaw. March was warm and gentle, without any lion to it at all. In the middle of March, the Professor told Jeff that Brother Thomas wanted to come down after Easter for the remaining week of the spring vacation.

"That's great," Jeff said. "But how come?"

"I don't ask him questions," the Professor answered. "What he said was, he thought we should do some planting. He wants to put in a vegetable garden. I think he's inspired by your Mrs. Tillerman."

That was a curious word, inspired. "He said she was strong," Jeff said. "He's pretty strong too, isn't he? I mean, you have to be, to be a brother."

"I think so," the Professor said. "Maybe it's like love; it's so easy to fall in love—the way you fall into the water when the weather is hot—but living in love is different."

"I wouldn't know," Jeff pointed out.

"Unhm," the Professor said.

One afternoon in early April when the Professor's vacation had begun but Jeff's hadn't, he got home to find the Professor vacuuming the kitchen. He shut off the vacuum when Jeff came in. He wore flannels and a regular shirt, with a sweater vest. His hair shone from a recent washing. He had tidied up the room and even washed the big glass doors. "Professor, what's going on?" Jeff asked. He took his books into his room and hurried back. "What do you want me to do now?"

"Make a pot of coffee," the Professor said. He finished the floor and coiled the vacuum cord around the machine. "It's not warm enough to sit outside, is it?"

"Too damp still," Jeff said. "Who's coming?" Brother Thomas wasn't due for another ten days, and besides, they didn't clean like this for Brother Thomas. He put water on to boil, then emptied the dishwasher. The Professor's nervousness was catching.

"A gentleman named Beauregard Jacobs," the Professor said. "Jeff, Gambo died last week. It was a peaceful death he told me."

Jeff didn't know what to say. "I'm sorry," he said at last.

"This Beauregard Jacobs is her lawyer. He said he had to see us, me because I'm your guardian."

"You're not my guardian, you're my father."

"He called this morning, he'll be here in about half an hour. I don't know, Jeff; does it look all right?"

"She can't do anything," Jeff told his father. "She won't. Don't worry." He knew that, for sure. He had finished Melody last summer, finished her for good and all. She couldn't get at the Professor again, not any more; and Jeff could only hurt himself.

"I just want to look as if I'm doing a good job," the Professor said, his eyes going around the room, to find anything he'd neglected. "Just in case."

But it turned out that Beauregard Jacobs wasn't interested in the Professor or the housekeeping at all. He had come to see Jeff. He came wearing a white suit and carrying a straw hat in his hand. His shoes narrowed to polished points. He was a big man, as tall as the Professor, but broad and heavy as well. He had dark hair with silver streaks in it and small brown eyes under shaggy eyebrows. He carried an attaché case.

They sat at the table, Jeff and the Professor at the ends, Mr. Jacobs in the middle so he could spread out papers, with a view out the windows. He had shaken their hands and presented his condolences, as soon as he came in. He had been grateful for a cup of coffee. It had been, he said, a long drive down from the Baltimore airport. This was surely, he said, the most secluded spot he'd ever seen, but then he guessed writers naturally hankered after seclusion.

"Is that right, Dr. Greene?"

"I'm not a writer." The Professor too had a mug of coffee to fiddle with.

"But surely Miss Melody told me—"

"Just a history book," the Professor said. "But you said you wanted to talk to Jeff?"

"Yes. Yes, indeed, I do."

Jeff waited attentively. He thought about getting a glass of water, so he too would have something to turn in his hands, but decided not to. The lawyer looked straight at him. He waited, listening.

"Your great-grandmother was a fine lady, very old-fashioned in many ways, which I for one find a rare virtue these days. A rare virtue."

Jeff nodded.

"My father was the man she originally consulted. I inherited her, as you might say."

Jeff nodded.

"I've administered her property for a number of years. I think you might say I'm more intimately aware of the structure of the estate than anybody else. She trusted me, I'm glad to say, absolutely. Yes, absolutely."

Jeff nodded again and saw the Professor's head going up and down at the opposite end of the table.

"That's by way of introduction. Preamble you might say. Because you see, young man, you are her heir."

"Her heir?" Jeff echoed, and the Professor at the same time sighed, "Oh no."

Mr. Jacobs chuckled at their reactions. "She did tell me you were an unusual pair, Miss Melody—I think I'll believe her."

"But what about Melody?" Jeff asked. "I thought she was going to inherit."

"Mrs. Melville has left her an heirloom ring, jade, and a portrait—not a valuable portrait, but it had sentimental value to

Mrs. Melville. She decided, however, that the male descendent should inherit the estate."

Jeff didn't know what to say. "But Melody thought—"

"She has had a hard time of it, you might say," Mr. Jacobs agreed. "Mrs. Melville had a hard decision to make. But she decided that it was better for the family if the property went through the male line. That was Mrs. Melville's choice. Miss Melody knew about it. She's had time to get used to the idea. Mrs. Melville told her after she'd drawn up the will."

But it wasn't fair. Even Gambo didn't like it.

"We ought to get the facts straight first," the Professor said. "Don't you think so, Jeff?"

"The facts, I must say, Dr. Greene, are going to be difficult to keep straight. Which is why I came up here myself, rather than trying to communicate to you by letter."

"But I didn't even go to the funeral," Jeff said.

"Miss Melody particularly asked that you not be told," Mr. Jacobs answered, but he looked at the Professor as he spoke. "You had, shall we say, protested for so long, Dr. Greene, all these years and so hard, she felt that it would be more of an emotional strain than she had strength for. She did say that since you finally agreed to a divorce and it has gone through, she hoped your bitterness has faded."

The Professor didn't say anything.

"He's not bitter," Jeff told the lawyer.

"Yes, well," Mr. Jacobs said. He cleared his throat, drained his mug of coffee, leaned down to open his attaché case and remove papers. He spread the papers around in front of him. "The estate consists of personal property (jewelry and household effects), the one piece of real estate, as well as some stocks. Much of the personal property can be sold at auction and the appraisers have given me an estimate of what they think it will bring. The real estate is, of course, the house, which is quite valuable in today's market. The investments represent only about fifty thousand dollars in capital. The difficulty is that much of the estate has outstanding loans against it. After taxes, depending on the markets, you should realize from twenty to thirty thousand dollars."

"I thought Gambo was rich."

"She had expenses."

Jeff thought about the big house down in Charleston and the proud woman with her black change purse and her rings and the sun-filled dining room in which they ate breakfast. "What about the aunts?" he asked.

"Fortunately, she had purchased annuities for them, several years ago, so they will move into a nursing home together. She has specified to each the furniture from her own room in the house. Miss Aurelia and Miss Belle will be able to end their lives peacefully."

"Had she mortgaged the house?" the Professor said.

"I'm afraid so, mortgaged it heavily. She also borrowed against the investments. Whatever real legacy there is will come from the personal possessions. She did make one specific bequest to you, which is the best single piece. I brought it with me. I've had it appraised so there should be no difficulty about giving it over to you now." He reached down and brought out a small black box, which he passed to Jeff. Jeff knew what it would be: Gambo's diamond ring.

He passed the open box to his father.

"Is that the one?" the Professor asked him.

"That's it."

The Professor stared at the diamond, glittering white in its black velvet setting. "It certainly is big," he said finally.

"It's worth—oh—you could probably get twenty thousand dollars for it. Her silver also is worth a fair amount, some of the china pieces, some of the furniture."

The Professor passed the ring back to Jeff. Jeff looked at it. Twenty thousand dollars, two or three years of college, Jeff thought; and it was his own. He couldn't imagine a hand that the ring would suit, but he could imagine the difference that much money would make to some people. The Tillermans, for example; if it was a question of paying for college. "Thank you," he said to Mr. Jacobs.

"Thank your great-grandmother. I was only glad to have some good news to bring, so to speak. Now, you'll have to instruct me. Unless you prefer your own lawyer to handle your interests? No? It's just as well. I think I really do understand just what needs to be done, to realize as much as possible from the estate. I'm not, Dr. Greene, the lawyer who handled the divorce. So we can work together without being hindered by whatever has gone on in the past."

"Fine," the Professor said.

Mr. Jacobs studied him for a long time. Then he put his pencil neatly across the top of his yellow pad and said, "I've known Miss Melody for years, of course. And I consider myself in a sense her lawyer now. But you aren't at all what I'd been led to expect."

"I can only hope the surprise is not unpleasant," the Professor answered.

"No, sir, it isn't."

Jeff liked this lawyer, the way he wanted everything set out clearly.

"But what about Miss Opal?" Jeff interrupted.

"Mrs. Opal Carter, yes. She wasn't specifically mentioned in the will. Miss Melody tells me that she can remain in the house until it is sold, but after that—she herself is in no position to pay Mrs. Carter's salary, much less support her. It is legally your house, so to speak; do you object to Mrs. Carter living there free?" Jeff shook his head. "There were only the four specific bequests, that ring to you, the items to your mother, the furniture to the two elderly women. The rest comes to you as single heir."

"Why didn't Gambo leave Miss Opal anything?"

"Perhaps she felt it would be possible for Mrs. Carter to find work. I would expect that is what she had in mind. Mrs. Carter will have social security."

Jeff got up from the table. The whole thing was wrong. He shouldn't inherit. It wasn't because Gambo liked him or anything. It was just because he was a boy. Miss Opal shouldn't be left with no pension, not after all those years of work. It should have been Melody's estate, or even her mother's, and there were other grandchildren as well, weren't there? He walked to the window and looked out, thinking.

"Jeff?" his father asked, after a while.

"If there are mortgages against the house, and she borrowed against the investments, where did all the money go?"

"As I said, she purchased annuities for her cousins. For that she sold a great deal of stock. Then, Miss Melody had an allowance of ten thousand dollars a year. There were taxes. Old loans came due and she would borrow again to pay them off. The maintenance on the house is costly."

"If," Jeff asked, watching the Professor's face, "if she borrowed against stocks, the bank wouldn't have given her their full value, would it? I mean, you have to put a deposit down when you buy a house even with a mortgage, so isn't there some money left on the stocks?"

"That's true, but it's only a small part of the value."

"But if the auction went well, would it be possible to pay off what's owing just against the stocks?"

"I think so. Once the house itself is sold."

"Then the stocks could be given to Miss Opal. Even if it wouldn't give her enough income to live on, it would give her some security, wouldn't it?"

The Professor agreed with Jeff, Jeff could see that. He turned his attention to the lawyer. He came back to the table.

"You're declining the legacy?" Mr. Jacobs asked.

"No. I don't mean to. I mean, I'll keep the ring, I'd like to."

"Have you considered what Mrs. Melville wanted?" the lawyer asked. "It is her will, her intention, that you receive it."

"But she did leave it to me, didn't she?" Jeff argued. "So it's mine to do as I want with, isn't it? I don't see really why she left it to me, but she did. Didn't she? I mean I see *why,* but I don't agree. But it is mine, isn't it?"

They argued for two hours, first over what Jeff wanted to do, then about how to do it. At the end, they invited Mr. Jacobs to stay for dinner, but he declined. They all shook hands. Mr. Jacobs said he would be in touch, would be sending all kinds of papers for Jeff to sign. Jeff thanked him, the Professor thanked him, and he left.

They had sandwiches for dinner. Neither of them felt like cooking or talking. Finally Jeff said, "It *is* hard on Melody."

"She won't be pleased," the Professor agreed.

"Boy, won't she," Jeff said.

"I think we may know now why she came by last summer," the Professor said.

"Yeah." Then Jeff grinned. "You said once you never knew what she'd do. Boy."

"What will she do now, I wonder," the Professor said.

"It's not right," Jeff said. "I mean, she really did think Gambo would leave her everything; she must have had some reason for thinking that; and she *is* the one who lived there, who stayed with Gambo. How could Gambo have done that to her? Except she did leave Melody the ring she really loved. She told me so, the first summer, she told me about that ring. It was jade, Professor, milky green, set around with little diamonds, like stars. It had the initials of the woman it was first made for worked into the setting. The jeweler had been in love with her. She died young, in childbirth. Gambo was left the ring by her mother. This one"—he indicated the closed box on the table—"was her engagement ring. It didn't mean that much to her. So she must have loved Melody."

"Oh, I think so. But you are the male descendent."

"Gambo couldn't have thought that Melody wanted the ring more than the inheritance, could she?"

"It depends on what Melody led her to think. She must have thought that Melody would cherish it."

"It was passed from mother to daughter, so she must have thought of Melody as a daughter."

"Yes, probably. I'm sure Melody tried to be what her grandmother wanted her to be. Or at least tried to appear to be. Don't you think?"

"Oh, yeah," Jeff agreed. "So it serves her right, I guess. But it's funny, Professor. Gambo loved Melody, so she gave her what Melody didn't want. She didn't love me, but—"

"It strikes me that love is just the beginning. If you think about it, Jeff. I think we can't help loving, but what matters is what we do about it. What we do with love. Do for it. What love does with us."

Jeff knew what his father was talking about. He could see what his father was looking at: the Professor was looking at his own love for Melody and for Jeff; the Professor was sitting up and away from them, studying them and trying to understand how they worked. The Professor was doing what he always did, using his knowledge and experience to try to understand things as they really were.

Jeff could do that too. He could look at what he'd done. In his imagination, he sat himself down in the Professor's seat and laid the facts out in front of him. He had been deliberately cruel to Melody, but—he saw—she had forced that on him, by her cruelty to the Professor. By the way she had taken advantage of Jeff's love for her and destroyed it. She had set him free from her, and as a free agent he had decided to hurt her so that she wouldn't be able to do damage to the Professor. Also, Jeff admitted to himself, because he wanted to get even for what she had done to him, Jeff. That wasn't all of his reason, but it was part of it, and it wasn't a pretty part.

Still sitting in the Professor's chair, Jeff looked around him, at himself: he had to make the choice he had, it was right for him and right for the Professor. It was just too bad that what he gave up, or gave away, in that choosing was hard on Melody. Not like Gambo's estate, which Miss Opal would be glad to have; that was an equally right decision, and one that hurt nobody.

The real problem with choosing the Professor over Melody came from Melody. She said she loved him, and he knew better; but maybe she believed herself. But that was her problem, not Jeff's. Jeff's problem was to accept what he'd done, and why. He could do that, he found: he could sit in the Professor's chair and see how he had to do it, and how he had to not like himself for doing it. He liked himself for not liking himself, he thought—swiveling up and around out of the Professor's chair. He looked at his father and had to stop himself from singing the song that was rising up inside him.

"I'm proud of you, Jeff," the Professor said.

Jeff didn't disagree, although he didn't think he'd done anything much. It was pleasant to make the right decision, just simply doing the right thing.

"Does this ring have sentimental value to you?" the Professor asked him.

Jeff laughed, partly from a sense of release, partly because it was over, really over. This inheritance, Gambo's will, was like bringing the whole question before the law. Like Gambo he had—under a different kind of law than Mr. Jacobs knew—decided against Melody. "No, none. I just thought—you asked me once if there was anything I wanted to buy and there isn't—but there are some years for college in here."

"You don't need to worry about that. You aren't worrying about paying for college, are you?"

"Not for me, I was thinking of the Tillermans. And Dicey. Just in case. I don't know if I could convince them, only for college, but—"

"I think, after this afternoon, you'd probably find a way. I didn't know that about you."

"I'm full of surprises," Jeff said.

"I think you are. There's a lot of your mother in you."

Jeff looked at his father.

"That's a compliment," the Professor said.

Jeff knew what his father meant. "And a lot of my father," he said. "And that's a compliment, too."

* * *

Dicey worked from nine to twelve on Saturday mornings, Jeff knew. The Saturday after Mr. Jacobs's visit, he stopped by the grocery store a little before twelve. Dicey's bike leaned up against the front window. Inside, he stood in line to buy a half gallon of milk and a package of English muffins. They were out of both, and Jeff had decided to drive past the supermarket and on into town, to kill two birds with one stone. When Dicey came out, wearing jeans and a boy's shirt, she was surprised to see him waiting. "I thought you might like a lift home," Jeff said.

She studied him for a minute before agreeing. She looked as if she was curious about him, as if he was unusually interesting. "Okay," she said. They loaded her bike into the back of the car. They pulled silently away from the curb.

"I wondered," Jeff said, keeping his eyes on the road, "if it would be okay for me to come over this afternoon."

"No," Dicey said quickly. "Gram's got some stuff she wants us to do."

"Oh, well," Jeff said.

"But after supper. We'd like it," Dicey said. "If you wanted to."

"I want to," Jeff said. They left the town streets, turning onto the long, winding road. He cleared his throat. "Actually, I really wanted you to come meet the Professor now. I thought we'd get a sandwich and pick up the guitar and you could meet him."

Dicey didn't answer right away. He looked over at her. She was turned so she could look at his face. She was getting ready to say no, he could see it behind her eyes.

"Look, he wants to meet you. I mean, does your grandmother plan to get you to work before lunch? I'll take you right home after, honest."

"I don't think so, Jeff."

"He won't complicate your life. He's not that kind of person, not at all."

Dicey laughed. "Then you are all right again," she said.

"What do you mean?"

"You know what I mean."

"Yeah, I guess I do. Yeah, I think I am."

"Maybeth will be glad. Are you going to tell me about it?" It wasn't like Dicey to ask questions, so Jeff told her the exact truth.

"Sometime, maybe."

She didn't crowd him, either. "Why do I need to meet your father?" she asked.

Jeff thought about this. "If I want to know you, I have to know your family too. I think families are like that, when they're real families. It doesn't have anything to do with being happy. I've been thinking about it."

The thing about Dicey, one of the things about her, was that she really listened. Jeff could hear her listening to him.

"You're right about me, if there's someone I'm going to know I always want them to meet my family."

"The Professor's my family."

After a while, Dicey asked, "What about your mother?"

"You've met my mother," Jeff reminded her. "Besides, she's not my family. I know that sounds strange." Although it didn't sound so strange to him, now he thought of it.

"Nothing much sounds strange to me," Dicey pointed out. She turned around again to look forward. "And I'd like to meet your father, I guess."

She sounded so doubtful that Jeff grinned.

"And Gram would tell me to do it. She likes you."

"Really?" That did surprise him.

"Really. She says you've got staying power and a gentle spirit. She says you're a rare bird."

Jeff didn't bother to try to hide his pleasure. "Wow," he said. Then, "She could be wrong." Then he didn't ask what he wanted to—what Dicey thought of him. If she thought anything, he guessed she'd tell him, sooner or later. He guessed she was telling him right now. He felt, turning off the road onto the shelled driveway that ran up to his house, as if he'd just gotten a letter, out of the blue, from somebody wise enough to know the truth, from everybody, or at least everybody who mattered.

"Hello," the letter said. "Hello, Jeff Greene, I've been watching you and I like you and I want to know you better. This is just to say I'm glad you're alive in the world." The list of signatures, he thought, would include his own.

CHAPTER 12

It was the first week in June, ten days before school got out. Jeff, his guitar on his back, walked the bike up the driveway. The air shone bright with sunlight, the shadows shone cool. May and June were his favorite months, before the summer heat began. And September and October. He didn't mind the rest too much, either. He sang as he walked, "Oh Lord, you know, I have no friend like you, if heaven's not my home, O Lord, what shall I do?" He sang the song happy because that was how he felt. Not for any particular reason, unless the shells sharp under his feet were a reason, or the patches of sunlight warm on his shoulders, or the idea for a slightly different riff to play between the verses of the song. He might, he thought, try to catch a few crabs for supper. He wouldn't succeed, not at this time of the year, but he'd like to get out on the water. That evening, he and as many of the Tillermans who wanted to, and Mina Smiths and a couple of her brothers, and the Professor, too, if he could talk his father into it, were going to see *Star Wars.*

He saw the car, Max's car, first. When he went into the house, he saw Melody, sitting cross-legged on the lawn. He stood for a minute, looking at her back. The sun shone around her, and her hair had grown long again. She wore it in one braid down her back. He slid the glass door open and walked out to find out what she wanted: he couldn't just ride away. He thought for a second he might, but the Professor would be home in an hour or so, and she was Jeff's responsibility.

She turned when she heard him, but didn't get up. "Jeffie? Are you angry at me? I wanted to see you."

He sat down in a chair. "Hi, Melody. Have you been here long?"

"Awhile. Awhile. It's poky, but it's quiet, isn't it?"

"Yeah." He cleared his throat. "What can I do for you?"

She shifted, to look directly into his eyes. She clasped her hands together in her lap, like a little girl. "Can't we put all that behind us?"

"All what?"

"Everything."

Everything. Starting when, Jeff wondered, and including how much? "I've already done that," he told her.

The beautiful eyes filmed with tears. "Oh, Jeffie, I don't know how to talk to you, you've changed so much. Grown up, I guess they call it, you're so tall, and handsome—and your voice—and I bet you've started to shave, too."

"Just once a week." She was flattering him, and he wondered why.

"But you used to love me. You'll deny it now, but you did. Men have convenient memories. But I remember, I remember that. What happened to us, Jeffie?"

Jeff couldn't take his eyes from hers and he felt—rising up within him—feelings so complicated he didn't know if he could stay cool, stay quiet. Anger, again, and guilt—he had been horrible to her. She looked so small and sad, he felt sorry for her. He thought he ought to apologize to her for what Gambo had done. And he had to get rid of her before his father came home. "What is it you want, Melody?" he asked.

"Oh, Jeffie, the way you say that. Nothing, I don't want anything. I just wanted to see you before I went away."

"You're going away? Where?" She'd let him know what she wanted, in her own time, in her own way. He could wait.

"Colombia. That's in South America."

"Why?"

Her hands separated, waved helplessly, then clasped together again. "You wouldn't understand, about the way people have to live in some places, about how ignorant they are. There's a village, in the mountains, and seventy-five percent of the children die before they're five. Diphtheria, typhoid, fever. Little children. And those that live—the girls marry at twelve and die in childbirth or are old women by twenty-five. In this day and age, Jeffie. They can't read and write, they just work, just to get enough to eat that day, they don't know anything about farming methods, or sanitation. There's so much that needs to be done. Nobody cares about them, and the young men go off to the cities and get ruined and the old are left alone. Brief, miserable, unhappy lives—and it doesn't have to be that way. We sit here like fat cats and don't do anything about it."

She was right, in her way. Jeff could think whatever he liked about her, personally, but she really wanted to help people who needed it. She really did feel for them, she really tried. "Where's Max?" he asked her.

Her eyes slipped away from his. "He's there already. He wants to buy a farm—land is really cheap. We're going to—to live with them and teach them."

Jeff was beginning to see. His lack of feeling about it surprised him, pleased him. He looked out over the creek and marsh. He guessed Max would be putting in a crop of marijuana, or poppies—that was his guess. But he guessed Melody really might love the guy.

Her voice went on behind him. "I can't ever be happy, knowing about them and not doing anything."

Happy, unhappy—Jeff was beginning to think that wasn't the question at all. The Tillermans never worried about that, they worried about . . . living right for each one of them, together. He guessed you might call that happy, but he didn't think that was it, he didn't think that was the half of it.

"You used to love me, I know you did." Jeff kept his eyes on the spacious horizon. "But you chose your father because he's the rich and famous one. Well, I don't blame you. I want you to know that I don't."

Jeff didn't need to argue.

"And you don't love me anymore, not even a little. I don't know why I came."

Jeff turned his face back to her at that. Because he did love her, or at least he felt tied to her, in a way; in a way as close as love would tie them. Poor Melody—she didn't know the first thing about love. "Why did you come?" he asked her gently.

He saw her face light up with hope. Poor Melody, he thought again, because she saw love as something that gets you what you want. She didn't understand at all.

"I need money. To get me there. And start work, for supplies and some books. So we can make a difference there."

"I don't have money, not that kind," Jeff told her. "I'm sorry, Melody, I gave what there was to Miss Opal, all I have is an allowance."

"You have Gambo's ring," she told him, angry.

He looked at her hand, then, and saw the green jade. She followed his eyes. "This one's not worth anything."

"Oh. Okay," Jeff said, hiding his smile. Oh, Melody, he thought. He went into the house to get the box out of the bookcase where he kept it hidden. He returned to find Melody standing up, watching for him. He passed her the little box, and she opened it. She slipped off the jade ring so that she could put the big diamond on.

"You keep that one," she said. "Really, I'd like you to." Jeff took the ring. Gambo wanted Melody to have it, but Melody didn't want it.

Melody had the diamond on her hand and held it out to catch the sunlight. "It's a pity to sell it." She sighed.

"Maybe you don't have to."

This was the ring she'd wanted when she married the Professor and was pregnant with Jeff. She'd finally gotten what she wanted; he didn't see why she should sell it—unless it was the money all along. Not the thing but its money value all along, in everything. Except Max, he remembered. There were always exceptions. The pieces of Melody didn't fit neatly together any more than the pieces of the Professor did, or of Jeff—or of anybody, for that matter, or anything. Even the blue herons nested in colonies, all of them together.

"Maybe you can keep it." He knew she didn't want to.

She laughed up into his eyes. "You are a goose, aren't you? But now I know you love me, whether you'll admit it or not, I don't need anything else to make me happy. And I better run, before your father catches me here. He'll be angry at you, if you tell him."

"No, he won't," Jeff said.

She wasn't listening to him, she was slipping her sandals onto her feet, bending gracefully over to pull the straps tight, her long braid falling over her shoulder. Jeff held Gambo's ring in his palm. You couldn't send anyone to college with it, he knew. But all the same it was the one he wanted. He hadn't known that and was surprised at his impulse to wrap his fingers tightly around it.

This was the ring that connected to what had been, to whatever it might mean to be a Boudrault of Charleston, where the tombstones stood in silent rows along crumbling brick walls, where tall houses looked over enclosed gardens, where so many lives had been lived out. Where the silent white beaches of the sea islands were washed by ocean waves, washed up, washed away. Poor Melody, he thought for the last time, watching her walk around the house and away; she never knew what the real treasures were.